DEDICATION

To my husband Colin, your love drives me to greatness.
To my beautiful children...Evandyr, Elianna, and now Kaelen,
your innocence is my inspiration.
To my amazing step-children...Holly, Pacey, and Mackenzie, you
are each loved more than you know.

To my beta-reader extraordinaire, Sherry, without you and your
enduring encouragement, the world of Pendomus might not exist.
Thank you.

PRAISE FOR CARISSA ANDREWS

"I have said it before and I will say it again The Pendomus Chronicles is one of the best trilogies of all time. The characters are all just as amazing as the world building."

— NANCY, THE AVID READER

"If you love films like Avatar or the Matrix, or books like Feed, Divergent, or Starters, then I'd definitely suggest picking up this one and giving it a go."

— KRISTIN, BLOOD SWEAT AND BOOKS BLOG

"I need book 2 ASAP! That's how good this book is!"

TANEESHA, A DIARY OF A BOOK ADDICT

"I'm a slow reader, I like to soak in all the details and enjoy the journey. However, I'm not usually a non-stop reader. The Pendomus Chronicles Trilogy changed all that! All the unexpected twists, turns, and detours kept me turning the pages! I read all three books in three days and loved every minute of it! Thank you Carissa Andrews!"

— S. JOESTEN

Original Copyright, © 2013 Carissa Andrews

Published in 2013 by Carissa Andrews

Cover Design by Carissa Andrews

Revised in 2018

All rights reserved.

ISBN: 0991055802

ISBN-13: 978-0991055807

PENDOMUS

BOOK 1 OF THE PENDOMUS CHRONICLES

CARISSA ANDREWS

AUTHOR
REVOLUTION

Behold, the beauty of this wretched world lies not in the contrast between light & dark...

But in the eye of the beholder.

1

R U N A

*a*long, abrasive, invisible tongue grazes the fleshy part of my left cheek. The creature snorts beside my ear, but I can't bear to turn my head. My mind plays tricks, rippling my memory until all that remains is an intangible, cold touch. I don't have the power left in me to fight.

How do you fight something you can't even see?

Hot breath flashes across my frozen cheek as a muzzle nudges along my neck, making me shiver. The creature takes slow, deliberate inhalations, edging to my ear, into my hairline. Repulsed by the intimacy of its touch, the burden of consciousness threatens to depart.

"Runa, you know what's waiting outside. You can't possibly be so stupid as to think you can live in the elements alone. I know you don't believe me, but the Morph is out there. With the way its evolutionary leap defied nature, no one can predict what it's capable of now. You need to respect that. Besides, RationCaps aren't hidden in the woods. Food doesn't grow on dead trees, you know."

1

The memory of Baxten's warning echoes from the past.

Regardless of my brother's admonishment, I had to take the chance. After everything that's happened, after all that I'd be losing … I knew he'd never understand, but unfortunately, now he never will.

The Morph's sticky tongue returns, paying particular attention to my eye socket, drenching the area in saliva. The viscous liquid pools in my eyelashes, cementing my eyelids together. Whatever its intention, it plans to take its time. I swallow hard and will death to claim me.

For a moment, darkness consumes everything. My eyes flutter open as my long white hair whips across my face. The delicate braids I'd taken so much time to arrange this morning would blend into the snow beneath me, if I weren't staining it crimson. The sweet stench lingers in the air, tugging my impulse to gag.

With no warning and even less fanfare, the Morph's claws slice through the flesh above my left eye. My skull screeches as claw contacts bone and an instant later squishes unceremoniously through my eyeball.

Suddenly, I'm four again. The smell of death carries from the present, clear through to the memory. But now, I can't take my eyes off my father's sunken face. The light in his warm brown eyes is gone, yet I clutch his hand, desperate to keep his essence somehow attached to his body. The room vibrates, pulsing with an energy that makes my skin crawl and my stomach lurch. The medics arrive, wrenching my hand from his without thought, and wheel him from my life. So I will move on. So we'll all go on as if he never existed … So we'll forget.

But I never did.

I still hear his deep, boisterous laugh echoing through the

main corridor of our Living Quarters. I remember the way my head bobbed up and down on his chest when he held me close. The way he always smelled like engine grease and electricity. I recall his last few moments, his last few breaths, as if I'd taken them myself.

To have him treated like that … his body destroyed without so much as a salutation to a life once lived felt wrong.

I blink away the memory, fighting through saliva, sweat, and blood.

The Morph's enormous paw dangles above me, covered red so it can take the shape of my would-be killer. He's massive, easily ten times the size of my frail body. My vision blurs, my head lolls to the side as I wait for the end.

Between the branches of this barren forest, snowflakes flitter through the air. They accentuate the blazing array of color from the sun as it hangs heavy in its locked region of the horizon. The halo is bright today, wrapping around the orb in a circular rainbow.

This place between life and oblivion is surprisingly peaceful.

Little gray birds gather in the trees. They call back and forth, seeming to be speaking to each other about me. A few scratch at the dirty snow beside me, looking for something. Their hops are odd, scritching back, a quick hop forward, just to start all over again. My memory download on animal resurrections from Earth called them juncos. Kind of a funny name.

One in particular hops closer, tilting its head from side to side, examining me, this dying bag of flesh and blood in front of him. The junco has beautiful black eyes and a white beak—an oddity, since the others' are yellow. A small smile breaks across my lips, and I chuckle.

He's just as different as I am.

The peaceful moment with the birds is interrupted as a ferocious howl snaps me back to the present. Seconds later, my body makes a crevasse in the snow and slams backward, hitting an enormous tree. What little vision I have blurs and takes on a brighter, more intense quality. The Morph pushes my upper body through a huge gash in the side of the tree, dangling me partway inside. My scalp tingles as the inner chamber of the tree resonates all round me.

The birds screech, and the one with the white beak swiftly dives in. His little gray body is so small, and his swooping gesture does nothing to distract my attacker. Pinned inside the tree under a dripping paw, I watch again as the bird circles in, and like a bomb, dives. The Morph grunts as the bird bounces off the *nothing* that should be its back.

The air ripples around us as the tiny bird lands in a heap beside the tree's entrance. Gray feathers ruffle in the breeze on an otherwise still body. Slowly, its white beak parts, to offer a final exhalation.

The unfairness tugs at my heart.

How could something so innocent give its life for me? What a waste.

My hair whips in circles, striking the sides of my cheeks, attacking my tears for even attempting to emerge. The tears burn, and I struggle to blink away the blood streaming into my remaining eye. The massive structure I've lived in my whole life comes into focus.

The Helix.

For the first time I can remember, disgust bubbles at the building's stark contrast of glass and metal with this forest of dead trees. Out here, the gnarly dark branches rise into the sky like they're orchestrating the celestial sphere. Some of the trees are ancient; their trunks command the space of a building, and for as long as I can remember, they've called out to me, whispering their stories of memories long forgotten.

It's unfortunate humanity never got to witness them in their glory. The Helix's history downloads tell us no life existed on this planet before the colonization happened. Yet, I'd hoped to be granted a way to study them as part of my professional appointment. With the way Pendomus is tidally locked, we know little can survive on its own. Humanity has been lucky. We've found survival on this temperate band between the desert and frozen tundra.

Supposedly, we brought the spark of creation with us. However, this remnant of the past, when life had sustained itself, is evident. Even in this landscape of hushed sounds and broken fragments of a life different from my own, life finds a way. This knowledge has always granted me comfort.

I'm probably the only one in all of Pendomus who thinks this way. These woods had been my place of peace. It's hard to believe only days ago I thought I'd been given a sign, a trinket from these woods. A simple blue crystal that held so much, a promise my journey ahead would be bearable, maybe even beautiful. I wish I'd brought it along instead of leaving it behind inside the Helix for Baxten to remember me.

The Morph snorts, evidently nonplussed by the bird's feeble attack. He bends in, lapping up the sticky red liquid from my face and nudging my head for better access. With no fight left in me, I blink slowly, allowing the intrusion to continue. Bright light pours into my vision, and I'm floating ... floating ... A pulse of heat spreads from my right side, and through me, all the way down to my toes.

The warmth surrounds me, cocooning me in a blanket of serenity.

Finally. The end.

The heat radiates again, just as I'm submersed in the creature's saliva. A bubbling sensation tickles at the side of my face but quickly becomes unbearable. Ripped from my peaceful death, my boiling skin itches. My shredded eye sears with an intense pain I didn't have the sense to feel moments before.

I pull as much energy as I can and desperately wipe at my face, trying to make the pain stop. My body submerges into something warm and wet. I flail, trying to get a bearing, but to no avail. Despite no unfrozen water being found on Pendomus, I'm floating deep inside the hollow tree, surrounded by a murky green substance with a remarkable resemblance. The frothing water sharpens my agony, and I realize my right calf has been damaged in the attack.

The edges of my vision crack and darken. As I slide out of this world, a white, five-petaled flower glowing bright in the middle of a green field flashes through my mind. The image contorts into a large bearlike creature walking beside me. Beyond, an enormous tree comes into view and I'm urged onward. The tree has an intricately designed door in the side of its massive trunk, which tugs at my memory. As I reach out to touch it, the tree vanishes and a little blue crystal rests in the palm of my hand. The blue object in my palm pulsates, expanding until everything in my vision is consumed, and my entire awareness is filled with the color blue.

2

RUNA

~24 Hours Earlier~

"℞u-na—" The word is disjointed, spoken aloud, but I pause, certain it's meant to be my name. With the eLink, no one fumbles with out-loud language anymore. There'd be no purpose. It's slow and clumsy ... not to mention, lacks definition and tonal equalizers for translation. Unfortunately, the eLink loses its integrity the further away from the Helix you are and I'm probably far enough away.

"Runa?" This time, there's no mistaking Baxten's call. It's been years since we practiced speaking out-loud to each other, but I still remember his voice.

I set aside the research I was working on to call out, "I'm here."

"Here, *where?*" He answers back, closer now.

"Trees. Near large rock—" I wait, watching the tree-line.

A few moments later, Baxten's brown, shaggy head pops out from behind a tree. The sun catches his ScanTech emblem and the creepy metallic-looking eye moving back and forth on its own accord. Always watching.

"See the Morph yet?" He asks, his words coming out slow.

I shake my head, ignoring his jab. "Not once."

"Lucky." He smirks. "Again."

"Poor you." I laugh, slapping his arm.

"Whatcha…" Baxten pauses, trying to find the right word to speak. "Learning?"

"Inside." I nod to the Helix. It will be easier to explain using the eLink.

He seems to understand as he nods and turns back the way he came. With a quick glance around at the trees I was studying, I follow him.

We walk for a few minutes in silence. It's interesting being with someone so close in proximity and not constantly being pinged for communication. It's nice, actually.

"Is it weird for you, too?" I ask, turning to him.

"Is *what* weird?" He says, scrunching up his face.

"Not being able to hear me in your head?"

"Yeah, I guess." He shrugs.

"You sound different, now. *Out loud*. Your voice has changed from what I remember."

"Okay." He shoots me a sideways glance.

"Not bad different, just … *different*."

"You sound exactly the same." Baxten nudges me with his shoulder. "*Annoying*."

His eyes crease in the corners and I push him back. He's been the one person in all of Pendomus who I've looked up to. The one person who's really been there for me.

"Why are you out here?" I ask. It's not often he'll come outside anymore.

His eyes sparkle and he says, "Your turn."

"Really?" I exclaim in excitement. "My professional appointment? Now?"

He nods excitedly.

"Will Mom— ?" I begin, but stop as the sparkle fades from his eyes before I even finish my sentence.

He shakes his head. "Too busy."

"Right." I nod, trying to hide my disappointment. There's very few things more important inside the Helix than being granted your professional appointment. This moment is what we work toward our entire childhood. To finally have our life's assessment back and our natural aptitudes read by the ScanReaders. I know I've never been high on her list of priorities, but I had hoped she'd at least make time for this.

Trudging in the knee-deep snow, we walk in silence back to the expansive building. Up close, the double-helix-inspired building looks like nothing more than a huge metallic complex. Even the mirrored glass gives the illusion its endless. For those who never step a foot near the trees, they wouldn't even see the way the large cylindrical tubes weave in and out of the ground. They know the stories, of course. Yet, they are perfectly happy living in complete ignorance of its true vision.

What a horrible existence.

When the shadow of the Helix looms over us, I hesitate. This is the hardest part of every day, going back inside. I sincerely hope my professional appointment has something to do with being out here. Studying the trees— or the perished plant life, or perhaps even the geological history of

Pendomus. How could it not? I've been exploring outside from the time I could be left on my own.

Excitement builds as we draw nearer.

Off to the right, a glint of light draws my attention. Not unlike the sun's halo, whatever it is scatters a rainbow of color across the shadowed snow. I leave Baxten's company to pick it up. A small, bluish chunk of ice seems to be the culprit of the array of color. Removing my glove, I pick it up and hold the ice in the center of my hand. The chunk pulsates, making my palm throb. The jagged edges glow eerily, illuminating the grooves of my palm.

"What's that?" Baxten asks, walking back to me.

"Ice?" I offer. Oddly enough, it doesn't melt against the heat of my palm. "Maybe a crystal?"

With my thumb and pointer finger, I hold it up against the low sun and see right through it. The clarity is amazing.

How did it end up out in the middle of nowhere?

Smiling at Baxten, I slip it into my NanoTech trouser pocket for safekeeping. "I'll take it as a good sign."

My brother nods and we take our last few steps to the door. Now within range, the familiar static of the eLink scratches at my brain as it connects. Baxten's face flashes through my mind and I frown, accepting his conversation. I've enjoyed our interaction better without it.

~You'll have to tell me all about your explorations later. You're kind of a mess. Take a few minutes to clean up and maybe even take a five-minute Lotus.

Baxten steps forward and pulls back the door to the Helix. My senses are assaulted with the manufactured air and backlighting.

Our reemergence goes unnoticed by those milling about the long cylindrical halls. Just outside our Living Quarters, I take my place in front of the small optical scanner to gain access to our residence. The eLink connects in conjunction with the scan and a reminder is prompted.

... Runa Cophem ... Congratulations. Our records indicate your professional appointment awaits. Check in with the ScanReaders within the next hour for this momentous occasion. Should you need further instructions, please visualize them now.

I briefly wonder where exactly I need to go to check in and a map, virtual images, and face are downloaded into my memory.

Opening the door, my eyes sweep the space as I stand in the main hall of our LQ. The dark grey walls are accentuated by two doors on either side and a large table at the far end. Same as always. The table is practically an extension of Baxten, usually filled with virtual blueprints and scanner parts.

~You should really go take a shower quick. It will help calm your nerves.

I turn my gaze to Baxten and he nods his head to the first door on my left. Reflexively, I run my hand across my hair and pull out a twig; a hazard of being outside. He chuckles to himself and walks down the hall to his quiet space on the right. We're both lucky enough to have a window view, not that he really ever notices his.

I can stare outside for hours, trying to imagine what life had been like before humans terraformed Pendomus. Most of the time, I ponder the life outside. Why the trees no longer grow leaves like the ones did on Earth. Or maybe they had been different on this planet? I've imagined different scenarios where the trees could produce leaves of fire or liquid leaves flowing in the breeze. I can see Pendomus in colors I've not seen in existence, but full of possibility.

The door to my mother's quiet space is partially open and I take a step forward. Her room is spotless with only the simple gray lotus chair placed in the middle of the three meter by three meter space. I click her door shut just she enters from the main hallway.

My heart lightens and I breathe a sigh of relief. She's come home to attend my professional appointment after all. Her dark brown hair stands out on the top of her head, however, the white lab coat looks crisp and clean as it drapes over her standard issue NanoTech garments. As a Ration-Caps Chemist, her position is highly esteemed. Without people like her, we wouldn't be able to survive. She creates the food that nourishes our bodies and keeps us healthy. I suppose that would be really impressive to most, but all I really ever wanted from her was love and attention.

Neither of which have been in supply, despite their demand.

Stumbling to the side, I wave to her. She briefly catches my eye and the corner of her lips curl upward, but falter. The crackling of the eLink alerts me of her intentions. The sudden juxtaposition of her smiling eLink photo flashing in the recess of my mind with her current expression is disheartening.

~Hi, Runa. Long day. I'm going to go redirect.

Entering her quiet space, she closes the door behind her without so much as a second glance.

I take another step backward, reeling from the brief conversation, and wondering if she's really here for me at all. She didn't even mention my professional appointment. For as long as I can remember, my mother has been distant and aloof. Even more so than other people inside the Helix. Baxten tells me mixed stories. Usually, how it's my fault she's distant. He enjoys telling me about what she was like when he was younger and it was just him and my parents. Supposedly, she was the most amazing woman he'd ever met. She was kind, loving, and affectionate. Then I was born and everything ceased. As if the life had been sucked out of her the moment I arrived. Other times, he tells me our father's death threw her over the edge. Either way, I don't ever remember a time when I felt her approval.

Most of the time, I'm not sure why her disdain should even matter? No one inside the Helix expresses many feelings for one another. At a very young age, we're taught emotions, particularly for other people, don't lead to rational thinking. Close relationships are discouraged, even inside our own family hierarchy. Yet, if you are passionate for your work, that's considered to be ideal. The whole thing has always seemed backwards to me. You can be passionate and excited for your role in society, but emotions are not helpful? Isn't passion for your profession still an emotion?

Needing to hurry, I walk down the hall, opening the second door on the left, directly across from Baxten's quiet space. There's not much inside, the walls are white with a tinge of gray, just like the rest of the Helix. Inside sits my own dark gray lotus chair and of course, some extra Nano-Tech garments in the small closet. Grabbing a dark gray and red set for my appointment, I walk to the allayroom to shower.

I set my new garments across the allay and close the door. In the mirror, the series of loose braids hovering over the rest of my white-blonde hair are somewhat messy, but overall, not terrible. Leaning forward, I stare into my amber eyes, trying for the hundredth time to imagine them deep brown like everyone else's. It doesn't work. Instead, I look tired. The bags underneath do nothing for me, but a little sleep therapy should take care of it. Baxten thought it may help calm my nerves before my ceremony anyway.

I'll go there next.

Turning the water on, I stand in the warm stream, letting the water flood over me. I take a moment, allowing the warmth and the texture to take over my entire perception as if the only thing in life at this moment is me and the water. I love the way it revitalizes me.

After a few minutes, I finish cleansing and hop out. Wrapping a towel around my body, I take my time combing through my hair and rebraiding the long strands before reaching for my new garments. Gray covers each piece of my attire from head to foot with only a few red lines at the seams to break up the monotony. My boots are standard black, but they're comfortable, reaching up to my ankles.

Something small tumbles to the floor when I pick up my used NanoTech Trousers. I kneel on the floor and find the small icy-crystal from earlier. Turning it over, it lacks the luster from outside, but sparkles none-the-less. When I place it in the palm of my hand, my skin still tingles.

My token is still with me.

Carefully placing the crystal in my new trouser pocket, I send my dirty clothes to be washed and walk back to my quiet space. Baxten towers over something at the large table in the main hall, his face full of excitement.

I can't wait to have a purpose like he does. To be granted access to learn more, do more. Until my professional appointment gives me privileges to more knowledge of the planetary history, I'm left struggling through without all of the known details. Excitement fills me again because soon I'll have that access. Taking a deep inhale, I close the door to my space and walk to my lotus chair. I take a seat, crossing my legs and placing my hands in my lap. The lights dim as the sleep therapy machine senses me and turns itself on. From behind, the brain calibrator emerges and encompasses my head. Resting back and closing my eyes, I wait. Seconds later, the familiar electrical charge tickles the top of my head. My hair follicles tingle slightly as my brain recharges, mimicking the primitive way humans had once slept. Luckily we no longer need to spend a third of our lives in stasis. Instead, our daily sleep therapy intake ranges from five, to thirty minutes per day, leaving more time to be productive.

Images of my day flash behind my closed eyelids and before I'm aware, the lights turn on again, signaling the end. I untangle my legs and stretch.

As expected, I'm clearer, calmer, and the day's events seem more manageable.

A smile breaks across my face as I remove the little crystal from my pocket. Taking a few slow steps, I place it on my window seam, allowing the natural light to pass through.

"Back soon, my good luck charm." I whisper.

Baxten's eLink photo emerges in the recesses of my mind.

~Are you ready, Runa?

~Yes, let's go. Is Mom ready?

I walk out into the main hallway to a confused expression on Baxten's face.

~Runa, I told you. Mom's not coming.

My eyes flit to her closed door.

~But she's in her quiet space?

Baxten shakes his head.

~No, she left when you were in sleep therapy.

I drop my gaze to my hands.

~Oh, I see.

Wrapping his arm around my shoulder, he leads me down the hall.

~C'mon, kid sis. Let's see what your future has in store... Just keep in mind, whatever you end up doing, you're not getting the large table to plunk sticks and rocks on. I've already claimed it.

I laugh with him as we leave our LQ behind, walking the bare corridor to check in with the ScanReaders. We don't have far to go. Since Baxten's professional appointment as a ScanTechnician, we were reassigned to a new LQ closer to the ScanReader department.

~This won't take long. It's really only a formality because they want to give you your department badge. You basically walk in and they hand you your professional badge and they'll eLink all of your assignments for tomorrow.

Baxten winks at me, ushering me inside the room.

~Great. I don't think I could handle much more suspense.

My pulse races as we reach the standard chrome counter inside the ScanReader lobby. A woman with short brown hair blinks, expressionless, at us.

According to the eLink broadcast in my mind, her name is Andrea Rupox.

~Proceed.

I bite my lip, but offer my information in return. She nods, already prepared for me as she pushes forward my badge. My smile beams as I take it from her and nod in appreciation.

~Thank you.

The moment I have the badge in my hand, it lights up and a series of maps, procedures, names, faces, and access levels are downloaded in my mind. My footing falters and I turn back to Baxten and the woman named Andrea.

~I'm sorry. There has to be some mistake. This can't be the correct appointment.

Andrea's expression is skeptical as I walk back to her, trying to hand the badge back.

Baxten grabs my wrist, confusion written across his face.

~Runa, what are you talking about? The scans are never wrong.

I shake my head, trying to fight the panic welling inside.

~I don't know what to tell you, Baxten. The scans are wrong. They have to be.

Grabbing his hand, I thrust my newly acquired badge in his palm. The emblem with a moving metallic blaze in the center puts a stop to his rebuttals. Instead his mouth drops open and he lifts his wide eyes to mine. Neither of us say the word etched across the top of the badge. I close his hand around it and shake my head.

~There's no way.

I walk out, leaving my brother standing in the middle of the lobby with the remnants of my childhood idealism. In that instant, I know what I have to do. They won't allow me to disavow their placement. There isn't precedence for something like this.

I need to leave the Helix.

Because after everything I've been through, there's no way I accept the role of Cremator.

3

TRAETON

*W*ho wouldn't love to explore more of Pendomus?

I'd be a fool if I said the thought wasn't utterly enticing. I've been hanging around Fenton on and off for nearly eight years now and he'll manage without me just fine. Besides, he and Kani have their thing going now. They need a third wheel about as much as I need to be one. It's not like I'll be gone forever.

Well, unless we manage to get ourselves killed.

The thought comes unbidden to my mind, but I shrug it off. I'll have Ash with me the entire time and that guy could pulverize someone with just a look. I know I don't know everything about Pendomus and we would be going far into the desert realms of the planet, but some things you can only prepare for so much. Eventually, you have to ignore all the worries or concerns and take the leap. I follow the last bend of the cavern system and enter the space leading out to the frozen world. The soft glow of daybreak illuminating the opening is like a magical portal to a new world. Outside, exploring—that's where I love to be.

I take a deep breath and walk out into the light. When the cool air hits, the breeze lessens my agitation instantly. Beyond the select few in the Lateral, I'm the only one who possesses first-hand details about the area around us. The topography of the planet. Of course Delaney would ask me to go on this mission.

Of course I'm going to accept it. There really was no other choice, but I couldn't let them know that. Still need to exert a little bit of free will, right? Keeps them on their toes.

The weight of the sonic resonator hanging loosely over my back reminds me of my current mission. I'm not just out wandering to clear my mind, I have to start my patrol of the area. There are people to protect and I'm not doing a very good job if I'm stuck in my own head.

Out here, you never know what might find you. Hundreds of animals were resurrected and released, few which behave in a friendly manner.

My lungs crackle under the coolness of my inhalation. The wind's scent is intoxicating, as oxygen courses uninhibited through my veins. The dank air inside a cave just isn't like this. The sky's amazing this morning as I start out, taking a moment to glance up through the trees. The branches are magnificent, covered in sparkling frost. Over my shoulder, a twig snaps, making me spin around. My eyes scan the area, but see only the awesomeness of the sundog hugging the Safe Haven's obscure entrance like a pair of parentheses. Pinks and purples contrast the white of the snow, making the edge where the rainbows meet appear to vibrate. Nothing is so awe-inspiring as the colors and wonder you never see inside the Haven. Colors even Kani can't replicate in her otherwise beautiful paintings. For some reason, they're too elusive.

As I continue onward in my circumference around our base, the woods are silent. The only exception is the sound of my feet trudging quietly through the snow. Focusing on the muffled crunching, I continue to put one foot in front of the other and create distance between the Haven and me. I watch for signs of predatory animals and people. We can't assume the Helix will let us be, if they find out where we've been hiding. Preparation is key and all that.

Somewhere through my rounds, the trees fill with the sounds of little gray birds. The sounds are cheerful at first, but after a while, start to grate on my nerves. A little peace, that's all I want. As if monitoring my progress through the trees, they follow me in the branches overhead.

I flick my hand at them, trying to get them to fly off. "Go away. Shoo."

Luckily, they get the idea and dissipate. Leaving the birds behind, I catch myself smiling again. I've been a bit self-reflective, but I know this is going to be a good thing. I've been in need of a damn adventure, anyway. I much prefer the wide-open spaces of the unknown to the suffocating close-ness of monotony. With a little luck, maybe I'll even be able to get to know Ash better. The man never talks.

A piercing howl slices through the trees, ripping me from my thoughts. The hairs on the back of my neck rise, causing me to crouch in a defensive position. The forest is suddenly silent and my instincts scream to run—which doesn't happen often. Usually I'm the first to run towards the fray. My only problem is, I've got not clue which direction the sound came from.

Frozen to my spot, my eyes follow the birds and the way

they're flocking—all heading in the same direction in the distance. Their irritating calls turn into horrifying screeches. In the distance, the sky blackens with their convergence as they appear to be circling a tree in the distance. I flick a switch on my vibration detector just as another howl invades the silence. This time, my instruments confirm the howl came from the same direction as the birds.

A sudden streak of gray and red whizzes through the air. Rushing forward to get a better look, the streak is actually a girl with long, white-blonde hair. Her face is bloody and her body limp. After a moment, her body slides across the ground and hits a large tree, as if something is maneuvering her. The only problem is, I can't tell what the hell it is. Or *where* the hell it is.

The thundering in my chest convinces me I need to take action for the sake of the girl. Without conscious effort, I run toward her and whatever is orchestrating her body's movements. I need to figure out what the hell is going on here.

Pulling the sonic resonator around to the front of my body, my fingers stroke the virtual keypad, giving the command to stun as I race through the trees toward her.

Could this be the Morph?

Stories have circulated for a long time about a killing machine no one can hunt. If this really is the Morph, now I know why. No one can see the damn thing.

After moments of stillness, the girl lifts her arm. Something glints in her hand and she swings whatever the weapon is above her. I curse myself for being so slow as I finally get close enough to be in range to stun the creature without hitting her. Not wanting to be seen, I flatten against the tree and clutch the sonic resonator tightly.

As I spin around to take aim, the girl musters a burst of

energy as she scampers up the tree trunk. Her struggles are evident, as she haphazardly reaches for a large branch and nearly falls back down. She manages to get a few feet up the tree before a gash on her leg splits open and paints the snow red. More horrifying, however, is the outline of the Morph as it appears in her blood.

The thing is massive. I take aim for the beast from behind the tree. Just as I'm about to pull the trigger, the girl is wrenched downward and lands in the snow with a quiet thump.

She didn't even scream as she fell.

Her body lies absolutely still, but I take aim at the blood soaked air above her and pull the trigger. The Morph shudders, but doesn't back away.

Am I too late? Is she dead?

The girl lies in a pool of blood, her face covered partially in her drenched hair. The outline of the Morph hovers over her, claws ready to attack again. The little gray birds screech and circle; some even attempt to attack the thing.

I release a second blast from the resonator and all the birds around the girl and her attacker take flight. Time itself stands still as the terrifying edge of the Morph's face stares straight at me. I pull the trigger a third time. The creature shudders again, but this time, picks the girl up by the front of her jacket. The girl's body is lifeless as the creature pulls her along. Blood-streaked hair and arms dangle across the snow like a ripped-up rag doll. Instead of coming at me, the Morph, along with the girl, vanish before my eyes.

As much as I try, I can't get my hands to stop shaking. The sonic resonator is locked tight in my grip, and my insides feel like they've been stirred and spat out. Instead of movement, only echoing silence is left of the attack.

"What the hell?" I mutter, flipping the sonic resonator to my back.

I will my legs to move and race toward the scene of the attack, stepping through the soaked snow. I round the tree, but the girl's not there. She's not anywhere.

"People can't just vanish." I whisper, my voice wavering. "Hello?"

Glancing from tree to tree, I watch for signs of movement.

What if the damn thing comes back?

The backside of the large tree has a huge gash in its trunk, so I grab the edges and peer inside. My eyes widen and my jaw drops. The tree is hollow—and drops straight downward into—*water?*

Floating on her back, hair like a crown of lightning, is the girl. She's a gory mess, and it's impossible to tell if she's alive. Removing my safety line, I jam the anchor to the outside of the massive tree trunk. Slowly, I drop myself inside; half climbing, half sliding down. The inner bark of the tree is covered in a green viscous fluid, making it impossible to get a good footing. Between that and my frazzled nerves, my hands and legs don't want to coordinate the way they should. When I reach the bottom, I take a deep breath and slosh my way to the girl. Her face is mangled, and her undamaged eye lazily closes as I near.

"Can you hear me? Everything's gonna be okay. I'm gonna get you outta here." My reassurance sounds false, even to me. She's dressed in standard NanoTech clothing, so I doubt she's going to be able to process what I'm saying anyway. It's not the eLink, after all.

Without warning, the murky water inside the tree bubbles around us and starts to rise. The water rushes around my body, warm and powerful. With extreme force, it pushes us both upward, back toward the entrance. I'm forced under a couple of times as it ascends. I claw at the sticky walls of the tree, but to no avail. Somehow, I need to find a way to get us both to the opening. In the depths below, the water begins to crackle and pop. The sound is like walking on ice and as the water reaches the opening, I begin to realize why. Beneath us, everything is freezing solid at a frantic pace. Grabbing hold of the girl's left arm, I struggle to get us over to the entrance before we're caught in the ice's progression. I clutch at the snow on the ground with one hand, and try to hang on to her in the other. When I gain some traction, I wrench myself out. Quickly spinning around, I grope for the girl's arms and tug. The water continues to rise and floods so fast, we're both flung backward as the tree regurgitates us. Seconds later, the entire entrance to the tree freezes solid.

Sprawled flat on my back, with the girl bleeding in the snow beside me, I blink hard to focus. The cold air attacks, making the warmish water inside the tree nothing but a distant memory as my clothing freezes.

What in the hell is going on out here?

Shaking the fog from my brain, I push up to my knees. The girl is limp, so I maneuver her body to pick her up. Her head drapes lifeless over my right arm as her gash across her face drains onto the front of my jacket. The contrast between the white of her face and the red of her blood is frightening. If she isn't dead yet—she doesn't have a hell of a lotta time. Without a second thought, I take off running. I don't know if she'll hang on until I can get her help, but I have to try.

Just meters beyond the tree, the girl breathes in a deep, garbled breath as she lurches forward. I fall to my knees, nearly dropping her. A bright, amber colored eye locks with mine briefly, but then begins to roll back in her head.

I place my hand along side of her face, trying to help guide her focus to me. "I'm taking you to get help. Hang on for me, okay?"

The girl regains a moment of clarity as she hones in on me again. A second later, her face lights up, and in that moment, I swear she recognizes me—but I've never laid eyes on her before. I'd remember someone like her. I'd remember a girl with hair as white as the snow and eyes the color of a blazing fire.

Oddly enough, the girl seems to be both in the present moment and inexplicably far away. She reaches out and places her right hand on my jawline, touching my lips with her thumb. The sensation is very intimate and I hold still, unsure of how to react.

Her voice is barely above a whisper. "You don't need to be sorry. I understand." She searches my eyes, a hint of a smile spreading across her bloodied lips, "I love you too."

All I can do is stare at her with wide eyes. Her words and the warmth of her hand are so purposeful, so *sure*, my insides constrict as she lets go and sinks back into oblivion.

Blinking away my uneasiness, I take a deep breath and slowly push back up. With her warm body cradled in my arms, I run. I don't stop when I realize how long this could take or when my lungs burn and my muscles cramp. I keep running, reliving the words... words not meant for me. Unfortunately, I can't outrun the strange, unexpected place in the pit of my stomach that kinda wishes they were.

4

TRAETON

"*Y*ou're gonna need to give me more time." I
mutter.

Ash peers down at me, crossing his bulked-
up arms over his enormous chest. His black shoulder-length
hair resting on his red Lateral Guard shirt looks like it needs
a good trim.

He's great at being intimidating; I'll give him that.

Ash doesn't say a word, but his dark eyes are black and
expectant.

"Delaney needs a decision. I know, I know." Pacing in front
of him, I spit, "Do you honestly think I'm not aware? I just
need more time. Maybe push it out a week? We've got—there's
a girl here who's healing from an attack. I can't just leave her."

The crook of Ash's eyebrow twitches.

"What?" I snort, making a face.

When a smart-ass grin emerges on Ash's face, I turn and
walk the other direction. I don't need to take his crap.

"Fine. Whatever." I wave my hand dismissively. "I'm in."

"We head out in twenty-four hours." His words reach me as I turn the corner of the tunnel.

Yeah, yeah.

I know what's at stake for this mission. If there *are* others on Pendomus living in their own society like us, we need to know. Maybe build an alliance against the Helix. Besides, I want to be there. I want to be on this mission. I just don't like the timing.

A few days. That's all I'm asking for. There's a deep sense of curiosity with this girl and I'd like to ride it out. I want to know what happened to her. Why the Morph attacked her. To get any of these answers, I need to be here for when she wakes up.

Will she remember what she said to me?

Even now, the impression of her hand lingers on my jawline, making my insides churn. Who were her words meant for? Was she outside to meet someone? A sudden wave of jealousy catches me by surprise. I have no right to feel this way—I don't even know the girl. She has every right to be meeting someone else.

Following the last twist, I enter the main section of the cavern tunnels we call home. The Haven. Outside our makeshift gathering room, Kani and Fenton are huddled together in conversation. The low lighting makes Fenton's hair appear to glow like the sun, but makes Kani look even more ominous than usual. Her almond shaped eyes turn into slivers as she notices my entrance.

"I still don't get what it wanted with her," she proclaims, shifting her weight to one side. "Or why she still needs to be here, instead of being moved to the Lateral. They have ways to deal with this sorta thing." Kani's fingers dance in front of her as she half-points in the direction of the girl in the other room.

Ignoring her, I step past them both and walk into the room where the girl rests on our bench. Her face blends into her hair, she's so pale. She lost so much blood, but at least we were able to bandage her up and stabilize her. Hopefully she'll come to soon.

"Don't ya think it's a bit weird, Trae? Coulda eaten 'er straight off. Why go for 'er eye? Doesn't make any sense," Fenton says, scratching his messy golden blond head.

"That I got no clue, guys. She was being attacked and I needed to get her out. All I know is, she couldn't be left to die."

"What if she's not sympathetic to our—situation? What if she wakes up and promptly turns us in to the Labots? What then, *Traeton?*" Kani huffs.

"There's no guarantee, guys. But she's injured, and she's not gonna be promptly going anywhere. Besides, she was out in the woods. Doesn't that tell you anything?" I pause, waiting for a reaction. Kani continues to look indignant, and Fenton sits quiet for a change. I continue, "Tells me volumes. If she were in league with the Labots, why would she be this far out?"

Pretty sure it's not the way those types roll.

"Trae's gotta point," Fenton agrees as he pushes up his yellow-tinted glasses he acquired on one of our explorations of Pendomus. "I don't think she's a threat. Look at 'er. She's so ... peaceful" He cocks his head to the side, smiling at the new girl.

Kani redirects her glare at him.

"There are plenty of what-if scenarios I can think of as to why she'd be out in the woods. You're kidding yourself if you think she couldn't be one of them. They're clever—you of all people should understand, Trae. With their mind control capabilities, they can be anyone, even pretty, dumb blonds. For all we know, she was playing up to see what idiot might come to her aid." She jabs a finger in my direction and makes a face.

"What would *you* have done, Kani? Left her to die?" I say.

"Of course not. I would've put her out of her misery and been done with it. Then gotten the hell out," she snaps back.

Well, that's pragmatic. I suppose she'd use that fancy sword she's so keen on bringing everywhere, or one of her knives.

Kani rolls her eyes, "Oh, don't make that face. If the two of you weren't so controlled by your hormones, you'd see sense too." She drops her arms and spins around to leave, her black hair twirling behind her like some sort of crazy fan. "You both gawk at her like she's some sort of new toy."

I open my mouth, trying to think of a good comeback, but nothing comes out. She's probably right. Despite the bandage over her eye, this girl is captivating ... and so different from the others. I've been outside the Helix for a long time and I've never felt this kind of magnetic compulsion before; and I don't even know her name.

Kani makes her escape down the hall, sputtering, "And now I'm stuck with her, because there's no way Delaney is letting her go back to the Helix. Super."

I sneak another sideways glance at the girl before turning back to Fenton. Hormones or not, I'd be a fool not to notice something special in her appearance. The Geneticists inside the Helix modify everyone to have dark hair and dark eyes. There are few anomalies who have light hair, like Fenton. But his family was never Helix born, so he really doesn't count.

I always thought the dark eyes made sense because of the ultraviolet light. But the standard hair requirement always drove me nuts.

Enter my blue-hair rebellion.

I don't want to be a clone of everyone else. I don't even *like* everyone else.

But with her... What's her story? Did she alter her hair or was she born this way? Was she treated differently inside? Was she quarantined too? Why was she in the woods? Why did the Morph attack her? Has she been on the outside long? Will she already be familiar with the ways out here? There's so much I was caught unaware of when I left the Helix. Humanity... ways of life. Natural courses.

My stomach flips. The biggest shock was learning about hormones and sex. If she's as clueless as I was, that'll be some kinda conversation for her. As much as I hate to admit it, Kani does make a point.

In the reflection of Fenton's archaic eyesight enhancers, the white-haired girl stirs.

Fenton notices too, as he cranes around my body and whispers, "Our mystery woman's wakin' up." His eyebrows twitch up and down suggestively.

My blood runs cold, and I hesitate. I need to talk to her, but I'm almost afraid of what she'll say.

I turn around slowly to face her. The bandage over her damaged eye wraps all the way around her head. I'm sure the whole thing is disorienting, but it was the best we could do with what we had on hand. Her shredded calf is suspended a couple inches off the bench so it's not resting on the wound. Looks like a weird contraption, hanging from the cave ceiling and looping around her foot, but it does the trick.

I raise my hand, silently motioning Fenton to stay behind,

and walk into the gathering room. It's a larger room along the cavern's tunnel system where we keep all the things that occupy our time—books, games, supplies, you name it.

Allowing a moment for her to catch her bearings, I stand off to the right of the bench. She appears so frail, and the bandage on her eye only adds to it. The wounds were deep— doubt she'll ever see outta it again. For sure she'll be scarred for the rest of her life.

Well, assuming she doesn't escape, then promptly turn us over to the Helix, and have the scars surgically altered. *Could happen.* I wouldn't admit it to the other two, though. Especially Kani.

"Hey," I whisper, leaning in.

Placing my hand on hers, I wait for her to come around. I can't even imagine what she must be going through.

Her lips part and she lets out a soft groan, but doesn't say anything intelligible.

Fenton and Kani aren't aware this girl can speak aloud yet. For me, it's another reason why I don't think she'll turn us in. People inside the Helix don't have a clue how to speak out loud. They learn once in the beginning of their download series and never use it again. Mostly because people are lazy. As soon as they've got the concepts in their head, the eLink is all they need. Why hang on to a fumbling language if you can instantly transfer your thoughts, feelings, and images through your mind?

The girl groans again, her hand twitching in mine.

Suddenly, my mouth is sucked of all moisture. Maybe *I* forgot how to speak.

"S-sorry. We, uh, aren't hooked in to the exchange-Link." I shake my head, and glance at Fenton. "If you're trying to connect that way, it won't work. We're kinda primitive here."

At the sound of my voice, she opens her good eye and slowly concentrates in my direction. As soon as we make eye contact, I take a small step back and release her hand.

The memory of her amber eye so purposefully fixed on me, the burn from her hand on my face …

Wetting my lips, I sputter, "My name is, uh, Traeton. Traeton Revasco. Trae, if it's easier to remember." I run my fingertips along my forehead. *Stupid. I sound stupid.* Set me up to explore unchartered territories and I'll be just fine. Set me in front of a beautiful woman and I'm a bumbling idiot. Great.

Fenton snickers in the doorway.

I take a beat and start again, "What's your name? How are you feeling? What were you doing out in the woods? Do you remember being attacked by the Morph?"

Way to overwhelm the girl, Trae. Good going.

Man, I'm no good at this. Where the hell's Landry when we need him?

The girl's fire-colored eye widens as she locks onto me. I didn't think it was possible for my insides to constrict more, but somehow they do. I shove my hands into my pockets.

Fenton's eyes bore into the back of my head. I wish to hell he weren't here.

The girl struggles a bit but surprises me by whispering, "Air?"

"Air? Is it hard for you to breathe?" I kick myself for not having the proper medical equipment. Maybe Kani's right—we should have moved her to the Lateral.

She shakes her head imperceptibly. A small, bony finger lifts as she points to the blue spikes on top of my head.

Oh. *Hair.*

My face flushes, and I scratch at my scalp. "Er, yeah. I altered it. Sort of a rebellion thing, I guess."

The corner of her lips curl slightly, and she croaks, "Nice."

Fenton huffs behind me. "Figures, she'd like blue."

She clears her throat and says, "Oona Copp-em."

Her speech isn't as clear as before, and I lean in. "Uh, *what?* I'm not sure what you mean."

"My—*name*." She swallows hard, taking a labored breath. "R-runa. Cophem." She closes her eye again and tenses her jaw.

"Glad to meet you, Runa." I nod, taking in her name for the first time. It suits her—it's unique, like she is. "I, uh, sorry to repeat myself, but why were you in the woods?"

"Where am I?" She shifts, ignoring my question.

"Safe. I found you pretty beat up out there."

Reopening her eye, she says, "I got attacked by the—the *bird!*"

She tries to sit upright but gasps and drops back down.

Even I wince at her pain. All the color she was regaining drains out of her cheeks.

"You okay? Lean back and rest," I tell her, offering a hand.

Kani snorts behind me.

Damn. I thought she left.

"A bird? Seriously? Those meds must still be working." Kani says.

Runa groans again and shakes her head. Then she lightly brushes my hand from her shoulder. The aftereffects of her touch linger on my fingertips as I pull back. Contact with her makes me uneasy. Like I've trapped her bird inside my body, and it's fluttering around trying to escape.

"I need ... to check on him," Runa manages to say.

"The bird?" I question, keeping my eyes locked on her. "You were attacked by the Morph."

"No—I mean, yes. But there's a bird out in the woods," she mumbles. "I need to find him. I need to know he's safe. He shouldn't have—"

"Yeah, see, I don't think that's gonna happen anytime soon. You need to rest up and heal. I'm pretty sure you about died. No offense, but you look like hell."

Runa smiles shyly and raises a hand to her hair, trying to smooth the strands. It's pretty useless, though. Her hair is a tangled mess of dead tree branches and blood caked into the damp strands.

I smirk at her and she quickly looks away. Her jaw sets, and her lips purse. A little color flushes through her cheeks, doing her some good.

"Looks like hell, but sure can talk. Interesting, quality don'tcha think, Trae?" Kani mutters. "Very Labot-like."

"Who cares how she manages ta talk?" Fenton interrupts, brushing past me. "Thanks, Traeton, for introducing us. Pft. Hi. Runa, righ'? I'm Fenton Tabet, and this's our other friend Kani Ling."

I blink hard as he actually extends his hand to her. Then, he jabs a thumb in Kani's general direction, as if they're *just friends*. I shake my head while Kani throws daggers at him with her eyes.

Runa tries to nod in acknowledgment, but doesn't accept his outstretched hand. Fenton doesn't miss a beat, pulling up a chair and taking a seat right next to her. "So, trying ta duke it out wit' tha Morph, eh? Not tha smartest thing ta do."

I take a step back to observe Fenton at work.

Was I this ridiculous when I talked to her?

I'd laugh my ass off if she can't even understand the self-enforced accent he's always been so hell bent on using just because he thinks the ladies like it.

Unfortunately, Runa bites her lower lip and says, "That was ... unintentional."

Fenton leans forward and places his hands on his knees. "Wow. I gotta say, ya *are* fantastic a' speaking. I mean, really? Unintentional? Took Trae three years 'fore he could say tha' word. Have ya been on tha outside long?"

"Check out her clothes, doofus," Kani interjects. "Nano-Thread. Issued. She's barely taken a baby step away from the Helix."

Kani, the ever-observant one. I'll admit, I almost forgot about her outfit. The gray and black Helix-issued attire lacks a certain flare but is form-fitting enough that, if left to my imagination ...

I blink hard, snapping myself back to the present.

What the hell is wrong with me? Damn. I hate when Kani's right.

Runa's eye flits from Kani, back to Fenton, and then to me. I quickly divert my gaze to my shoes, my cheeks burning.

"I go out to the woods sometimes. I had hoped— It's peaceful out there." Runa regards Fenton tensely, but adds, "I practice speaking. I didn't want to forget."

"You're very good," I say.

The corners of her lips twitch, and her eye sparkles as she regains more of her faculties. "What is this place?"

"We're your pit stop between trying to get yourself eaten and going to your next destination. Don't get too comfortable." Kani proclaims.

Way to make her feel safe, Kani.

She seriously doesn't play well with others

Runa's eyebrows pull in tight, and her smile tugs downward.

"Ignore her," I say, glaring at Kani. "You don't have to worry. We'll take care of you until you're better. Then we'll help you get to where you need to go. How's your pain?"

"I'll live," she whispers, flinching as she tries to sit up again.

I reach for the stash of medicines we have on hand, and pull out the best pain reliever we've got. Works almost instantly when it comes in contact with skin and enters the bloodstream. Pushing back her sleeve, I shake my head. Why wasn't this the first thing I offered? Shoulda been. She's gotta be in a world of hurt. I run the medicine along her hand and up her wrist. She sighs, and her eyebrows release.

"Better?" I ask.

She nods, and sinks back into her pillow.

Nodding in return, I look at the others. "Okay, guys. Introductions over. I think Runa here needs more rest." Her name rolls off my tongue, making my heart skip a beat. I don't know whether to try to get to know her or run as far away as possible.

Kani says, "Don't you think we should check to see if she needs to find the allayroom? I for one don't want her peeing on the bench."

"Good idea. Let us know how that turns out." The shock on Kani's face is gratifying as I walk by, pushing Fenton along with me to the kitchen.

I glance at Runa as Kani steps forward to hash things out.

The bench can't be all that comfortable, but it's the best I could do. Originally, I had suggested we have her rest on Kani's bed. Just about got my head bitten off. Kani's particular about neatness—nobody messes with her space. Not even Fenton is allowed in there.

If Runa's coming from the Helix, it'll be a while before she's able to sleep anyway. Passing out and going to sleep are two completely different animals. One requires a conscious decision. She's most likely used to those Helix sleep contraptions—they zap your brain so you feel like you've slept, but they're not the same. All they really do is mess with the natural cycles a human body is supposed to undergo.

I swear, the Helix wants to zap *all* the natural cycles out of humanity. Make us nothing but robots, running around doing whatever the Helix deems acceptable, all the while we think we're living and fulfilling some higher purpose.

But real life, the unmanufactured kind, isn't like that. Things are complicated and messy. People make no sense, and there are no clear answers. You have to stumble through, hoping you make it to the other side in one piece.

With Fenton by my side, we walk to the adjacent cavern space we use as a kitchen.

Fenton sits at the table and leans forward on his elbows. "I like 'er!"

"You *would*," Kani huffs as she enters behind us.

A smile spreads across my face, and despite myself, I admit, "I do too. I think we can trust her."

"Trust her? *Like* her?" Kani points at each of us consecutively. "Were the two of you dropped on your heads? You don't even *know* her. I'm going to get a thrill when she kills you both in your sleep." She turns on her heel and stomps out.

"What's 'er problem?" Fenton asks, scrunching the side of his face.

I shrug. "Hormones?"

We both chuckle.

"I HEARD THAT!" Kani yells from the tunnel.

Before we can stop ourselves, we burst out laughing. Kani can be a pain in the butt, but I've never seen her jealous before.

It's kinda funny.

5

RUNA

*T*he woman with narrow slits for eyes disappears as quickly as she can, and I'm left in my solitude. My body aches terribly, but hope trickles into my veins, tempting me into a lull of excitement. It's hard to believe others live beyond the Helix. When I'd left, I didn't have a plan. I didn't know where I was going to go, or how I was going to survive. Part of me even wanted the Morph to come.

My fingertips trace the bandage on my eye. I wish I could see what it looks like, but I already know I won't like the answer. What I wouldn't do to bathe right now, though. My garments are crusty, and I'd like to at least rinse the hard lumps of blood from of my hair.

Without a word, the girl named Kani returns, walking up beside me with her arms crossed. She's tied her black hair into a loose ponytail, and bright green streaks peek through the strands. They're not as vibrant as the man—Traeton's blue hair, though.

"You better not even *think* about turning us in," she hisses, one hand drifting to her side. Absently, she taps the hilt of a knife strapped to her leg.

I close my eye, unsure how to respond. Of all the things happening, turning anyone in is the least of my concerns, especially someone who keeps knives on them.

"It took us a long time to feel safe. To make a life of our own out here without feeling trapped. I'm not going to let you come in and ruin everything. I know you just about died, or whatever, but it doesn't give you license to do anything you want. Because if you're one of *them*—I will end you." She takes a step toward the door and turns back. "Just so we're clear."

I can't process fast enough for a response, so I stare blankly as she spins around, her ponytail bobbing from side to side as she exits.

One of them?

A repetitious tapping comes from someplace farther away. Kani stomps past the entrance to where I lay, and a moment later, Traeton and Fenton whisper to each other in hushed tones.

"Blood…"

"Feathers…"

Rolling to my right side, I curl up as best I can and put my hands over my ears. If they went back out to where I was attacked, I don't want to hear any more. I don't want to hear how mangled the bird was, or how much blood I lost.

The next thing I know, a rough, cool hand removes my hands from my head. Traeton's dark eyes are clouded with worry. Behind him, Fenton adjusts the strange yellow band covering his eyes.

"You okay?" Traeton asks, taking a seat.

"Fine ... fine," I lie. My uninjured leg starts twitching of its own accord.

"Yeah, you're the spitting image of fine," he chuckles. "Fenton and I went out to search for the bird."

"I figured by the way you were talking." I sigh.

"Tha' was one crazy mess! All tha' blood ya lost. Still looks fresh ... Snow'll do tha', ya know." A bushy brow arches above the yellow rim on his face. "It'd be pretty easy ta assume tha' whatever tussled didn't make it."

I knew it. The bird's dead.

"So, if he's not there. Was he ... eaten?" I squeak. I try to hold back the imminent threat of tears in front of complete strangers, but it doesn't work. Traeton's eyes narrow as he watches me, and my insides recoil.

"Not necessarily," Traeton says matter-of-factly. "We didn't notice any stray feathers or anything else indicating a bird was even in the area. Perhaps he flew off?"

"Are you just saying that to make me feel better?"

The corner of his mouth tips upward, revealing a dimple in his cheek. "Depends. Did it work?"

"No," I say, stifling a tiny smile. "Okay, maybe a little."

Traeton's eyes twinkle. He coughs and pushes up to a stand. "Good. I, uh ... I wouldn't worry about the bird. They're stronger than you think."

"So, why are we assuming something didn't make it?"

"Fenton meant *you.*"

Fenton grins. "I assume ya were out in tha woods for a reason. Not too many people are willin' ta do tha'. Maybe you were lookin' for a way outta the Helix. Am I righ'?"

"I ... I was out—" My head spins. "

Fenton steps forward and puts a hand on my shin. "There are options, ya know. We can help ya find a place of your own. Or," he continues, "ya might consider staying here."

Kani curses not far away.

Traeton shifts to cross his arms. "But we'll help you get to wherever you wanna go. This has to be a lot to take in."

"That would be great." I nod. "My brother, Baxten, he might be looking for me. But I doubt …"

Traeton leans back. "Were you in the Helix before?"

"Yes." I reply, swallowing hard.

"Well, if he was gonna come out searching for you, he probably did already. You were unconscious for nearly thirty-six hours."

My jaw pops open. I've never been unconscious, let alone for so long.

"Do I have to decide what to do now?" I whisper. "Not that I'm not grateful. I just have a lot to think about."

So much has happened. Of course I'd like the option to stay, but according to Kani, I no longer have the option to leave. As unhappy as I am with my professional appointment, do I really want to *never* go back to the Helix? What if I never see Baxten again?

"Take as much time as ya need. In tha meantime, would ya like some supper?" A mischievous glint flashes in Fenton's eyes as he raises his yellow band to the top of his head.

"What is that yellow thing covering your eyes?" I ask, unable to help myself.

Fenton removes it from his face. "Wha'? This?"

"They're called glasses." Traeton shrugs. "They used to be for blocking sunlight, or maybe correcting vision before the technology we have. Fenton here just thinks he looks better with them on." Taking a step forward, he messes Fenton's yellow hair. "Anything that hides this lunatics face is good by me."

Fenton covers his heart. "Thanks, Trae. I feel tha love."

"So, what this supper thing?" I question.

They both burst into full-on chuckles.

"What's so funny?" I giggle with their infectious laughter.

"Yeah, Trae, wha'so funny?"

Traeton raises his eyes to the ceiling. "Nothing—just, you'll see. This will be a whole new experience for you."

I try to sit up, but the movement sends shooting pain up and down my entire body.

"Here, let me help you. You shouldn't be trying to get up on your own." Traeton reaches up and unhooks my leg from the contraption holding my bandaged leg up. Not waiting for a response, he scoops me from the bench. My muscles flare in the momentum, but calm almost instantly. I wrap my arm around his neck, trying to make bearing my weight easier for him. He doesn't even seem fazed. His body is so warm, and his pulse beats against my rib cage.

"I coulda done tha'," Fenton mumbles as we walk by.

I search Traeton's profile, trying to figure him out. He's been so kind, and he doesn't even know me. After a moment, the faintest hint of his dimple appears, but he keeps his eyes straight ahead.

We enter another cavern room adjacent to the last one. The space is brightly lit and open. A large rectangular table sits in the middle with low-lying benches on either side. Kani glares at me from the far end of the table, but I smile back as sweetly as possible. A pungent odor fills the air, and I wrinkle my nose.

Fenton takes a position near the odor and shifts things around inside some sort of container. None of what he's doing makes any sense, but then, that's been the case from the moment I woke up here. Traeton sets me on a bench and

I shift my bandaged leg outward. Spikes of pain shoot through the surface of my skin, and I flinch.

"Be right back, guys." Traeton ruffles his hand through his blue hair and smiles at me. "Fenton, don't bore her to death, okay?" He hesitates a moment, like he wants to say something to me, but he turns and walks out.

As I watch his frame leaving the room, a sudden wave of disappointment washes over me. I hope he's coming back soon. Something about him makes me feel safe. My eyes flit to Fenton, who smiles broadly in return.

The muscles in my shoulders and back groan as I struggle to keep myself upright. I wish I could lean back. I set my hands on the table and take a tense glance around the room.

Kani frowns at me from the other end of the table, and abruptly stands. "Does she have to eat with us too? Can't you just bring her a dish? It's not as if she'll stomach the soup, anyway."

"Eat? As in … food?" I gape, the inklings of recognition dawning on me.

My mother's a RationCaps chemist, so I've grown up my whole life hearing about the perils of food and how her way is better. No one is ever nutrient deficient or overweight from her RationCaps. Evidently, that was not the case before they were perfected.

Kani frowns again and fiddles with the ends of her green blouse. It's zipped halfway up, revealing an off-white shirt underneath. The white one is low cut, exposing the upper part of her collarbones in a graceful loop. I've never seen such beautiful clothing before. I peek down at my dirty, damaged NanoTech garments.

Bleck.

"She's notta dog, Kani," Fenton replies and glances at me

over his shoulder. "'Sides, she could probably use a break from tha' bench she'd been restin' on."

"To what? Sit on another bench?" Kani huffs. "I'm losing my appetite. She hasn't even washed the blood out of her hair yet." She shivers noticeably, and my face instantly flushes.

"Is there someplace I could go to wash up?" I ask, swallowing my pride.

She rolls her eyes and drops her mouth open. "Of course. We're not animals."

"Well, can I get some help?"

"The sooner the better," Kani mutters under her breath.

Fenton says, "Hang on, we go' time. This soup's gotta sit anyway. I can help ya, Runa." He sets down some sort of utensil and wipes his hands across his blue pants.

"The hell you will," Kani sputters. "Traeton, *you* do it."

Pausing mid stride back into the room, Traeton examines each of our faces with wide eyes. "Do ... what?"

"Take *Ruin*-a to the Oasis to clean her gross self."

Traeton's chin drops open for a second, and he shakes his head. "Yeah, I don't think ... I mean, shouldn't we wait? Supper's gonna ... C—Can't *you* do it?" He points back at Kani.

"Do I look like I can drag her butt all the way down to the Oasis? I mean, honestly, Trae. You'll live." Kani nudges him toward me.

My face sears with humiliation. Am I so gross no one even wants to bring me to get cleaned up?

"Seriously, guys, I go' no problem bringin' 'er down there," Fenton offers again.

"No, but you will." Kani's jaw sets and she places a hand on her hip.

Turning to Fenton, Traeton says abruptly, "No ... no, it's fine. I was just ... doesn't matter." He shakes his hands dismissively. "I'll take her. Kani, can you find a change of clothes for her? We should really fix up her trouser leg." He closes his eyes and pinches the bridge of his nose.

"You—want—me—to—what?" Kani's eyes narrow to laser beam precision.

"Don't be so melodramatic," he retorts.

Kani gives me a once-over and heads out the door. "She'd better not stretch them."

Traeton's shoulders drop and sits down across the table. "Sorry about all that."

I attempt a smile, but I'm pretty sure it's more of a grimace.

In this light, Traeton's hair is a brilliant blue and the color stands out against his black shirt. Like Kani's, his shirt is partially zipped, revealing a gray shirt underneath.

Traeton places his hands on the table and taps his fingers lightly against the wood. His eyes wander, landing on everything but me as we sit for a long, awkward moment.

Kani finally saunters back with a stack of clothes in her hand. She plunks them down unceremoniously on the table in front of me. "Do *not* wreck them."

"Come on, Runa. We should get going. We have a fifteen-minute walk, or so." Traeton shifts out of his seat and moves around the table. Once again, his arms slide around my body and he hoists me out of my seat. With one arm still around me, he grabs the clothes Kani brought in. He places the folded clothing in my lap and smiles awkwardly.

If circumstances were different, I'd love to be in his company for a walk. Instead, this is going to be the longest fifteen minutes of my life.

6

RUNA

*T*he longer I'm here, the more questions rattle around in my head.

Why are the three of them living here? What made them leave the Helix? How did they discover this place? What is it like to live here? What's the Lateral I keep hearing about? Why do they eat primitively? Why does Fenton speak weird? Is Kani *always* so—crabby? Why *blue*?

Traeton's focus is solely on the walk ahead—he hasn't spoken a word. Not one.

An interrogation would be better than this.

Tunnel sconces light up every ten meters or so as he takes me to wherever this Oasis thing is. The shadows show how rocky the cavern walls are, drawing my eyes to the dark crevices leading off in new directions. I can't believe the size of this place.

"How big are these tunnels?" I finally break the silence and crane around to view Traeton's stoic face.

He keeps his eyes straight ahead, "Fairly big, I guess."

"This place is amazing. If I'd known about *this*—"

"If you had known?" Curiosity plays at Traeton's tone, and for the first time in what feels like forever, he looks at me.

I bite the inside of my cheek. "Things are ... less than perfect for me inside the Helix."

"Ah. Is that why you left?"

I sigh. How can I explain everything that pushed me to leave? Would he even understand?

"I've always been different, as you can probably see. I'm the only one I know who likes being outside." I steal a glance at his face, watching his eyes for any sign of disapproval. When he offers none, I add, "Well, until meeting all of you."

"I can't imagine not being outside." Traeton offers. "It's my second home, really."

A grin creeps across my face and I pull myself a little closer to him.

The minutes tick by like hours as he continues walking in silence.

"Traeton, if you set me down, I'll try to hop along on my left leg. I might need you for balance, though."

He shakes his head and winks. "Nah, I got this."

My cheeks flush, but I smile again.

There's no way I could carry another person fifteen steps, let alone fifteen minutes.

"Sorry about all the confusion earlier," he says.

"I'm sorry too."

"For what?" he asks, surprise playing in his tone.

I wrinkle my nose. "For being gross. For needing someone to help me get cleaned up. I'm sure it's not what you want to be doing."

I look away, letting my hair fall between us like a curtain.

"Honestly, it's no big deal. I don't mind. Besides, you do have a pretty good reason for needing help," he chuckles.

"Well, thank you anyway."

In the distance, I make out the faint hum of running water. However, as we get closer, the sound is more like a hundred Helix showers, all running at the same time.

"Stay here. I'll trigger the lights. It's a little rocky and if I can't see where I'm going, I'm liable to drop you." Traeton sets me down and steps into the darkness. "I'm sure you could do without that."

Instead of doing as instructed, I hobble behind him, holding the wall for balance. He's done enough for me, the least I can do is manage a few steps on my own.

The lights flicker on as I enter the space they call the Oasis. Five sconces illuminate the upper part of the walls, and they cast deep shadows in the grooves of the natural rock formations.

It's breathtaking. From what seems like everywhere, water pours into two large pools, one on either side of the walkway.

"Uh, well, okay. That's the bathing side." Traeton points to the left. "Soap and such should be over there." His face turns white, and he starts backing toward the entrance. "You should have a towel with your clothes here. I'll just—I'm gonna be—yeah—out there," he points out the way we came. "Yell if you need me."

My head is spinning and I'm suddenly overcome with fear. What if he leaves me here? Would he? Could I find my way back?

"Will you be far?" I blurt, making an attempt to smile.

"No. Not too far. In the tunnel here." He shifts his eyes and backs out farther. "I'll give you some privacy."

"Thanks," I mumble, wishing I could voice more of my concerns. It's ridiculous to question his motives, but I'd never survive in here if he left me alone.

On the opposite side of the walkway to where he pointed is another pool of water. Though he didn't mention what it's for, on the floor are large containers. Suddenly parched, I hop over to it. Water trickles down, running over the stones before free-falling into the standing pool below. I reach out and let the chilly water flow over my hands.

Cupping the water, I drink in some of the cool, deliciousness. It's better than anything I've ever tasted, and I can't seem to get enough. I drink until my stomach aches, which doesn't take long.

I scan over my shoulder, using the nearest rock for balance. This task—bathing in open water instead of a shower—it's a little daunting. The area is so exposed. A few days ago, I had no idea water existed like this on our planet. Does this come in on its own, or is it somehow created by Traeton and his group?

The scent of wet dirt surrounds me, a clean sort of smell that settles some of my anxiety. Smiling to myself, I take a tentative hop to the bathing water's edge and glance down into the mirrored reflection.

My smile instantly evaporates.

I look awful.

My hair's a tangled, bloody mess, and the bandage covering my left eye is worse.

Slowly, I sit on the nearest rock and struggle to get undressed. It's a relief to free myself of the ripped NanoTech garments, but everything aches, despite the medicine.

I remove the bandage around my calf and pieces of the absorbent fabric stick to the dried gash, reopening the wound. Blood slowly trickles to the ground, darkening the stone at my feet.

There's no sign of Traeton in the black void.

I remove my undergarments and clumsily make my way into the water. Colder than I expect, I'm not sure I can even bathe in it. However, the longer I stand, water up to my ankles, the warmer it seems. I hop along the rocks until the water is deep enough for me to submerge most of my body. My injured calf itches, and I'm unsure if I should even be getting it wet.

Trying not to get the bandage on my face wet, I bend forward slightly to rinse the blood from my hair. My footing falters, and I fall face first into the frigid water. My hands instinctively reach out, but I don't find the bottom. Instead, bubbles surround my body and the current is so strong, I can't tell which way is up as I flail against the water.

I'm blinded by a fierce white light blasting through my entire perception—even my damaged eye senses it, sees it. I want air—I *need* air.

A woman's voice rings out clear and crisp, as if she were in front of me.

"Runa, Daughter of Five, please don't be frightened. We are here to protect and guide you. Your place in this world is more important than you realize and we are doing all we can to prepare you for what comes next. Even now, from this great length, we are helping to speed your regeneration. Allow the affects of the water around you to sink in. At this moment, it is imperative you listen closely, for we don't have much time.

When you vacated the Tree of Burden, you initiated the seal— the gateway to us needs to be reopened and you must return to us. The Tree holds everything you will need to protect yourself and

Pendomus from the oncoming storm Videus is stirring. He is ruthless and he will stop at nothing to acquire you. We must not allow this to happen.

This won't make sense now, but it will. In order to regain access, you must reacquire the key, which will be a most difficult task, as it remains inside the Helix. Until you are strong enough to retrieve it, stay hidden amongst the shadows. At this very moment, you are being sought after by those who wish to do you harm. Be watchful. Your guardian will connect with you when you are ready. There is much you don't understand about this world. But above all else, you must be protected. At any cost."

I break the surface and fill my lungs deeply with fresh air. My arms thrash against the water, groping for something to hold onto. A high-pitched noise reverberates off the walls, stinging my ears. In the same instant, Traeton bursts in, an expression of complete shock—no, *horror*—on his face. He immediately spins around to face the other way, his hand flying up, shielding his eyes.

My heart vaults into my throat, and as quickly as I can, I dive behind the nearest rock outcropping. The high-pitched noise goes silent as I close my mouth.

"What the—Are you okay? Why were you screaming?" he calls over his shoulder.

I watch him closely, waiting for any sign of a shift in his demeanor. When nothing changes, I allow my shoulders to unclench.

"I ... yeah. Sorry. Don't turn around, okay?"

Shaking, I don't let my eyes leave his silhouette. He stands stone still. Taking a deep breath, I move toward the towel.

What just happened?

Daughter of Five? Tree of Burden? *Guardian?* Did I bump my head when I fell? What do I tell him?

I chew on my lip.

"Sorry I screamed. Just now, when I was under the water, it was like it … *reacted* and I got disoriented. It reminded me of when I was floating in the tree." The last sentence slips out unintentionally, and I scrunch my face.

Great. I'm sure he's going to think I'm insane. Heck, *I* think I'm insane hearing voices this far out. The constraints of the eLink require proximity and even if we were right on top of the Helix, the rock alone would block the signal. So how someone could enter my mind—I just don't know.

Dropping the towel to the ground, I keep my eyes on his back and pull on my undergarments swiftly.

"Reacted?" he says, his voice arching higher.

With trembling hands, I hold up the white shirt Kani gave me. I don't understand how I'd possibly stretch the fabric. It has to be at least two sizes too big.

"It was like the water was boiling around me," I tell him, sliding the shirt over my head. "Maybe I was out of my senses, but it felt like the water did the same before when I was in the tree. Boiling hot … and then … I saw you. Or at least, I think it was you."

I yank up the brown trousers and survey how they fit. They, like the shirt, are large and the fabric flows loosely around my legs. They aren't necessarily pretty, but they do have a nice flow to them.

"You uh, saw me at the tree?" Traeton's voice is gruff and he rubs the back of his neck.

"I think so. Well, your blue hair, at least," I say. I point to the top of his head and drop my hand to my side.

He can't see you, Runa. Back turned, remember?

"Is that all you remember? About me, I mean."

His question catches me off guard, and I look up. "Yes, just blue."

"Ah." He shifts to one side.

My encounter moments ago circles around in my mind. Despite having no visuals to connect to, the sensation was extremely real—as if the woman was right beside me. Or connected to the eLink...

"Traeton, what do you know about the tree you found me in?" I ask.

He shifts slightly and says, "Uh, not much. That was the first time I'd noticed the tree before. It was sorta weird, though."

"How do you mean?" I ask, sliding my foot into my boot and letting it constrict to my size.

"Well, besides the obvious of standing water—" Trae raises a hand to his forehead and taps it gently as he thinks. "The tree itself, though... There was something unusual about it. Like it had a mind of its own."

I stop in mid-step of the next boot. "A mind of its own?"

Relief floods my body as my curiosity piques. He's had his own experiences with the tree.

"Yeah. When I was trying to get you out, the water rose and basically flushed us out of the tree. Then it froze solid."

"*Really?*"

"Truly. I've never seen anything like it." He nods. "Can I turn around yet?"

"Sure. I'm decent." I say.

Traeton continues to stand still for a moment. Then, with a nod of his head, he turns around.

"I need to go back there again." I confide. "To the tree. It's important."

His mouth drops open slightly, but he doesn't say anything.

Why is he not saying anything?

I rub my hand across the fabric of my thighs in an attempt to make the wrinkles lie flat. "Does this look okay? Seems a little big."

"Oh, yeah. Very fine," he swallows, then continues, "So the tree, huh? Okay, I can help you find it from here. Was this a special place to you before the attack?"

"Yeah. Something like that."

"Alright, it's settled. As soon as you're better, I'll take you back to the tree." He grins.

Smiling back, I push a wet strand of hair behind my ear, but it brushes against the wound on my face, making me flinch. I took no notice that the bandage must've fallen off in the water. With my fingertips, I touch the swollen flesh and cringe. In a swift movement, I pull the same strand forward again.

"My bandage—I was trying to keep—I think I may have lost it." I say.

Shrugging, he says, "No big deal. We can get you a new one. You probably needed to rinse your eye off anyway. Let your wound heal fresh."

With the extra role of bandage Kani slipped in with the clothing, I'd love nothing more than to cover my face. Unfortunately, the wound on my leg is trying to adhere to my trousers.

Picking up the roll, and lifting my trouser leg, I turn to Traeton, "Do you think you could help me get this around my calf?"

His eyes widen. "I don't think I'm the best one to—it might be better to let—"

Wonderful, I'm insane *and* incapable. "N-never mind. I can do it," I stammer.

I sit down and pull back the fabric on my right leg again.

"No, here. I'm sorry. I can help. I'm just … no good with this sort of thing." Traeton kneels and takes the roll from me. He takes my leg in his warm hands and places it on his bent knee.

My cheeks burn, and I hold my breath. His head is so close, the varying shades of blue and black sparkle as they stick out in all directions. An odd sensation washes over me. I'd like to touch his hair—run my hands through it.

He raises his eyes to meet mine, and I blink away my wildly inappropriate thoughts. The way he observes me from under his eyebrows makes me bite my lip. He has nice eyes. For a moment, it's like we're magnetic. Slowly, his face inches toward mine. My breath hitches, because I don't know what this means. I'm drawn to his mouth, as his tongue once again grazes his lower lip.

The connection is abruptly broken as he shakes his head, his lashes fluttering.

"Whoa. I … uh … Ready to head back?" He breathes out, and pushes to a stand, brushing off his knees.

What was that all about?

"Uh— if you are," I say.

The dressing on my wound is hardly noticeable as I stand up, letting my trouser leg fall back into place. I set my dirty garments inside my towel, the way I would back home, to make them easier to carry.

He helps me through the narrow passage before picking me up again. Trying to make things easier for him, I reach around and pull myself closer. As I do, Traeton inhales sharply.

"I'm sorry. Am I hurting you? Do you need me to shift?" I ask, acutely aware of how heavy I must be.

Clearing his throat, he says, "No, I'm fine."

Shadows play across his face, and I wish I knew what was going on in his head. So much about him baffles me.

"Why did you do it?" I ask.

His footing falters a little, and he replies, "Sorry, do—do what?"

"Pull me from the tree. Save me. Bring me here. Take your pick." I shrug.

I'm not sure what it is, or why I need to understand his motives, but I can't help myself. The indifference in his face evaporates briefly, and he sets me down.

"I don't know. I couldn't let you die," he says, pacing back and forth.

"Why not? You don't know me." I try to understand things from his perspective, but he doesn't make any sense.

He stops pacing and says, "You're right, I don't know you. Does that mean if roles were reversed, you woulda let me die?" His intense brown eyes burn into mine and the corners of his mouth curve upward.

The thought of leaving *anyone*—but for some reason, him especially, to die ...

I shake my head. "No. Absolutely not." Refusing to be helpless, I turn and hop along the tunnel of my own accord. On the floor to my right is a detailed set of spirals that have been etched across the dirt. I tilt my head and move closer, but Traeton steps in front and brushes them away with his foot.

"Erm, okay. So, what's the deal, then? Why did you ask?" he questions, his eyebrows knit together.

"I don't know. You seem so ... *different.* Hard to figure out. You know?" I offer.

Tilting his head slightly, he faces forward and walks along side me.

"Yeah. I can kinda relate."

I search his eyes. "You do?"

"Well, you're way more interesting than me, for starters. Your attack—whatever just happened back there," he points back at the Oasis. For a moment he seems distant, then he blinks rapidly, color creeping into his cheeks as he looks away.

"Yeah... that was weird." I concede, my cheeks flushing.

"So we're in agreement, then. You're way more confounding."

Without any further discussion, he steps forward and scoops me back into his arms.

7

RUNA

"*C*ome on Trae, couldn't you re-bandage her eye before you brought her back in here? It's all gooey." Kani moans as we enter the kitchen space.

Traeton gently sets me in the spot I vacated earlier and turns to her. "All things considered, I think you should handle that, Kani. Where's Fenton?"

"Mainframe checkups." She spits back.

Traeton places a hand on my knee, "I'll be right back, Runa. Kani will take care good care of your eye."

A deep level of disappointment sweeps through me as he exits. I don't want Kani to tend to my eye—I'd much rather have him do it.

Maybe it was the water, or the strange voice that invaded my mind, perhaps even being around Traeton. I'm not sure— but I feel different. On top of everything, there are nuances I can't make sense of and body language I can't interpret. I'm missing things, and I desperately want to understand. This place is so different from the Helix. There's a mystery at every turn, and I want to unravel them all. But I don't even know where to start.

Mumbling something to herself, Kani leaves the room right behind Traeton. A moment later, she returns and throws down a metallic tray with some sharp-looking objects placed in the center.

"Don't move. I'm gonna make this quick."

My eyes widen as she takes a seat in front of me, and a soft, powerful light illuminates my face.

"What is that?" I shrink back, blinded.

"Hold *still*," she commands, reaching toward my face. Reflexively, I lean further back.

With little need to be gentle, she tilts my head back and rubs a smelly ointment into the lacerations. Her hands are steady and sure of themselves, as if she's done this a thousand times before. The expression on her face is determined and almost pleasant, like she's in her element.

Why didn't I realize this before? *She's their medic.*

"Oh, don't be so proud of yourself," she warns, as if reading my mind. "You should've figured it out eons ago."

I shrug and manage a sincere smile. "I figured Fenton was the one to bandage me up. Though, to be honest, I'm not sure why. He seems more the doctoring type, I guess." I cover my mouth, trying to hide my laughter. "You would have been my *last* guess."

"That was the plan," she tilts her chin up and examines my eye. "I was hoping you would be on your merry little way by now, never the wiser. So much for that."

With a cleansing wipe, she rubs gently at my face and her expression borders bewilderment. Finally, she says, "What the hell?"

Anxiety rushes through my veins. I shudder when she sets

down the cloth, which is completely covered in brown sludge. "What's going on? Is my eye—how bad is it? Never mind, I don't want to know."

Kani hops up and runs down the hall. "Oh shut it. You've got to *see* this."

When she returns, a small handheld mirror is clutched in her fingers.

"Look," she says.

The mirror spins around in her hands and shines directly at me. Three long, angry scabs run from my scalp, over my eyebrow and eye—all the way down to my jaw. Everything's red and puffy.

"I'm hideous," I say, diverting my eyes from the mirror.

"Well, yeah. Yeah, ya are," she concedes, "However, not what I'm talking about."

"Would you say what you want to say? I don't get where you're going."

"Okay, I'll keep things simple, brainless. You have scabs." When my expression remains unchanged, she repeats, "*Scabs.* It's been three days. When I bandaged you up, the wounds on your face were enough to gross me out. Which, for your information, takes a lot. Skin was flapping around everywhere," her hands flap back and forth, "But this—should have taken *weeks* to heal this well."

I take another look at the dark lines puckering on my skin. "What does this mean?"

"Means I am *damn* good!" she says, bursting into laughter. "Let's check out that eyeball of yours."

Despite what she says, the memory of the voice in the Oasis comes to mind.

... we are doing all we can to speed your regeneration ...

Could this be someone—or something else's doing?

Shaking a small tube and emptying the contents into a clean cloth, she wipes at my eyelids. The cool, tingly sensation of the cleanser is nice as she uses small, gentle swipes.

"Okay, I'd like to see the damage to your retina. It was too crazy before." She edges closer, slowly dimming her light. "Besides, I don't have the medical tools to deal with that kind of trauma."

The muscles around my eyelids don't want to cooperate, as she gently pulls them apart. After a couple of sticky attempts, she's able to get the eye open, but only a slit.

"Can you open it any further? How do the muscles feel?" Kani watches me with an ardent expression, but she doesn't force anything.

Surprisingly, there's some vision in the damaged eye. I bend forward, trying to focus through my eyelashes. Everything is blurry but becomes clearer the longer I keep it open, and the more I blink. Both eyes start to work in unison, and things I hadn't seen a moment ago emerge.

The room is filled with little orbs of light.

"*So?*" she asks.

"I have some vision, but I think the eye is damaged." I squint, trying to make sense of what I'm viewing. The little orbs float in and out around me, almost dancing happily. The stone wall appears to undulate, making my insides flip. I close my eyes and steady myself on the bench.

She sighs, "That we already knew, Princess Obvious."

"I mean—I'm *seeing* things—little specks of light all around us. I wasn't seeing that before."

"Well, you eye's heavily damaged. I'm surprised you have any sight at all. My guess is the photoreceptors in your retina are probably damaged," she offers, leaning in for a closer look.

"I'm gonna pull your eyelids apart so I can examine the reaction. This is probably gonna hurt a little."

Not giving me time to respond, she uses her thumb and forefinger to separate my eyelids. When our eyes meet, she yanks her hand back, and gasps.

"Is my eyeball—*gone?*"

My hand flies up to cover my face.

"How would you be able to see out of it, dufus?" She rolls her eyes. "Um... no. I've never—Have you always—? Oh, just look." She spins the mirror around again and focuses it on my damaged eye. Gleaming between the scabs is a swirling bright blue iris where my amber color should be—but beyond that, my eyeball is intact.

My chin drops open and I touch my face with the tips of my fingers.

"How can this be? I felt it squish—felt the claws." I say.

"So you're telling me this eye wasn't always a freaky blue?" She places the mirror face down in her lap.

I roll my eyes.

"Wow. That, *was creepy.*" She stands up and sets the mirror on the tray. "I don't know what to tell you. Maybe you just thought that had happened? I'm sure an attack like this is pretty disorienting."

A lopsided grin graces Traeton's lips as he enters the room. I rake my hair forward, trying to hide the damaged side of my face.

"Everything okay in here?" he asks, his eyebrows wrinkling.

"Yeah, Runa. Everything okay?" Kani's tone is bordering playful, and I shift uncomfortably. A slight smirk spreads slowly across her face.

"I—uh." I mumble, still trying to wrap my head around what's going on.

Kani leans toward Traeton and says, "I think you better have a look at Runa's eye."

There's no way to avoid this, so I sit still and wait. A part of me wants to tell them about the voice at the Oasis ... but I doubt it's a good thing to hear voices when you shouldn't be connected to the eLink.

"May I?" Traeton is suddenly in front of me with his hand outstretched. Those deep brown eyes sparkle with a mixture of concern and curiosity.

I nod and find a spot on the floor to stare at. I'm surprised he can't hear my heart thumping as he gently pushes back my hair, and tucks the strand behind my left ear.

When I meet his gaze, his sudden inhalation is all the verification I need.

I raise my hand and shield my face as I turn away. "It shouldn't look like this. I don't know what happened ... As if I needed to be more of a freak."

He places a warm hand on my shoulder, and I shudder away the goose bumps.

"No, Runa. Your eye is—well, *amazing,* actually. I'll admit, the color surprised me. But look at how you've healed," he takes a breath, "astounding."

"Wha'sup wit 'er eye?" Fenton asks as he enters and cranes around Traeton. I stare directly at him. "Oh. *Whoa.*"

"What about your sight?" Traeton asks.

I shrug, trying to give an air of nonchalance. "I can see out of it, but I'm seeing orbs of light."

"I already told her the photoreceptors are probably messed up." Kani says.

"Does anyone else in your family have two different

colored eyes? I'm curious because I've never seen this before."

"No, this isn't— " I shake my head. "I wasn't— "

"She wasn't born with two different eye colors. Yeesh." Kani finishes for me.

"Oh." Realization spreads across Traeton's face. "*Oh,*" he repeats.

"How'd tha' happen, then?" Fenton muses.

"I wish I knew." With a quick hand stroke, I release the bangs from my ear and let them fall forward.

"Don't we all?" Kani's expression hardens slightly as she starts cleaning up the used bandages and her supplies. "This will have to do for now. Just let it get some air and breathe. Should continue to heal up fine."

Elsewhere in the cavern, a loud beeping pierces through the tunnels.

"That'll be Landry again." Traeton says, "I'll go see what he needs."

Without another word, he walks out again.

"Who's Landry?" I ask.

"That'd be me obnoxious brother." Fenton winks.

"He's actually pretty cool." Kani admits with a grin. "But we can't have the two of them in the same room or they'll go off on a tech-talk that will last a week."

"Tha's 'cause he think he knows ever'thin'. Time ta eat, ladies." Fenton walks back to the counter, clanking around, until four steaming containers slide across the table. I pull the closest one to me and glance down. A brown, gelatinous goop not unlike what came off my eye puddles inside.

I raise my eyes, and lean toward Fenton. "What is this?"

Fenton beams, "Only the bes' soup in all a' Pendomus. Okay, now here's a li'l etiquette, 'cause I betcha don' know if ya were in tha Helix. This—is a spoon." He lifts a metallic object and waves it in front of me. "Use this ta scoop up tha soup. Behold," he demonstrates by shoving the spoon into the soup and cramming a large lump into his mouth. "See? Easy. And *delicious*."

Kani takes a seat beside Fenton and rolls her eyes. "Okay, wow. You don't have to eat like this slob over here. It can be done a little more ... Delicately," she dips her spoon and takes a small sip. "Truthfully, it's a million times better than the RationCap crap."

My face flushes with an unexpected desire to defend my mother.

"What's wrong with RationCaps? I've never had a problem with them," I respond.

They both stare at me wide-eyed.

"I don't understand why you'd think this is better." I shift my gaze back to the soup, leaving it untouched.

"There's a whole hell of a lot you don't *understand*." Kani says, a touch of animosity resurfacing. She taps her fingertips across her lips.

"Then explain," I offer.

"You crash-landed into our world with your freaky attack and strange eyeball. Not the other way around. Since we're on topic, I think we *should* have an open discussion? Just not on your terms. Sound good?" She leans forward, resting her chin on the top of her right hand. "What the hell were you doing in the woods? *Really?*"

"You wouldn't understand," I say, dropping my eyes to my hands.

"This is complete crap. Admit it. You're one of them," Kani spits.

"One of who? Who do you think I am?" I slap my hand on

the table and point to my face. "Take a gander at my eye. Did I do this to myself?"

"Maybe you did. Wouldn't put it past your kind," Kani says, crossing her arms over her body.

Fenton turns to her and whispers, "Come on, doll. She's no' in league with 'em. She's no decoy."

Kani stares at the wall behind me and whispers, "How do you *know*, Fenton?"

"Kani," his voice is soft and he places a hand over hers. "Ya already know it too."

Instead of pulling her hand back, she visibly relaxes under his touch.

"What does the term *Labot* mean to you?" she asks, her eyes burning into mine.

Both Fenton and Kani watch me closely.

"What?" I scrunch my face, confused.

"Labot. It's a simple word. What does it mean to you?" she repeats.

"Nothing," I shrug, "I've never heard the word before."

Kani scrutinizes my every move, but something in her face noticeably softens. With a sigh, she leans back. "I'm not saying I believe you—"

"I think wha' Kani's tryin' ta say is, she's sorry," Fenton says, nudging Kani in the shoulder. "Righ'?"

"I'm confused." I reply.

Kani sets her spoon down. "Time you listen up, and learn something, then. There are people inside the Helix who are *not* good people. Technically, I'm not even sure they're people."

"We needed ta be sure you weren't one of 'em," Fenton finishes.

"Well, I'm *not*," I tell them. "These people—Labots? Who

are they? What do they want?"

A mixture of unreadable emotions play out across their faces.

"Depends on their mission. Mostly, they want to keep you silent," Kani laments. "To protect the secret."

"The secret?" I ask.

"Everything you think you know is one big lie," Kani states. Her jaw clenches, but she doesn't elaborate.

"What do you mean?" I lean forward.

"If ya ain't one of 'em, ya can't go back. They'd kill ya on sight, Runa. Labots are tha' bad."

Fenton reaches over and rubs Kani's back in small circles, but neither of them say anything else. Instead, she leans into him and closes her eyes. They're so—intimate. It's unheard of in the Helix—and yet, they share this moment. *Together*. I divert my eyes, contemplating what makes them behave this way. My whole life I've wanted to reach out to people like this—but according to the Helix etiquette, it's wrong.

Isn't it?

"Soup's gettin' cold," Fenton nods at my bowl.

I raise my spoon to my lips. All eyes are on me as I do so, and immediately I regret putting the viscous brown goo in my mouth. The soup is lukewarm and tastes like feet smell. I drop the spoon back into the bowl and my body shudders. Wishing I could get the taste off, I stick out my tongue.

Both Kani and Fenton burst out laughing.

"Pretty good, eh? You'll get used ta tha'. The more ya try, the more ya'll be able to pick out different flavors. Tha's wha' your tongue's for, didn't ya know? Well, amongs' other things, but we'll wait to regale you with those types of tales." Fenton says, wiggling his eyebrows.

He's so absurd, and yet I can't help but giggle.

"Ha! Did ya catch tha'? I got 'er ta smile," he says triumphantly.

Unable to help myself, I admit, "It tastes *awful*."

Kani laughs. "Here, try this." She pulls a hunk off what resembles a rock and hands it to me. "This is bread. Try dipping it in the soup, and take a bite."

"Will it improve the taste?" I ask, sniffing at the bread.

"C'mon, now. My soup's *amazin'*," leaning in to me, Fenton says, "You're body just has ta ge' used ta eatin'."

"I'm telling you—that'll take a while. RationCaps take their time weeding from your system." Kani swallows another spoonful of soup.

Fenton rolls his eyes. "*Women.* Food is wha' your body wants. Not tha' synthetic crap inside the Helix. They like messin' with people. If ya stick around, you'll notice a big difference. You'll see."

"What do you mean? Why would they mess with people?"

"Because they *can*," Kani says bitterly.

I shake my head. "Like I was saying earlier, my mother's a RationCaps chemist. Her profession is highly esteemed. If this were true, why would she do it? Our survival depends on them."

"That's just what they want you to believe, brainless. Remember what we were just talking about? Besides, she wouldn't have any idea. People inside do as they're expected to do. They aren't trained to search beyond the surface," Kani says, rotating her spoon in little circles. "People are drones of society. They like to be told what to think rather than think for themselves."

Even to me, that was evident.

"So, you gonna run back to Mommy and turn us in, then?" Kani's accusatory tone resurfaces.

Her words sting; she doesn't know me, let alone my nonexistent relationship with my mother. Even if I did choose to go back, I would never bring up this group to her. There would be no point. She wouldn't listen.

"I won't say anything, if that's what you're worried about," I say. "Besides, I—I don't want to go back."

Conflicted relief flickers across Kani's face.

"Why do you want to be out here, Kani?" I ask.

"Because it's better than the alternative," she admits, taking another bite. "People inside don't really have a life. They're servants to the system, nothing more. They just don't have the sense to realize it. At least out here, I'm in charge of my destiny. If I wanted to live in the Lateral, I could. If I want to live here, I can."

"C'mon. You're no' gonna eat any more o' my soup? Try again. Make a guy feel special, would ya?" Fenton asks, pointing at my bowl.

"What's in this, anyway? It looks like mashed up tree bark."

"Probably better if ya don't 'ave all the details," he mumbles, stirring his own soup sheepishly.

Kani's head bobs up and down slowly.

That's not very comforting.

"If our bodies respond better to—*food*," I wave my hand in front of my soup, "what made us stop? Why create Ration-Caps at all?"

"May 'ave something to do with tha supply," Fenton explains. "Easy for us ta gather enough organic food fer *our* meals. Bu' on a larger scale, tha' would be next ta impossible on Pendomus. The hot side of tha planet burns up just abou' anything edible, and the cold side ... well, no' much can grow there, either. You 'ave ta be resourceful."

"Okay ..."

"Or, on a simpler level, by pushing RationCaps, they can control what everyone consumes," Kani says, tossing down her hunk of bread. It bounces off her plate and rolls across the table.

"But still, why would—" I begin.

My stomach rolls, and my vision starts to blur in and out of focus. I shake my head, trying to clear the peculiar sensation away, but it doesn't help. The light in the room tilts, and I put a hand to my mouth. "I don't feel very—"

Fenton's voice is far away. "Uh—Kani, does she seem a l'il *green* ta ya?"

"Already? She can't be going through transition yet? We gotta get her to the allayroom—*now,*" Kani responds.

Transition?

Someone hoists my arms in the air, and my feet drag along the floor. The searing pain in my leg is no match for the nausea bubbling up, and I try my best not to be sick on both of them.

Hushed whispers surround me...

"I don't get this"

"'This is way too early."

"What if she's been on tha outside longer than we though'—"

"I don't like this. Not one bit."

Kani and Fenton lug me down the dimly lit tunnel toward a dark offshoot. The lights blur by in strange streaks, and it's all I can do to keep my wits about me. They prop me up on my knees in front of an allay and back away. Without fail, I lean forward as all of the recent contents of my stomach abruptly hurl themselves back up.

8

TRAETON

I am the worst human being ever.

I glance at the urgent message from Delaney.

Ash tells me you're having second thoughts about the mission. You need to regain some focus. We need you on this one, Traeton. Come see me if you need reminding on why.

I swipe away the message and close my eyes. I *should* be focused on this upcoming mission. Or at least, getting my head in the game now that Runa's awake. Instead, the more time I spend with her, the more I want to get to know her. Things are starting to get muddy and it's only been a few hours with her. On top of everything, I have a million inappropriate images embedded in my mind, and no matter what I do, I can't give them back. Worse yet—it's not as if I hadn't considered them all *before* I saw her naked—the curse of being a guy outside the Helix. She has no idea and as soon as she learns about this stuff, she'll freak right out. Everyone does.

Ash would have a field day. Fenton, too.

Maybe the best thing for me—hell, her as well—is getting as far away from her as possible.

I stand up from my rocky outcropping and meander back through the twists and turns of the cavern tunnels. It takes less time to return than it did to get away. Isn't that ironic?

Up ahead, Kani and Fenton are standing outside the allayroom, and Kani's arms are flailing wildly.

What the hell is she so excited over?

My chest clenches, and I take off running. "Runa ... is she—?"

Kani glares at me and sticks out her tongue. "Barfing up a lung? Yes."

My body relaxes. "Oh, is that all?"

"Is that *all?* Are you *kidding* me, Trae? Her body shouldn't be going into transition for another twenty-four hours by our calculations. Am I the only one who sees the problem here?" she says.

"Maybe she's been outside longer than we thought?" I offer.

From the other side of the door, Runa heaves.

"Yeck." Fenton sticks out his tongue. "I don't miss havin' ta watch ya all go through tha' a' all."

I tip my head to the allayroom door and ask, "How much did she eat?"

"Not enough to still be going," Kani says. "Was I this bad?" Her eyes dart between the two of us. "Don't answer that."

I smile. She wasn't a pretty sight, either. Chartreuse would be an accurate description.

"Trae's righ'. Ya musta miscalculated on how long she'd been ou' there," Fenton says.

"Doesn't matter anyway," I tell them. "The sooner Runa

gets better, the sooner she can decide where she wants to go. Regardless, she can't go back to the Helix. The Labots won't let her back in now without an interrogation. Or *worse*." My mind wanders back to my sister, Ava, and a shiver runs up my spine. "Alina will help her."

Fenton's eyes narrow, "Why ya want 'er outta here so bad all of a sudden? You're not still plannin' on leavin' with Ash, are ya?"

"Yeah, Fenton, I am. I'm the only one who makes sense to send out into the field. And it's not that I want her out of here." Though, if I was honest with myself, the thought of Runa here alone with Fenton doesn't sit well with me at all. "It's just—she has—she seems more a Lateral type to me. Besides, Kani doesn't want her here."

Kani cocks an eyebrow and a lopsided grin sneaks across her face.

"What?" I glare back.

Fenton tilts his head and stares at me through the bottom edge of his glasses. "So, if she decided ta stay, you're *not* against the idea?"

"She can do whatever she wants." I shrug nonchalantly.

"Well, tha's good, 'cause I wanna convince 'er ta stay wit' us," he pats me on the chest and winks. "Ya can thank me later."

"Let's not get ahead of ourselves, boys." Kani props herself against the cavern wall and continues, "She's not in the position to give a crap about staying or going when she's heaving up everything she ever ingested. At the rate she's going, she'll be closing in on her momma's breast milk soon."

I snort. As if that could even happen. No one in the Helix nurses babies.

Fenton opens his mouth to say something, but the door to

the allayroom swings open. Runa's face is devoid of color, and she's visibly shaking as she holds the door for balance.

"Are you okay?" I ask, taking a step toward her.

Kani shakes her head and chuckles.

I ignore her and keep my eyes trained on the white-haired girl in front of me. Runa sways, and I close the distance to pick her up before she passes out. The second I have her, she sinks into me, completely relaxed.

This is starting to feel way too familiar. Hell, it's almost comfortable.

Still leaning against the wall, Kani says, "She's going to go through the fever next. Best thing for her is rest. We gotta pump her full of fluids."

Fenton snickers to my left and hunches forward, his hand over his mouth. "Pump her wit summin'."

My eyelids slam shut, and my face flushes. "Fenton," I groan.

Kani rolls her eyes and says, "I'll find something for her to *drink*."

"Oh, right. *Drink*," Fenton snickers.

A mischievous glint emerges from the depths of Fenton's brown eyes as he stares at me. "Kani, all things considered, love, I think you an' I should share a bed. Don't ya think?"

"What?" she utters, confusion crossing her face.

"Runa can sleep on my bed," Fenton says. His eyes cross over from her to me. "Should be more comfortable than tha bench she's been on."

"So?" Kani snorts.

I stand frozen, slack jawed.

I see where this is going. Fenton hasn't overly wanted me to go with Ash from the beginning and he's seen an opening.

Not to mention, he loves any chance at making me uncomfortable.

Fenton's smirk widens at my recognition. "Tha'll work ... right, Trae?"

I swallow hard in response. He knows me way to well.

Sighing in defeat, Kani says, "Be sure to change the bedding. Who knows the last time that lump of fabric has been washed." Shuddering, she takes off toward her bedroom. "Then again, why do I care? Do what you want."

The wattage of Fenton's grin is so bright, we could use it to light the entire Haven. When Kani is safely out of earshot, he says, "I'm no' blind, an' certainly no' stupid. Do ya think I can't see tha way ya look at 'er?"

"So what? Is there a law against it? Besides, you look at her, too. Don't say you don't."

"Yeah, bu' fer some reason, ya feel the need ta defend yerself about it and I'm tryin' ta figure ou' why. Runa's awesome, I won't lie. But when 'ave you ever known me ta hurt tha girl I'm with by bein' with another one?"

I raise my eyebrows, knowingly.

"Okay, except tha' *one* time. Doesn't count," he waves his hands dismissively, "Tha's not tha point. Tha point is, Kani gets me. I dunno why, but she does. And as much as I think Runa's got some amazing womanage goin' on, I'm not gonna hurt either o' them. 'Sides, Kani'd stab me dead in my sleep."

I nod in agreement.

"Furthermore, I ain't about ta go traipsing in on my bes' friend's source a infatuation." He raises his eyebrows and glances at Runa's limp body. "When were ya supposed ta leave?"

"Twenty-four hours, well less, now."

Fenton tips his chin toward Runa. "She'd be devastated."

"You don't know that." I start walking down the corridor toward our room. "She's so new— There's so much she doesn't—"

"I'm telling' ya, something's stirrin' wit her. She's diggin' ya as much as I see ya diggin' her. Yer always off on missions, searchin' fer summin'. Wha' if it's her—an' ya just gotta give 'er time?"

"That's a bit presumptuous." I snicker.

"Nah. Tha's one possible hypothesis, an' jus' as likely as any other ya migh' cook up." He follows along side me and pats my shoulder. When we enter our room, Fenton immediately goes to his bed and strips away the jumbled mess of blue fabric covering mostly the floor.

"Ya know, why didn't I think a this sooner?" he says, throwing everything into a heap next to him.

"Dunno," I mumble. My thoughts revolving around possibilities and varying futures only Fenton knows how to make a person consider.

With a flick of his wrists, the new fabric for the bed flutters open. Fenton haphazardly tucks in the edges and grunts, "I dunno how ya've managed all these years, I really don't. Off galavanting tha planet an' other such nonsense. Yer practically impervious to tha power a women."

I glance down at Runa's sleeping form. Oddly enough, the scabs on her eye don't seem as angry as they had before and the color is slowly returning to her face.

Especially to her lips ...

Oh, yeah. Impervious, all right.

Fenton finishes replacing the covers and steps aside with a flourish of his hands. "The bed ... is remade."

I laugh at his idiotic behavior and step forward to lie Runa down. She barely seems to notice the change but moans softly when she sinks into the pillow. I tuck her in, pulling the quilt up to her chin, and take a seat beside her. Her white hair seems to glow against the dark blue pillowcase. I sweep a few strands caught in her healing skin and I gently push them aside. Droplets of perspiration pearl across her forehead, and I place my hand on her burning skin.

"An' ya wanna leave." Fenton says, his watchful eye trained on me.

"I … I just wanna make sure she's doing okay."

"Is tha' *all?*" Fenton asks, his smile sliding into one of triumph.

"That's all. Dammit. I just—*we* just met her, Fenton," I reply.

He grunts, and the middle of his eyebrows upturn. "Tha' doesn't mean nuthin'."

"Well, it should," I fire back.

Kani walks in with a small box in her arms and sets it on the night table between the two beds. "Water. It has added electrolytes, so when she wakes up, give her some," she tells me. Her eyes rest on Runa, and she lets out a soft sigh. "She may not be as bad as I originally feared. Doesn't mean I *like* her, though. And sure as hell doesn't mean I want her lurking around."

"She's no' tha' bad, Kani," Fenton protests.

"Regardless, Trae's right. She'll do better with Alina," Kani says, "and we need more medical supplies now. Fenton and I can make the trek. Then we can stop by and ask Alina what she'd like us to do."

"Good idea. That would be great, Kani, thanks." I tell her.

Kani tips her head in acknowledgement and grabs Fenton by the hand. "We'll head out in a couple minutes. I, for one, need to finish eating, since we sort of came to a screeching halt with all the puking going on. Still can't believe she's going through transition so soon."

"Everyone's a little different," I offer.

She gives Runa a once-over, "Some more than others."

My eyes return to Runa. For me, being different's not a bad thing.

Sighing, I follow the two of them to the kitchen. From the stovetop, I fill a bowl and take a seat. Fenton's soups are the best.

"Mushroom chowder? I love this one," I tell Fenton, shoving a spoonful into my mouth.

"Can ya believe she didn't like my soup?" Fenton says indignantly. "How do ya no' like this?"

"Well, I like it." I take another big bite and savor the taste. If I leave with Ash, it will be months before I get a meal like this. Universe knows, I can't cook.

We sit in silence for a while, enjoying our food. No talking. No arguments. Everyone seems to be wrapped up in his or her own thoughts.

Even Fenton quietly scarfs down a second bowl before speaking up. "I dunno wha' tha two of ya are so afraid of, ya know."

"I'm not afraid of anything," I say, probably a bit too quickly.

Kani wrinkles her nose. "We don't need another person messing things up. You two are enough to contend with."

"C'mon, guys. Tha's it? Really? Tha's all ya got? Wha' if I just walked on by when I saw ya and yer family in the woods, Trae? Or you, Kani? Wha' makes 'er so different tha' ya wanna dump 'er off?"

"What's wrong with the Lateral? As I recall, we *all* started out there," I say.

"Yeah, but it migh' be nice ta 'ave 'er 'round," Fenton counters, dropping his spoon into his bowl. "Once the RationCaps are flushed, and 'er moods regulate, tha' is."

Kani snickers. "That'll be hell. As it is, we have her injuries to deal with. When her hormones spike, she's going to be like a pregnant lady on whack. Besides, what's in it for you?"

Fenton wiggles his eyebrows and says, "Wha's wrong wit wantin' another sexy beast in our band of studs?"

Kani shakes her head and pops a piece of bread into her mouth. "Oh, *please*."

"Guys, I don't know why we need to go around and around about this. Let's just talk to Alina and get her take on things. Nothing wrong with inquiring, right?" I say.

"Right," Kani snaps back.

"Fine. But I'm no' gonna give up tha' easy," Fenton adds.

"I didn't expect you would." I chuckle.

Shortly after eating, Kani and Fenton set off for the Lateral and everything in the Haven becomes eerily silent.

I stay nearby, in case Runa wakes up, which could be anytime. Unfortunately, I don't have a whole lot I can do, and I sure as hell don't wanna be stuck alone with my mind. Aimlessly, my fingertips trace the desk beside my bed. My woodcarving tools and my beat-up copy of *Across the Multiverse* all lay where I last left them. I really should be packing them up so I'm ready to go. I glance at my watch. A little over fourteen hours.

At least I haven't gotten another reminder message from Delaney.

I pace back and forth in my bedroom, sneaking glances of Runa more often than I should.

I need a new book.

Reading the written word is an acquired taste, but I love it. The eLink breaks concepts down, gives you the words without needing to view them, but everything is more abstract. Thank goodness Fenton's a good teacher.

Kneeling down in front of my shelf, I stare into the sea of colors and vertical spines. I stand for a few minutes before I realize I'm not even taking in their titles.

"Eh, doesn't matter," I grab the first one my hand touches.

I flop down on my bed, trying to ignore the fact that I can hear Runa's soft snores a few feet away. With the book clutched a little too tightly, I take in its cover. The hardbound book has faded blue edges and metallic print. The binding groans as I open it and stare at the black blobs on the brittle pages. Fifteen minutes pass and I have absolutely no idea what I've just read.

I throw the book aside and sit up on the edge of my bed. I grope at the soft fabric of my quilt and my eyes drift yet again to Runa. Her breathing has become labored; sweat clings to her neck and forehead.

Screw it.

I push off the bed, walk over to her, and take a seat.

Even with the puffy scabs down her face, she's beautiful. My eyes fall to her lips, and my heart thumps loudly in my chest. They're the perfect shape for—

Oh, this is so not good.

Runa's lips tug downward, clearly unhappy with whatever she's visualizing. Or perhaps she's uncomfortable even in her sleep? I wish I could make this easier for her.

Maybe I can.

I get up and walk to the allayroom. From the small shelf in the corner, I grab a rag and soak it with cool water. The excess seeps out when I squeeze, trickling through my fingers. In a weird sort of way, it grounds me. Calms my nerves a bit.

When I get back to her bedside, I place the chilled cloth on her forehead. A sense of satisfaction sweeps through me when her frown begins to dissipate. I should have thought of this sooner. Instead, I was too busy trying to ignore the way she's consuming my thoughts.

When Kani went through transition, Alina played music to ease the tension. I glance around the room, looking for the music player I took from the Archives, but it's nowhere to be found.

I make my way back to the gathering room to see if I've left it behind. I'm about to leave empty-handed when I spot Kani's player tucked in the chair cushions.

"Excellent," I clutch the small device in the palm of my hand. "This'll work fine."

The only problem is, I need to figure out how her music player works. The music was loaded centuries ago, back before creativity gave way to technology and sterilization, so each one has a different music selection and vastly different controls. We're lucky we figured out how they were powered and how to recharge them.

I fumble with the controls until I remember Kani's device is meant to sense the music best suited to your mood. You can also manually adjust the songs, but I have no clue how. Kani's used it a number of times, trying to clue in Fenton during his more oblivious moments. Never helps, though.

In my left hand, I hold the device and wait for it to analyze the chemical compounds in my skin and the impulses of my brainwaves. It flickers brightly and the room fills with a song I've never heard before. I suppose that's the point. The male vocalist meshes with a myriad of instruments, and I take a moment to listen to his words. A hint of sadness hugs his tone, but something else hides in the undercurrent.

Loss. Desperation. Confusion.

Longing.

I set the device on the table between the two beds and lie back. The themes resonate with me, as I suppose it should, and as the chorus loops around, I sing along. Feels good to release some of what I feel into words. I gotta hand it to the inventor of this device—it's good at what it does.

The song ends too soon and I reach over to find a way to replay it. I'd like to listen to it again. Instead, the music player crashes to the ground as I'm caught off guard by the two different colored eyes peering up at me.

9

RUNA

*S*omewhere in the distance, a voice beckons me. A real, honest-to-universe voice.

Masculine, *magnetic*.

I've been sitting here for so long. I'd like to follow the voice, but I don't. Not yet.

My lotus chair hugs my legs, and if I get up now, I may fall over. My quiet space is barren, as the Helix prefers. Yet, on my windowsill sits the mesmerizing blue crystal I found in the woods days ago. It pulses with an odd energy, glowing. I've stared so long, the rough edges of its shape are embedded in my memory.

An image flashes in my mind, disrupting my concentration.

My mother's forlorn face warns me she's entering the Living Quarters. The exchange opens up to my brother Baxten and I as my mother's thoughts intrude upon my own.

~ *I'll be in my space.*

She's brief, as always.

I sigh, wishing for once she'd come down here to find out

how my day was. She'd never believe me if I told her I'd tried to escape the Helix—and if she did, she wouldn't care.

Baxten's smiling face flashes in my mind next.

~ That was quick. Are you going to tell her what you found today?

Inwardly, I cringe. I can't stand the thought of making it real.

I push my thought back to him over the eLink.

~ Not yet.

Without meaning to, I begin thinking of the woods. Of leaving the Helix once and for all.

I've forgotten to release my eLink connection to Baxten.

~ Runa, you know what's waiting outside. You can't possibly be so stupid as to think you can live in the elements alone. I know you don't believe me, but the Morph is out there. With the way its evolutionary leap defied nature, no one can predict what it's capable of now. You need to respect that. Besides, RationCaps aren't hidden in the woods. Food doesn't grow on dead trees, you know.

My eyes drift to the trees, and suddenly I'm beside them.

Electric fire rains from the sky, and my beautiful world is burning around me. The trees are shriveling and dying. Desperation fills my heavy heart, and I kneel in a pile of ashes. The air is sweltering.

"Within the ashes of the old, something new emerges. You emerged, Daughter of Five. Your time to make a difference is nearing. Your healing is nearly complete. Remember to get to the Tree of Burden with the key. You cannot fight ignorance with ignorance. Open your eyes and your heart to this new world. Funny thing about endings ... they are cleverly a beginning in disguise."

The scene shifts. Large snowflakes descend in fluttering

luminescence, and the fires from before are gone. The intense heat is now a cool steam, the sky a deep purple.

The quiet, peaceful trees are dormant in the snow-covered ground. Waiting.

The forest I remember. The forest I love.

The masculine voice is still with me, echoing through the trees like a haunting remnant of the past. Standing up, I follow the melodious pull, and it draws me outside of myself.

I'm surrounded by the rocky embrace of cavern walls.

A wonderfully cool, damp cloth rests on my forehead, and beside me, the voice still beckons. I remove the cloth and roll to my side, unsure where I am. Across the room is Traeton. He's lying on a similar slab, his eyes closed. Words gracefully escape his lips, and I can't look away—I've never heard someone use their voice in this way. He's *astonishing*.

The words are powerful, and they intermix with emotive waves in other sounds. Ones I can't place. I'm not even sure where they come from. Abruptly, the mixture of sounds ends, as does Traeton's voice. He rolls to the side and reaches for something on the table between us, but when our eyes meet, the device in his hand clatters to the rocky floor.

He turns scarlet and bends down quickly to retrieve it.

"I'm sorry," I tell him. "I didn't mean to startle you."

"It's ah—okay. I didn't realize you were awake. I—I didn't wake you, did I?"

"I'm not sure. I've never slept before," I admit.

"Yeah, well really you—sorta passed out." He scratches at the back of his blue hair. "Are you feeling any better?"

I shudder, remembering my moments in the allayroom. "Remind me to never eat Fenton's food again."

Traeton's face brightens and he chuckles. "It's not that bad."

"So says the non-sick one," I reply, pointing at him playfully.

"Good point." The deep grooves in the middle of his cheeks appears.

Silence falls between us, and Traeton's eyes shift to the small device now on the table.

"What is that thing?" I ask. "Your voice sounded amazing."

"Uh ..." His mouth falls open as he blinks wildly.

I try to stifle a laugh, but it's too late. Uncontrollably, my giggles burst at the seams, and for some reason, the upturn in his eyebrows only makes me laugh harder.

"What's so funny?" he asks, a hint of a smile on his confused face.

I giggle through my fingers. "You. I mean—I'm not sure. No, no—it's definitely you."

"Okay ... I'm glad my singing is funny to you."

"Singing?" Birds sing. The wind sings ... But people? I struggle for air between giggles. "Well, it was amazing."

"Oh, please," he shakes his head, "It's the first time I've heard the song. I was only singing the chorus."

I laugh again. "What are all these crazy words you speak?"

He chuckles. "I'm not even sure anymore. What are we talking about?"

"No idea," I chuckle.

"My guess is this would be the transition talking. You should probably drink some water." Traeton crosses the room in three huge strides and kneels down. From a small metallic box he pulls a bottle of water and hands it to me.

I place my free hand on the slab beneath me and aim to push to a sit. Traeton's strong arms wrap around my shoulders and he helps me the rest of the way up. My mood shifts in an instant. I should be grateful, but something in the proximity, his touch—it irritates me. I feel good—better than good, I feel *normal*.

"I'm not incapable." I say, my nostrils flaring. "I can sit up on my own."

I bite down on my bottom lip. *What's wrong with me?*

Traeton's eyes are wide, but he takes a seat next to me.

"Sorry," I grab the container still held out for me.

"Runa, I think we need to—there's a lot you don't—out here, things work differently than they did in the Helix," he begins.

"Yeah, I get that," I snap at him, and my eyelid slams shut. I don't even sound like myself— I sound like Kani! What is wrong with me?

He sighs and runs his fingertips across his forehead. "You might—*feel* a little different."

"What's that supposed to mean?" The lighthearted mood all but a distant memory, agitation sets in. I'm sick of getting the runaround.

"It means—uh, your body will be—it's gonna—" he stammers. "You're going to be up and down for a bit. You're also gonna need to *sleep*. I'm sure you figured out we don't do Lotus machines here. We do things the old-fashioned way."

"What do you mean?" I ask, taking a long sip of water.

"Basically the way they did on Earth."

"I figured." I look to the ceiling, and he makes a face.

"Takes longer, though. Well, a lot longer. About seven and a half hours, to be exact," he says, scratching at his temple, one eye squinting. "Unless you're Fenton. Then, nine."

"How often?" My voice is a growl. This is nothing to be upset over, I get that, but the idea still unearths something buried inside.

He places a crooked finger over his mouth before saying sheepishly, "Every day."

My mouth drops open. "Wow. You're telling me a *third* of my day, everyday, I'm going to be unconscious?"

"Technically, yeah. But look at it this way—without having to work sixteen hours a day, you're actually *up* on free time."

"Funny." I flop back down on the bed and notice the thumping behind my left eye is gone.

Could the voice—be real? Could my eye really be healing so rapidly? If so, what does it mean? I look at the box of medical supplies and dismiss the thought.

"Sometimes less is more," Traeton continues, "It won't seem so bad once you've gotten used to sleeping. I just wanted you to be aware," his voice is wary, "So, anyway, this —um—this's where you'll be sleeping for a bit. We thought you might—well, the bed's more comfortable."

"Is that what it's called?" I say, trying to reel in my sudden anger flare. "It looks like a medical slab."

"I could see that," he agrees.

"It is more comfortable, though."

"That's … good," he says, walking to the other side of the room and takes a seat on the other bed.

"And you'll be …"

Traeton chews on his lower lip. "Here," he pats the fabric beneath him.

"So, this is … *your* space?" I sit up and glance around again, this time paying closer attention. For some reason, understanding this is where Traeton spends a third of his day makes it more interesting.

"Yup. Well, it's Fenton's too."

"Wait. What? Then this is his—I can't kick him out—" I

say, "I should go back to the bench. That'll work fine ... It's not right to dislodge him." I push aside the fabric, trying to stand up.

Traeton is at the edge of my bed in an instant, and he places his hands on my shoulders. "Sit. Please, Runa. It's okay. Fenton and Kani are going to share a bed for now. No big deal. You need to be comfortable too. Your injuries need—"

My eyes widen, and I cut him off. "They're going to share a bed?"

This one is barely wide enough for me—how can two people rest properly?

"Yeah. They're kind of—a long story," he shifts to one side, "It's just—it's not a big deal."

My chin begins to quiver and tears emerge. I feel completely out of control, but I can't stop the sobs, "Poor Fenton. He shouldn't lose his bed because of me. Or share with Kani. She's so ... so ... *mean!*"

Traeton chuckles and tries to hide behind his hand.

"This isn't funny!" I roar.

"Nope, it's not. Not at all funny," his lips take on the shape of a straight line, but his eyes are still smiling. I bury my face in my hands.

I feel so out of control.

Taking my hands in his own, Traeton kneels in front of me. "Runa, listen to me. This is all normal." His eyes are way too empathetic and accessible.

"*Normal?*" I complain. "I'm so far out of my element—Nothing is normal. I feel completely clueless."

"You're not clueless. You're *uninformed*," he answers.

"Oh, that's better."

"Just the way the Helix likes it. Here's the thing—those

RationCaps do more than just meet nutritional require-
ments. They've got—" he stumbles for a moment, his eyes
distant as he searches for something to say, "They've got
hormone agents in them. Hormone-*suppressing* agents. What
you're going through, the mood swings you're having right
now, while they might seem strange, it's all normal. We call it
transition out here. Your body's trying to regulate itself. You
need to realize that's all this is, and it will pass."

"That's *all* this is? What's that supposed to mean? What
I'm feeling isn't real? How could you say such a thing?" I cry,
pulling my hands from his.

"No. It's not like that. Everything is amplified, that's all,"
he says.

"Why can't I just be normal?" My lip quivers again, and I
bite down to make it stop.

"No, you're—" he starts.

"*Look at me, Traeton*—white hair, mangled eye—have you
ever seen anyone who's as strange as me? I haven't," I sputter.
He waits until I stop talking and raises a single finger to
point silently at his own head of hair. I stick out my tongue
at him and continue, "Well, until I met you. But your hair's
not even actually blue, is it?"

His eyes are sympathetic, "You're not strange."

"I'm not, huh? You chose your hair color, and everything
else about you is *perfect*. What if you were born like this?" I
lift a strand of hair and let it fall.

He stands up and turns away. "I understand more than
you think."

For a moment, he stands still. I watch his shoulders rise
and fall slowly.

I blink furiously at his silhouette and finally say, "I'm
sorry. I shouldn't—"

Traeton turns around, his eyes now guarded. "You don't need to be sorry. But you do need to rest. You'll need to get your sleep cycles in line with everyone else's. Kani and Fenton are at the Lateral checking on space. Do you need anything else? How's your pain?"

Recognition dawns on me. He doesn't want me to stay here with them. Tears well up again and silently fall to my lap.

"What's wrong, Runa?" he asks.

"Nothing, I'm fine." My cheeks are flaming as I lie down and turn away from him. I can't let him see me like this. I need to get myself under control.

"If your pain gets worse again, let me know. In the meantime, try to rest. You'll feel better once you do. I'm gonna shut off the light, but I'll be right over here if you need me,"

A moment later, his bed creaks and the light is extinguished. Until now, I had no idea how dark it was down here. I can't even locate my hand in front of my face. My whole life, I've never experienced this kind of emptiness.

Lying still isn't easy, and this sleep thing is even more elusive. Being here, experiencing life outside the Helix with them is just a slap in my face at how unprepared I was when I ran out. I roll to my back and stare into the black abyss.

Baxten was right. I wouldn't last a day on my own. I hadn't even considered I may need sleep. He probably already assumes I'm not coming back. Mother probably hasn't even noticed I'm missing. Grief surfaces and compounds with everything else as the cool, stinging tears puddle on the fabric beneath me. Even now, her lack of empathy or care has the power to wound me, I hate it.

Only a few feet away, Traeton's breath is rhythmic. I roll over again. I'd love to go out into the woods for a little while, clear my head. The voice said I need to go back to the tree anyway. But more than that, somewhere in my core, I'm drawn back to where my old life was ripped from me. I need to come to terms with it in order to accept a new future.

I don't know how to do this—any of this. Live away from all I've been brought up with. I thought I was so brave before. I was such a fool. I'm ignorant, and it makes me vulnerable. Susceptible to all the horrible things in this world I've never even imagined. I only need to walk by the mirror to prove my point.

This hormone thing—if what Traeton says is true, what role does the suppression play? Why were the hormones suppressed? Maybe because they make humans crazy?

I sure feel crazy right now.

Traeton grumbles, and the light flickers back on. I roll over to my side to meet his surveying eyes.

"Couldn't sleep, either, huh?" he asks.

"I guess not."

"The first time I slept, without the exhaustion consuming me, it was the strangest sensation," his eyes take on a distant quality as he continues, "I found myself dreaming and it took some time to realize none of it was real. Such a strange concept, really. To view something in your head so vividly— every one of your senses are activated—yet, it's just a fabrication."

I stare at him, perplexed. Is that what was happening to me earlier?

"You'll have them too. *Dreams*. Sometimes they're peaceful, even wonderful. Other times, not so much."

"What causes them?" I ask.

"The best explanation I've stumbled upon is we're

processing the day's events. Our subconscious is working out a solution to whatever happened," he says.

"My brother Baxten would find a way to somehow make them seem like I'm at fault," I say.

"Isn't that what brothers are for?" Traeton's cheek twitches and his lips upturn. His face is bright, light, and his dimples shine triumphantly.

"I suppose." I frown. "Do you have siblings?"

"Actually, I do," his smile fades, "My sister woulda been close to your age."

"*Would* have been?"

"I, uh … it's really …," he says, rolling to his back and sighing, "complicated."

"I'm sorry. I didn't mean to pry."

"It's okay. I shouldn't—it's not bad to ask questions," he props himself up on his elbow, "Life was hard for us in the Helix. Ava was an amazing person. But she suffered. Every day. Ours wasn't an ordinary life. We had constant Medic visits checking on her improvement. They wanted to test if she was still a value to society, I guess to find out if their treatments were working."

"I'm—I don't think I'm following," I sit up and watch him intently.

He wets his lower lip and continues, "When someone in your life has a mental disorder, like Ava did, there's sorta this undercurrent of fear running through you. She was probably the most intelligent person I've ever known, but she was unstable. I guess they figured that out too. Sometimes she'd see things that weren't there and predict the future. Sometimes she had voices in her head not connected to the eLink. Other times she would just go into a deep depression. Which, as you know, is unheard of. Wasn't much they could do for her."

My eyes widen.

She could hear voices in her head.

"What happened to her?" I lean forward.

"Labots broke into our Living Quarters and took her."

"Oh, Traeton, I'm so sorry." My guilty conscience for attacking him gnaws at my insides.

He shrugs, "When it happened, my father ordered me to take my mother and my middle sister, Cecilina, out of the Helix. He told us to go to the woods, and he'd meet us," he pauses, looking away, "I never saw him again."

His eyes fill with such sorrow. I wish I could comfort him somehow.

"Labots. Kani thought I was working with them. What *are* they?" I ask.

"The Helix's version of civil order. On Earth they'd be the law enforcers. Only why are there law enforcers for a *perfect* society?"

"Why don't I know about them?"

"Unless you had some reason to, they don't want you aware of them. Be glad you've never encountered one. They're not nice."

"What do they look like? How would I know if I met one?" I ask.

"*You'd know,*" his eyes go distant, "They're faceless."

"What?"

"I don't know how or why. But when you look at them, they're completely blank. Like all their features were wiped clean. Maybe they never actually had faces. Hell, maybe they're not even human."

"How is that possible?"

"Your guess is as good as mine."

"I can't imagine what that was like for you," I look deep into his somber eyes, "What became of your mother and your younger sister? Why aren't they here with you?"

"They're fine—together. Fenton and I came out here to the Haven a few years ago," he says.

"Are you glad you left the Helix? Knowing all you know now?"

"I suppose. Life wouldn't be the same inside, after Ava. Honestly, I'm surprised they allowed her to stay with us for as long as they did. If I were them, wanting to hide any evidence of mental illnesses, I woulda taken her away much younger. Before she had any impact on others."

"Seems harsh," I say, surprised.

"Not harsh. Just—easier. At least, considering the outcome."

The silence that falls between us is deafening.

"I wish I could change it. The past, I mean. Things shouldn't be so complicated," I offer.

"And yet, sometimes they are. Even in its most simplistic form, life is utterly complex," his eyes dart to the floor, "You do need to rest, Runa. You've had a crazy few days. You need to heal."

"Okay, I'll try again,"

"Good night, Runa."

"Thanks for—talking with me, Traeton," I smile, wishing we could talk more.

His dark eyes burn into mine for a moment as he searches my face, "Call me Trae."

"Okay, *Trae*," I smile.

Trae grins sort of a lopsided grin in return, "Not the best of circumstances ... how we met. But I'm really glad we have."

"So am I."

He holds my gaze for a moment, then extinguishes the light once more.

I roll over, feeling the inklings of something I've never felt in my whole life.

Wanted.

RUNA

"*R*una—Runa, wake up!"

Traeton hovers over me, distress written clear across his face. His hands are strong on my shoulders as he shakes me. I blink hard a couple of times, trying to make sense of what's happening as dust flies everywhere, peppering my face, and making me cough.

The last thing I remember is being happy. *Did I fall asleep?*

"Whats going on?" I ask, shielding my eyes.

"We're not sure, but we need to get outside." Trae says, pulling me to a stand. "It's not safe here. Get dressed. Your boots are beside the end of your bed."

He shoves my NanoTech jacket into my hands and puts his own jacket on.

"Nuthin' on tha mainframe. Tha Lateral's no' reportin' anythin' either. Doesn't appear ta be seismic, though. Which way ya wanna go?" Fenton calls from the doorway.

I struggle to put my jacket on as Trae scavenges his space, picking up things and shoving them into his pockets or slots on his trousers. "Okay, that tells me it's localized.

Were you able to isolate where this is coming from?" Trae asks.

"Nah, nuthin' conclusive." Fenton shakes his head.

"This might be our only chance. If the Lateral's not experiencing it yet, we need to be their eyes and ears." Trae says as he continues to outfit himself.

"Bu' if summin's attacking from tha outside—tha' pretty much blows. We'd be face'n whatever's causing tha mayhem in tha firs' place. I kinda don't like them odds. Do you?"

"Not really, but we don't have a choice."

"Attacking?" My eyes widen as I look between their faces. "Who's attacking?"

"We dunno, Runa." Fenton says, shooting me a look of condolence. "Trae, wha' if we head on over to tha Lateral? Migh' be tha safest bet."

Trae stops for a moment, considering. "You're right. You should take Kani and Runa— but I gotta get topside. You know that."

Fenton nods. "Yeah, okay."

"No. I'm going with you, Trae." The words escape my mouth before I've had time to process. I'm not sure what we'll find, but something tells me I need to stay by him.

"Runa, you're hurt already. Fenton's right, you should go to the Lateral. They have safeguards for cave-ins we don't have here."

I jut my chin out and stand firm. "I don't care. What if I caused this?"

"Oh fer heaven's ta pete." Fenton sighs. "Why would ya be tha one causin' this?"

I bite my lip. I hadn't really given much weight to the strange voice's warnings until now, but I'm beginning to think I should pay attention.

"Kani seemed to think the Helix could be looking for me." I offer.

There. We'll just ignore the fact I've had a voice unrelated to the eLink telling me I'm being hunted. They'd think I was crazy if I told them. Especially after what Trae said about his sister.

"Yeah, bu' even if tha' were tha case..." Fenton begins.

I cross my arms and frown. The cavern shakes again, sprinkling dust and rock from above us.

"We don't have time to argue this." Trae says.

Fenton exhales, deflated. "Fine, fine. We'll *all* go. Trae, ya better 'ave Jane with, tha's all I gotta say."

"Jane?" I ask, grabbing my boots from the edge of the bed. My body moves more easily than I expect and glance between the two men to see if they notice. When neither of them seem to register, I slip my feet inside my NanoTech boots. They autoconstrict to my measurements and I stand up, ready to go.

"That's what Fenton calls the sonic resonator." Trae snickers, picking up a gadget from the table between us. As I walk closer to get a better look, the tiny device fitting inside the palm of his hand flips open, expanding to ten times its original size.

"I got her now." Trae says to Fenton as he hooks a strap from one end of the device to the other, then throws it over his shoulder.

"It looks like a blaster." I admit.

"It is," he tips his head and grins, "of the *sonic* kind."

"I knew it. The Helix found us." Kani affirms, an air of panic in her voice. She places a sharp object into a holster on her hip and enters the room. Kani is already clad in outdoor gear from head to toe as she steps over chunks of rock. "Are they trying to flush us out? Or worse—bury us alive?"

"Either?" Fenton offers.

"Super." Kani says.

"We're going topside, Kani. You ready?" Trae asks.

"No, Trae. I wanna hang out here and meet an untimely death," she says sarcastically.

A giant fracture rips open a fissure in the ceiling, dropping a cascading stream of rock and dust all around us. Kani screams, running out of the room and down the tunnel, with Fenton close on her heels.

"Come on—we need to get out of here." Trae exclaims as he reaches out to pick me up.

Instead, I grab his hand. "No, I can run on my own."

His eyes widen, "You were just attacked, Runa. There's no possible— "

"Yes I can. You'll have to trust me for now." I drop his hand and run in the direction of Kani and Fenton, leaving Trae standing in the middle of his room with his mouth gaping open.

My muscles surge with new strength as I make the twists and turns of the cavern tunnels a few meters behind the other two. After what feels like an eternity of stone walls, a crack of daybreak bursts into the tunnel. Kani and Fenton run straight outside just as another surge roars around us, making me shield my eyes from the debris.

"Come on, we need to follow them," Trae grabs hold of the back of my jacket and pulls me into the searing white light.

As my eyes adjust, I spin around, searching for the source of attack, but there's nothing except the trees and our low hanging sun.

"How's this possible?" Kani exclaims, "There's nothing out here."

Fenton takes out a small ocular scanner and sweeps the horizon. "Nuthin' on tha readouts. No heat signatures or anythin'."

"I thought you said it wasn't seismic." Trae mutters, pulling out his own ocular scanner.

"Didn't appear ta be."

"Then how do you explain this?" Trae fires back.

In the distance, a voice bellows over the wind. The same two syllables repeat over and over.

"What is that?" Kani asks, her eyes wide.

With our feet frozen in place, we crane our necks to figure out what's being said. Even with a cupped hand behind my ear, the sounds don't make sense.

"It could be a warning, for all we know," Trae suggests.

"Or a trap," Kani laments.

Fenton taps a keypad on the top side of his glove, "I migh' be able ta amplify tha sound. Give me a sec."

All the possibilities jumble up in my mind. Who would be out here at the same time we're experiencing such strange things inside the cavern? Could it be this Videus person? Or someone working with him trying to get ahold of me?

The amplified words erupt from a speaker engrained in Fenton's glove. "Runa—Runa, can you hear me? *Runa!*" There's an edge of panic in the young man's voice.

Surprised to hear my brother Baxten's voice, I take a step forward, searching the trees. A hand wraps around my forearm, pulling me back.

"You can't go out there, Runa," Trae shakes his head.

"It's my brother. I have to— "

"Kani's right. This has to be a trap," Trae states.

"How do you know?"

"Because, if the Helix *is* trying to locate you—it's how I'd draw you out."

I shake my head. "Why would Baxten go along with it? That's not like him."

"He may not have a choice," Kani states.

My mind reels. The perception I had of the Helix has been so drastically altered since the day of my professional appointment. How could it be only a few short days ago?

I hold Trae's gaze for a moment, then push past him, searching for Baxten one last time. I need to know he's okay before I go.

"If you're gonna search for him, keep low," Trae latches onto my arm, making me lower my stance. He gestures to the others to get lower too. Then, I follow his outstretched pointer finger to a spot in the distance. Baxten's body comes into view and I following his movement through the trees. He's cradling his left arm and leaving what looks like a trail of blood behind.

"He's hurt. We need to go out and get him— "

Trae opens his mouth to speak, as a black creature slinks out from behind a tree, then wraps itself around Baxten's feet.

"Help! Someone help me— " Baxten screams as he thrashes about wildly.

I shake myself free of Trae and surge toward him. Even as I get closer, I can't make out what the creature is at his feet.

"Runa— " Trae takes hold of my wrist, pulling me up short.

I clutch at his fingers, trying to pry them loose. "Let go, Traeton. I need to get to my brother. He needs help."

"And what if the creepy black thing comes after you?" Kani says in an urgent, hushed tone from a few yards back.

"Well, I can't stand here and do nothing," I spit back.

Suddenly, right before our eyes, electricity zaps back and forth, encircling Baxten and the creature in a great big ball.

"What the— " I yell, struggling to get closer.

The electricity arcs get more fervent as Baxten struggles in vain.

Finally, I slip my wrist free from Trae's grasp and run toward my brother. Just meters away, Baxten's face lights up when he recognizes me. The black serpent-like creature at his feet squeezes tighter, binding his legs to the point of utter immobility. I reach out for Baxten as his fingers extend outward to me.

"Runa— Help me," he screeches in panic.

In the next moment, electricity arcs around the creature and fire materializes from the ground upward, consuming Baxten completely in the blaze. The intensity of the heat knocks me back with force. I shield my eyes with my arms, but the stench of burned flesh and hair floods my nostrils. Then, just as quickly as it arose, the fire dematerializes, along with everything else it had consumed. In the blink of an eye, all that's left is the blackened, sizzling hole in the snow where my brother had just been standing.

"No— " I scream, rushing forward, "No. He can't be— "

I drop to my knees, clawing at the scorched ground.

"C'mon, we can't stay, Runa," Trae says, placing a hand tentatively on my back, his eyes searching the trees.

"He can't be …" Tears stream uncontrollably as I struggle to get away. "He can't be."

"Wha' tha hell is goin' on ou' here? Firs' Runa's attacked,

now this?" Fenton says, rushing toward us. "We need ta ge' outta 'ere and ge' some recon goin' on."

"I second that," Kani states, grabbing Fenton by the hand tugging him backward. She also scans the area with wide eyes.

"I couldn't agree more. C'mon, Runa. I know it's hard, but there's nothing you could've done for your brother," Trae yanks me up to a stand, but all I can focus on is the lingering stench of burned flesh and the echoes of my Baxten calling out to me for help.

"He was looking for me …" I mutter, "This is all my fault."

"This isn't about you, Runa. This is something else. We need to figure out what," Trae drags me backward, away from the scene of my brother's demise.

The voice said they'd be after me—but this has all happened so quickly. I've had no time to heal, or to process.

Did Videus do this? Did he attack my brother?

A familiar howl erupts, piercing through the already tense moment. Kani and Fenton halt their progress, and turn back around. Every hair on the back of my neck stands on end as I flashback to my attack in these woods.

"No, no … This cannot be happening. Not this, too," I cry, freezing in place.

Fenton spins around and asks, "Wha's tha' now?"

"Shhhhh," Without moving a muscle, I whisper, "That's the Morph."

Panic floods the faces around me. At the same time, an electric crackle shifts through the breeze making the tree branches around us groan.

"What the hell are we supposed to do?" Kani exclaims, "We can't stay here. I don't wanna end up like Runa's brother, nor do I feel like being eaten by the Morph, thank you."

"Then run—run as fast as you can," I exclaim, turning to run toward the cavern entrance. Kani pushes past me, running faster than any of us, as the electric crackle emits again, much closer than the first time. The Morph lets out a strange howl, nearly a cry.

"Is it being attacked?" Trae asks to no one in particular as he looks over his shoulder. "This would be a good time to hit it from another direction," he twists around and stabilizes his elbow against his knee, then takes aim with Jane. He fires in the general location we last heard the Morph.

There's no way I'm stopping to watch. Instead, I race for all I'm worth beside Kani and Fenton into the tunnels, scrambling over the frozen, slippery rocks. I know exactly what the Morph's capable of. Seconds behind us, Trae follows us in and another vehement howl from just outside the exit reverberates off the walls inside the cavern.

"What the hell?" Kani repeats, "What the hell? It's going to follow us in."

"Not if I can help it," Trae says as he takes aim again, pointing the sonic resonator toward the opening. He pulls the trigger and blue dots along side of the barrel light up from the trigger to the end.

"Did it work?" I ask, scrambling backward further.

"We'll find out," Trae says, holding his position.

We're a few meters from the entrance, but the cavern begins to rumble around us again. The force is more fierce than it was before and an avalanche of boulders and snow flood into the opening, effectively blocking the way out. Ice chunks the size of my head skid across the cavern floor, coming to a final halt directly in front of us. The cavern goes deafeningly quiet.

"Well, there goes tha' way out," Fenton says matter-of-factly, "On tha upside, a' least the Morph can't ge' in."

"C'mon, we better head out. Who knows how long before the rest of the entrance collapses. We need to get to the Lateral as quickly as possible. I need to debrief Delaney ASAP," Trae stands up, offering me his hand.

I take his offering and stand up, unsure what to say. Everything inside me is screaming for my brother. To have the last ten minutes of my life turned back so I could save him. Call to him before the creature got to him. *Something.*

Trae pauses for a moment, searching my face. Then he reaches out and slides his hand in mine. "I know this is all a lot to process. But you're not alone. You've got us. Okay?"

"You don't know me, Trae. You don't know anything about what I'm going through," I release his hand and start walking.

Trae stands in place with a wounded expression, but he let's me continue on my own.

Kani steps forward, her eyes glinting with determination. "I don't know about you, but I need more of my knives before heading to the Lateral. If any of those damn things come for us, I'm gonna be ready."

A low tremor begins again and none of us stop to question what to do next. We start running toward the Haven. We don't get far when my insides lurch and an eerie déjà vu creeps over me. The tunnel, the lightning, my worries, all of it fades away and white light consumes me.

The feminine voice from the Oasis is now an urgent calling in my mind.

We know you need answers. Videus has claimed your brother and he's coming for you. We are working hard to protect you, but you must leave the confines of the underground. It's time you come to us at the Tree of Burden. You and you alone must enter the Tree and put an end to this. Videus has been hunting for the Tree through the millennia—you must reach it before he does, or all knowledge regarding your purpose will be forever lost. The safety of all you cherish, and the world at large, depends on you, Daughter of Five. Find your Guardian— Tethys will help you complete your mission and get to the Tree. Trust her.

The Tree has your answers.

"*D*o something, Kani" Trae's strained voice reaches me first.

"For crying out loud. Relax, Traeton. She's alive. Pupils are dilating. Pulse is strong," Kani replies, "Other than her crazy fast healing and creepy eye, she's the spitting image of normal."

"I'd like ta know wha' tha H-E-double Helix jus' 'appened?"

The ground rumbles quietly beneath me, stirring me from the depths I've been lingering in.

"From what I can tell, she's had a syncopic episode," Kani says.

"Kani, *please*. Use English," Trae moans.

Kani sighs, "She fainted."

"Well, she picked a fantastic time ta fall unconscious. A' least tha tremors are startin' ta subside," Fenton says.

"Yeah, super," Kani mutters, "We still need to get out of here to let the others know the entrance is blocked. Amongst other things."

My eyes flutter open as Trae places his hands on my shoulders, but everything feels unreachable as I struggle to regain my equilibrium. His forehead is etched deep with lines of worry.

"Runa. Are you okay? Wow, I feel like I ask that a lot," Trae shakes his head and takes a seat on the ground next to me. He props his elbow on his bent knee and runs his hand through his disheveled blue hair.

"I—I'm okay, I think," I begin, struggling to push myself to a seated position.

The Tree has answers ...

My mind swirls with a new sense of purpose. I can't let Baxten's death mean nothing. I need to get back to the Tree before this Videus has a chance to get *anything* else he wants. He's taken something from me I can never get back and for that, I will stand in his way.

"Did you get hit on the head by falling debris?" Traeton's eyes narrow and he asks Kani, "Should she be moving?"

Her shoulders inch toward her ears, "She'd be the one to ask."

"I know you don't believe me, but this is all my fault," I blurt out, staring at the rocks spattered across the floor, "The attack on the cave system. My brother. All of it."

I place my hands on the ground, attempting to get up, but Trae grabs hold of my forearms and helps me stand. I glare at him, wishing for a moment I could be left alone to grieve in peace.

"How do you figure?" Trae asks.

"When I left the Helix, it wasn't under the best circumstances and I have reason to believe someone's hunting me," I confess. "This isn't going to stop. They'll be back."

"I knew it," Kani mutters, pacing back and forth.

"Ya mean tha Labots?" Fenton interjects.

"I'm not sure," I admit, tracing a fingertip on my unscathed eyebrow. As far as I know, they could be involved, "Have any of you ever heard of someone named Videus?"

I search their faces as I say the name out loud for the first time.

"I've heard the name before, but can't place where. Who is he?" Trae asks.

"Someone I've been warned to be cautious of. Unfortunately, I don't even know what he looks like," I reply, "I could use a Helix mainframe search …"

Kani steps forward and says, "Even if you could connect out here, the Helix would surely have flagged you by now. Your presence has been gone too long from the system."

"So?"

"So … Remember what we said about the way the Helix doesn't particularly like that sorta thing?" Kani spits.

"Yeah, but Landry can crack into just about anything without being detected," Trae offers, "Including the Helix."

Kani raises her hands and walks away, "Your burial, then."

"Hey— I could crack in, too … If I 'ad tha equimen' he has," Fenton moans.

"Now there's something to be proud of," Kani says sarcastically as she turns the corner.

Fenton makes a face and shrugs, "Well, I could."

"And you think he could go in undetected?" I ask. If we can get more information on Videus, I could be forearmed before going to the Tree. I'd know what to look for.

"Tha Helix operates within an authentication system. If we can find a work 'round ta trick tha eLink into believing tha access is legitimate, it'll work. Then again, been a while. Landry'll know more," he concedes.

Trae turns to me, his dark eyes surveying me closely. "If you're good, Runa, let's head to the Lateral and we can do some digging. Whatever's going on, we need to sort this out."

"Thank you," I breath a sigh of relief, "I'm sorry for getting you involved, though."

"Technically, I got us involved by bringing you here."

"Good point," I tell him.

More than anything, I wish I could get the sickly smell from the fire out of my nostrils.

"Well, I suppose we should follow after the others. Lead the way." I sweep my hand out, allowing him to go in front.

"Nah. We go together," Trae says, tipping his head to the way the others went, "Let's go."

We walk together in silence for a few minutes. Even the cavern system has gone eerily quiet and I keep expecting another rumble to happen at any moment. I stare blankly ahead of me, drained from everything that's just transpired.

Eventually, Trae turns to me, "Just so you know, it's gonna take us nearly an hour to get to Landry's. If you start getting tired, you tell me, okay? We'll take a break."

"Okay," I agree.

We reach a large metal door and gain access to the recognizable section in the cavern's inner workings they call the Safe Haven. Truthfully, I hadn't even noticed the door when we had been running to escape to the outside. As we cross the threshold, I inhale the familiarity deeply. If I follow all of the expectations laid out by the voice, this could be the last time I'm in this space.

The glow from two holographic screens in a room on the right illuminates the space and floods into the hallway.

"This is the Control Room," Trae says.

I step into the room, as Trae places the sonic resonator on a standard rapid-charging port on the table inside. Kani is busy strapping two more knives to her body. She offers one to Fenton, who flashes his hands in dismissal in front of him.

"Nah. Tha's yer thing, love."

"Suit yourself," Kani gives me a stern expression as she walks out.

Fenton winks as he follows after her.

I lean into Trae, "What's with the knives?"

"She's just comfortable with them as a means of protection. Kani's never been big on technology because she says it can malfunction when you need it most."

"Makes a certain amount of sense," I say, "Has she always been so … terse?"

Trae laughs, "Pretty much, but she means well. She had a hard life in the Helix, too."

"Why?" I walk to the door, watching her black ponytail bob from side to side as she continues down the hall.

"Now, that's *her* story to tell," Trae smirks at me.

The path we continue on is familiar and will eventually bring us to the Oasis. As we walk, all I can think about is my brother. And retribution. If Videus is behind this—he will pay.

Finally, we reach the Oasis. The cool, clean smell in the air cleanses away some of the fire and reminds me of so many things. It was the first time the voice invaded my mind. But more than that—it reminds me of Trae's consistent desire to help me.

My heart constricts. These new feelings I have for him—they're strange and strong. What will happen if I listen to the voice and return to the Tree? Will I see him again?

We continue onward and after a while, the tunnels all start to appear the same to me. Finally, as we round another twist, we come face to face with an extremely tall, muscular man. He's clad in black trousers, and his shoulder-length black hair rests against his fitted red shirt. As we approach, he straightens, giving the appearance he'd make a great wall. His dark eyes immediately rest on Trae, who shifts beside me, and mutters something under his breath.

Kani and Fenton step aside, allowing us to approach the man. His black eyes are murderous, but he doesn't say a word. Instead, he steps up in front of us, blocking us from traveling further.

"Ash," Trae says, standing toe-to-toe with him, "We're on our way to see Landry."

Ash raises his eyebrows, but maintains his silence.

Ash ... what an appropriate name after the recent events.

"Yes, yes ..." Trae continues, not waiting for Ash to respond, "I will go see Delaney, too."

I glance between the two of them, trying to figure out their body language. Trae's certainly intimidated, but holding his own.

The muscles in Ash's neck bulge and his massive head tilts toward me, "This the girl?"

"Yeah," Trae swallows hard, glancing my direction, "Runa, this is Ash. Ash, this is Runa."

Ash's eyes search me up and down. I raise an eyebrow and channel Kani.

Turning back to Trae, he steps aside and says, "Ten hours."

"I know. Do you need to keep reminding me?" Trae spits, running his hand through his hair and stepping around Ash.

I stumble on Trae's heels, wanting to get as far away from Ash's dark eyes as possible.

"What was that all about?" I ask when we are far enough out of earshot.

"Oh, you gotta be kidding me. You haven't told her?" Kani says from behind us.

I look over my shoulder and ask, "Tell me what?"

Trae blows out a slow burst of air. "I'm leaving soon."

"You are?" My voice cracks unexpectedly, "What happened to finding out what's going on? Or bringing me to the Tree?"

Trae's lips take on the appearance of a thin line and I turn to the others.

"Trae's s'posed ta go on a mission fer tha Lateral soon," Fenton offers, "In ten hours, I s'pect."

"Oh." Disappointment sweeps over me and I ask, "Will you be gone long?"

The silence growing between us elongates, making my stomach clench in knots. I didn't realize how much I was leaning on his support until this very moment.

"Yeah. The mission could take a while, unfortunately," he finally offers.

"More like months," Kani says.

"I see," I breathe. The wind feels like it's been knocked out of me. Of this new group of friends, Trae's been the one I feel most connected to. The one I felt I could trust to help me. With Baxten gone now, I'm utterly alone in this world.

"Don't worry, Runa. I'll stick this thing out with you first. The threat happening to the Lateral is more pressing than the mission. I'm sure Delaney will agree," Trae offers, "If this Videus is a part of it, then we are all on the same mission for answers."

"It's okay, Trae. I appreciate what you've done so far. Don't feel like you need to stick around for me." I tell him, trying to sound sincere.

I turn, continuing to walk down the tunnel.

Our trip to the place they call the Lateral feels like it takes forever as we each walk in silence. Eventually, the lamps carved into the walls flicker softly and light our way to a larger, open area. Trae stops, allowing me to go out first.

I stand at the top of a large staircase meandering back and forth down an enormous cliffside, to what I presume is the Lateral—hundreds of feet below. Our little Safe Haven is nothing in comparison to this—this is an underground city.

The Lateral is encased within a large circular boundary, which had to take some work to build. The high walls arc around the main part of the city made up of small buildings. They sprawl out across the circle in green geometric patterns with walkways in between. The walkways link to a central location in the middle part of the city—almost like spokes on a wheel. The lights of the city seem to be a combination of electricity and natural candlelight and it's breathtaking.

"It may be pretty from up here, but after all these steps, you're gonna wonder what the hell was so terrific about it," Kani mutters as she pushes past and starts down the stairs.

I follow after her, but the woman is on a mission to complete all the steps in record time. Eventually, Fenton pushes past me, too, trying to keep up with her. After a few minutes of step after step, they stop at the nearest landing and wait for Trae and I to catch up. So far, I've counted four hundred twenty-three steps—and we're just past the halfway mark. Kani's toe taps a rhythm on the rock.

"Newbies," Kani says, leaning against the sculpted half-wall encasing the stairs.

116

The closer we get, the more details spring out of the city. I don't know what most of it even does. The rooftops are full of plants. There's so much green. People, too—walking from place to place. Some sitting on benches or near —trees?

"Green trees? How is this possible down here?" I raise a finger and point.

"Special lights. See those?" Trae points at some large fixtures hanging from the very top of the cavern ceiling, suspended within a couple hundred feet of the city. "Those are high-intensity discharge, multi-spectrum lights, but we call them HDMs. Basically, they mimic the sun's light, allowing us to grow things. Things like trees and food. See all the green on the rooftops? Those are gardens."

I stare in awe, my troubles temporarily suspended. "That's *amazing*."

"Yeah, kinda is," he says, "The lights are timed to turn on and off in a pattern sustainable to the plants—basically, one like Earth. It gives some hours of light, and some hours of complete darkness. Helps set circadian rhythms to a more normal level, too. If you watch carefully, you'll notice they're dimming. It's closer to evening, and the light should be waning."

I never thought about the difference between light and dark. With Pendomus being tidally locked, it's always perpetual daylight.

Once again, Kani takes off, prancing down the stairs while the rest of us try to keep up. When we finally reach the bottom, another man with a red shirt stands at the entrance to the city's circular encasement. From the stairs, you don't get an accurate gauge of how high the walls are, but they're immense—a good thirty feet high or more. The doors are enormous metallic beasts, and I wonder how they could possibly open.

"Hey, Patric," Trae waves.

Patric is carved from the same mountain as Ash, but his dark hair is cropped short. He blinks and doesn't say a word. His deep cheekbones reveal black eyes in the flickering torches on either side of the entrance.

He sighs and steps aside to let us pass. No awkwardness or questions about who I am.

There's a loud metallic thud, followed by a ticking sound, and the doors pull apart on their own. Once inside, the circular walls are like a gentle hug wrapping around you. The buildings inside are primitive in their design, built with stone and wood. They're angular, and square, with the uppermost levels open to the artificial sunlight. Everywhere I look is the color green. Green trees, plants, and flowers.

The air is fresh and musky. Sweet and bitter. Yet all of the smells blend together perfectly.

Deep shadows are cast by the candle-lit lanterns hanging across the pathway of polished stones.

"Trae," I tap him on the shoulder, "why aren't most of the lamps electric?"

"The generator isn't big enough for the kind of power it would take. Besides, we wouldn't want the Helix to discover us," he says, "They'd notice a huge power draw like that. Besides, more important things need electricity."

"Do you have one at the Safe Haven? A generator?"

He nods, "Yeah. Ours is a lot smaller, though. With only three—*four* people," his eyes flash to me, "we don't need much."

"Where did the generators come from?"

"The original one came from Earth," he says, "Our engineers dissected it to figure out what made it tick. From there, it's been adapted for the specific needs of the Lateral based on our energy accessibility. At least, that's what the engineers tell me when we play cards."

Wow.

My mind was so set on just acquiring the knowledge I need to get inside the Helix—to protect myself. It had never occurred to me the Lateral was something this spectacular.

"Runa, before we go to Landry's I need to stop and talk to Delaney. Either you can come with— or Kani and Fenton will take you straight there. What do you prefer?" Trae asks.

"Who's Delaney? Is he the leader of the Lateral?" I ask, my insides suddenly jittery.

Kani snickers,"Yes, *she* is. The one and only."

"Oh, whoops," I respond, considering. The Helix has always given the illusion the people are in control of themselves. So an antiquated system like government seems a bit hard to comprehend. "Let's see Delaney."

The outdoor torchlight accentuates Kani's cheekbones as she says, "People know what they can do to help, but no one is forced into any roles they don't agree to. We need a leader to keep us united. People, as it turns out, are unpredictable. Even the *normal* ones."

Kani and Fenton wind us in and out of buildings before turning up a set of stone steps. Fenton smooths the side of his head, winks at me and raps on the door.

After a moment, it swings open, and a small woman steps out. She's dressed plainly, but elegantly. Her cream-colored shirt contrasts nicely with the rich, dark brown of her skin and the dark curls of her hair. She's quite tall and exudes a commanding presence.

"Hello, *everyone*. Ash told me you were on your way," she has a twinkle in her eye as she nods to me.

Trae takes a step forward and the two of them embrace. "Hey, Delaney. This is Runa. She's—gonna be sticking around," he sighs, "She's the one I found out in the woods, being attacked by the Morph—but I'm sure you know all of this already."

"Hello, Runa. Won't you come in? We have much to discuss," Delaney extends her hand to me.

I accept, and she ushers us into the small house. After walking through an extravagant entry way, the main room she leads us to is open. It has a small seating area with large cushy chairs set predominantly in the room, and a large wooden table off to the left side.

The walls are adorned with objects on the walls. Large, inner parts of colorful flowers. The sun, set into the dead trees outside. A pair of hands—they're worn, like they've worked hard in their years.

"What are these?" I ask, taking a step forward.

Kani's the first to speak up, "Paintings."

"Paintings?" I repeat.

"I didn't stutter. Yes, paintings. These are mine. It's a form of artistic expression—which I suppose means nothing to you, being from inside the Helix," she smacks her forehead with the butt of her hand, "When I can't find a way to express myself in words, I paint."

"Seems like you can express yourself in words just fine," I reply.

The guys cover up a snicker, and Kani scrunches her face.

"Yeah, well, you don't know me very well yet, now do you?"

I step forward and take in the vibrant colors. I had no

idea people were capable of making things like this. Creating such—beauty. With our voices, with our hands.

For ourselves.

Everyone takes a seat in one of the oversized chairs and Delaney sweeps her hand out, "Please sit, Runa."

I take the seat nearest Trae, sinking in further than I anticipated.

Delaney smiles and sits in a large wooden chair with red, gold, and black woven through its upholstery. "Traeton, Landry tells me you were experiencing seismic activity in the Haven. Did you figure out what caused it?"

Trae shakes his head, "No, not conclusively, but the Haven's exit has been collapsed. We need to do some recon topside. Things aren't right out there."

"How do you mean?" Delaney asks.

"Fer starters, we jus' watched Runa's brother burst inta flames," Fenton says, leaning forward with wide eyes.

"He did what?" Delaney's eyes darken and she turns to me, "My goodness, child. Are you okay?"

An upsurge of emotion wells inside me and I bite my lip to keep it from quivering.

Trae leans forward, resting his forearms across his knees, "We're not really sure how it happened, to be honest. There was some sort of creature out there— it attached itself to her brother's legs and … well, incinerated them both."

"Unbelievable," She whispers.

"We need to invest some time at Landry's researching into a possible lead to the seismic attack, as well as Runa's brother's attack. As much as I think the mission with Ash is important, I believe whatever is happening right outside our door poses a bigger threat. We've now had two attacks in under a week."

"Perhaps. Runa, can you explain to me what happened to you? Why would the Morph attack you?" Delaney's dark eyes are serious as she waits for my answer.

"I don't know. I was in the wrong place at the wrong time, I guess."

Kani flits her eyes at me and leans toward Delaney, "Did anyone tell you Trae found her inside a hollow tree filled with water?"

Delaney looks to me and I nod in confirmation.

"The Morph has some unusual characteristics you and the rest of the team should know about," Trae says.

Delaney places her fingertips over her lips and leans forward, "Go on."

"It's now my belief that the reason no one has ever seen the Morph, is because it's invisible," Trae says.

"If that were true, how would you know it was there?" she asks.

I sweep my bangs behind my ear, "It was hard not to take notice, since it did this to me."

The creases in her forehead grow deeper as Delaney stands and walks closer to me. The intensity in her examination is overwhelming as she takes in my wound, the colors of my eyes. She never inhales or acts surprised. She just —looks.

"It also got her leg. Right here," Kani points to my right calf.

"How long ago was this?" Delaney asks.

"Four days," Kani answers, awe tinting her voice.

"Hmmm," Delaney's lips tug downward, "Runa, I find your story particularly fascinating for two reasons. The first, obviously your miraculous healing. The second, the attack itself. It brings about some very problematic results."

"Problematic? I don't understand—" I shake my head.

"What do you mean?" Trae asks.

Delaney returns to her seat and sighs. Her fingertips flutter against her lips as she looks between the four of us. "It's problematic … because the Morph doesn't exist."

"*H*ow can you say the Morph doesn't exist? Take a gander at her," Kani snickers, pointing at my face.

Delaney stands up and walks behind her chair, clutching onto the back.

"Lane, what you're saying makes no sense. Runa's proof —" Trae begins.

"What I'm about to tell you is strictly confidential. The only reason I'm telling you any of this is because these attacks," she points in my direction, "*your* attack, Runa, comes as a complete surprise. I don't like surprises. I'm going to need your help to figure out what actually did this to you."

"Spit it out, Lane," Kani retorts, "What are you saying?"

"The Morph, or rather, the *mythology* of the Morph— came from us," Delaney blinks deliberately, and her lips press into a thin line, "Trae, you know better than anyone in this room why."

Trae's face is completely expressionless, but he tips his head in response.

"Whoa, whoa … Wha'?" Fenton says.

"I wasn't attacked by a mythological creature. This is real." I shine the damaged side of my face at her, my anger bubbling to the surface.

"Precisely," Delaney raises her eyebrows in acknowledgement, "Which is why I'm going to need you to show me where this attack occurred. Come to think of it, can you draw me a map?"

"We don't have time for this. I need to get to—" I stop abruptly, unsure how much I want to divulge to this woman who's evidently been lying to everyone.

"Runa," Delaney starts, trying to sound reasonable, "I understand you may be on a different mission, but I'd appreciate your help. The safety of everyone here—including you and your friends—depends on it."

Well, this sounds familiar, doesn't it?

I hang my head in defeat. I need to find out more information on my brother's killer— not wasting time here.

Kani stands and puts a hand on her hip. "I can draw you a map to the area where it happened, but that's as good as it gets, Lane."

Delaney's back is ramrod straight and she pulls at the bottom of her shirt. "I see. Well, a map should suffice—for now. However, if we can't locate the creature in question, we will come find you for more information."

In a swift movement, Delaney reaches into a drawer on the underside of a small table to her left. She takes out a small flat object and passes it to Kani.

I watch in awe as the blank paper goes from nothing to explaining the terrain and location of the Tree. Kani's hand flits back and forth with precision and speed as she pours out her knowledge through her fingertips.

A few moments later, Kani's hand comes to a stop, and she tries to pass it over.

"No, I need details too," Delaney says, "Details only Runa can offer. Can you write for her? I assume she's never done it before, based on what you've explained."

"Uh, what kind of details do you need from me?" I ask.

"Do you remember anything specific we should be aware of?" she urges.

"Well, the sonic resonator Trae used made it release me. At least, we think that's why." Kani's hand scribbles furiously at the paper and Trae nods in agreement. "I remember three huge claws on its paws—drenched in my blood," I shudder.

"It was completely invisible?" Delaney leans against the table and crosses her arms.

"I had no idea the Morph, the *creature,* was beside me at first. It was deadly silent. For some reason, it took a particular liking to my eye. The attack didn't happen right away—"

Delaney listens to the rest of the details. When everything has been written down, Kani gently folds the paper and places her hands over top.

"I've been thinking. Before I hand this over, we deserve more answers," she tells Delaney, her eyes flashing, "For example, how did the mythology of the Morph come from you?"

"Kani's right. This ain't tha sorta thing ya jus' go aroun' hidin' an' think we're all okay wit it," Fenton says.

"Kani, there are some things you don't need to know," Delaney states calmly.

"If I wanted more cryptic, I would have stayed in the Helix, Lane. You can't tell us something like 'you made up the Morph,' and not expect me to ask why?" Kani laments.

"Delaney taps her lips with her pointer finger, "It was for security reasons. We needed a cover."

"For what? Making sure everyone obeys you?"

"No, Kani," Delaney whispers, her eyes narrowing, "People go missing from the Helix all the time … and never go back. Why?"

"Because they end up here," Trae says calmly. So far, he's the only one taking this news with complete stride.

"Precisely. It was a cover so those inside didn't come searching any farther than they had to. We needed something to keep the wrong people from finding us. Is that so hard to understand?"

"More like keep people in line," Kani snorts, "We've been just as afraid of the damn thing."

"No, Kani. That's the Helix's job. We have more insight into human psychology. We knew people would latch onto our story, inside the Helix or not. Those in charge behind the scenes needed a way to keep people in the hive and attached to their machines—just as much as we needed a viable reason for disappearance," Delaney offers.

"How is their goal any different? The outcome is the same for you."

"Kani, I understand your concern. But we did what we thought was best."

"I'm *sure*," Kani stands and flicks the paper between her fingers, "Take it. Are we ready?"

With a final tip of her head toward the door, Kani turns and stomps out.

"Unreal," Fenton says, following after her.

"Traeton, can you stay a moment? I'd like a word."

Trae nods, "Of course."

"It was nice to meet you, Runa. I'm glad whatever

attacked you didn't win," Delaney's lips take on a slight smile, "Thank you for your cooperation."

"No problem," I say, turning to the door.

"I'll meet you guys at Landry's," Trae says, his blank expression resurfacing.

I halfheartedly smile and follow the other two out the door. Kani and Fenton stand huddled together with tight lips. The lights are dimmed to a flicker and the shadows in Kani's eyes look ominous.

The moment the door closes behind me, Kani shoves a finger at the house. "That—*woman!* All this time, lying to us. I knew it. I *knew* something wasn't right. That's why I went with the guys when they splintered. Everything's about control. *Her* control."

"You said she was the leader. Isn't control supposed to be part of the job? You know, by *definition*."

A part of me wants to be reasonable, but the tension is cause for concern. Truthfully, I'd like to be inside with Trae, hearing what's going on.

Kani chews on her lower lip, "You would side with her. Whatever, doesn't matter. Let's go."

"Lead the way."

Kani's black braid whips around as she and Fenton take off. Trees, buildings, people—they blur together as we speed walk our way through the crowd.

So many people linger out on the streets, and they turn their heads, watching as we stride past. Some of them even smile, as if I'm any other girl walking around.

A woman sitting on a step leans in and tells a young boy next to her, "See, honey? More people find us every day."

While I'm sure my white hair stands out, I'm not the only one in NanoTech garments.

Sitting on the ground near a tree, a young woman cradles an infant in her arms. The baby is so tiny. The woman leans in, her dark hair hiding her face as she blows on the baby's belly. The child flails, making a sound so similar to a giggle. Can a baby so young giggle?

The corners of my mouth twitch upward.

So lucky.

Parents and children—happy together. The thought stirs something inside and makes my heart ache. I wish I had such an upbringing. Now the only person in my life who has ever been kind to me inside the Helix is dead.

The lights overhead continue to dim, and the flame lanterns on the street cast more light than before. The darker it gets, the more prominent the strange little orbs dancing in my vision are; as if they have a mind of their own. I blink, but nothing seems to deter them.

Will they ever go away?

We turn a corner and a tangle of arms and legs move like spiders on a bench, nearly hidden in the shadows of the impending darkness. Their odd shape makes me stop short. They move as if they're all part of the same object. I take a step closer, trying to get a better understanding of what I'm seeing.

"What the hell? Don't be *rude*!" Kani grabs hold of my arm and yanks, "Let's go."

Fenton chuckles. "She'll hafta learn about kissin' sooner or later."

"Let's go with later," Kani spits back.

I stumble after her, but can't tear my eyes away. For a brief moment, a face emerges, and I gasp. The tangle of arms and legs is actually two people, lost in their own world. A woman is seated across a man's lap, his arms wrapped around her waist. Giggling, she throws her head back and he takes hold of her arms, pulling her closer. His mouth traces the curve of her neck and lingers on her exposed shoulder.

My pulse races, and I suck in a quick breath. The interaction appears both ridiculous and absolutely fascinating. The two of them don't even notice as we move away.

Kani spins around, eyes blazing, "Geezus. You can't just gawk at people like that."

"I'm sorry. I just—they were …" I point behind me.

"Yeah, so what?" she flares her nostrils, "Look, I get it. I do. But out here, you can't just stare at everyone."

"Right. I'm sorry."

I fall in line again, but my heart pounds loudly in my ears. What's the purpose of kissing?What would it be like—being tangled in that way? Would it be awkward? They seemed so in tune with each other. Does kissing like that come naturally? How do they *breathe*?

We finally stop at the base of a set of stone steps to a moderate-size building. The doorway is a bright blue and light shines from the windows, cascading in large rectangles across the lumpy walkway.

Kani raps her knuckles across the wood three times, and takes a step back. A moment later, a set of brown eyes peer out of a crack in the door. With an audible sigh, the door slams shut. Fenton smirks as a series of clicking sounds go on behind the door. When the door reopens all the way, the oddest-looking man I've ever seen steps out.

Nearly the same height as Fenton, Landry is more muscular in build and has absolutely no hair on the top of his head. Instead, three small wavy lines of hair are shaved into both sides of his jaw, and he has the tiniest hint of a triangle under his bottom lip. Running down his neck and under his black shirt, a spiral pattern is etched into his skin.

If I wasn't aware Landry was on our side, I'd assume something was seriously wrong with him.

"Ladies," his lips flicker, making the wavy lines on his jaw flow like water.

"Hey— " Fenton says, pushing his brother aside, "Watch it."

Landry smirks and steps away from the doorway so we can follow inside.

The main room is dark, lit only by a series of holographic screens in the back. There are two large plush chairs in the front.

Taking a seat near the monitors, Landry cocks his head, "Runa, I presume."

I smile and nod, unsure of what to say.

Landry's laugh is deep and unexpected, "I've heard a lot about you the past few days."

My face flushes, and I fiddle with one of my braids.

"Super," Kani says.

"I can see why Trae's so enthralled," Landry steps forward, and my eyes go to the floor.

Trae's what? Did I hear him right?

"Tha's an understatement," Fenton says under his breath.

"May I take a gander at your eye?" Landry asks.

I lift my jaw to meet his inspection. He's much older than all of us with an air of maturity about him. It seems out of place for someone who looks so peculiar.

"Isn't that something?" Landry's eyes narrow, and he tilts my chin to the side.

"Yeah, yeah. Freakin' awesome. We need to do some

research. Delaney's on our butts about helping her, and we have other plans," Kani taps the floor impatiently.

"So, quakes, huh?" Landry says, starting the conversation off.

Fenton plops himself down in one of the plush chairs, "Our exit is blocked."

"Blocked? With what?" Landry asks.

"Snow. Ice. Rock. The whole thing sorta caved in after Trae shot Jane at the entrance," Kani shifts her weight, but doesn't take a seat, "But that's not the worst of it ..."

"We go' some bigger problems ou' in them woods," Fenton says, "First off, tha Morph ain't tha Morph. There's black, creepy lookin' serpent or salamander things as big as a person and they can incinerate you if they ge' close enough ..."

"Whoa. Huh? Slow down," Landry says.

"Fenton's right. Plus, turns out Lane's been lying about the Morph all this time. Evidently it's some big rouse. So we have no clue what's actually attacked Runa," Kani says.

Landry scratches the side of his jaw, "Okay ... not surprising on Lane's part. I've wondered about the Morph for a long time, since no one has ever been attacked. But the serpent? What's up with that?"

"We don't know yet. My brother was just killed by one and I could use a Helix mainframe search. Are you able to get in?"

"Damn, sorry, Runa," Landry begins.

"I don't really want to talk about it. I just want to find answers. Can you do it?"

"Sure. Easy peasy," Landry says, turning around to face his monitors. With a few flicks of his fingertips an access point to the eLink appears. It looks just as it would in my mind when I've reentered from outside.

"Okay. Who do we want to be today? Erbert Redlin or Erma Bombeck?" Landry asks.

"Who cares?" Kani says.

"Go wit Erma," Fenton snickers, "Ya look like a Erma to me."

"Erbert it is," Landry says, ignoring his brother.

"Can I take it from here?" I ask, edging closer as the access is granted.

With his thumb, Landry rubs the triangular patch under his lip, "I dunno about that. I don't usually let other people play with the equipment."

"Oh."

"But ... I s'pose I could make an exception," Landry scoots aside, giving me access to the holographic screens.

I flick through the prompts with my fingertips. It's a strange sensation to use physicality for such simple tasks, where the intention in my mind was enough only days before.

Entering in the data for Videus, I'm surprised to see a slew of information come up, but much of it doesn't make sense. Words are out of order, whole sentences seem to be missing.

Trae opens the door to Landry's house and steps inside.

"Hey everyone. Find anything so far?" he asks.

"I'm not sure. Landry, why is so much of it jumbled up?" I ask, then point to the screen. "What's this about an engineer?"

"Where?" Landry peers closer, "Videus? Why are you searching for him?"

"I've been told to be wary of him—and I suspect he may be the one behind the attacks," I tell him.

"Runa, have you ever gotten details on the engineer in charge of the mission to colonize Pendomus?" Landry asks.

"No." I tell him, "My downloads gave no credit to an engineer. We've been taught our colonization was the inspiration of many. The general cooperation of all involved, with no one standing out more than the other. Which is why we operate the way we do in the Helix."

Landry nods, "I suspected as much. Well, despite that theory … I stumbled on something in the Archives a while back which I found interesting. There *was* an engineer and based on this inquiry, I think his name may mean something to you—it was Goddard. *Videus* Goddard."

Sucking in a breath, my pulse quickens, and I stare at him. "Are you sure? Why is it not listed here? Why were we never told?"

"Who knows? It looks like whoever's been in here has done a good job confusing the trail. I don't even see a last name attached to— "

Whole sections of data suddenly start erasing in front of our eyes until the entire list of results is gone and we're left staring at a blank holographic screen.

"Quick—log out of the system," Landry reaches around me, flicking commands until the Helix encrypted eLink is gone, "That was close."

"What just happened?" I ask.

"Someone caught on ta tha search and apparen'ly didn't like it," Fenton responds, adjusting his glasses.

"There's clearly something up with this. Why don't you guys go to the Archives and search for yourselves? The system out there is primitive, but as far as I've been able to tell, it isn't linked to the Helix in any way. The data should be more secure, maybe even more intact. If someone out there's using the founding engineer's name to wreak havoc, understanding his namesake would be a good place to start. Means he's an inspiration of some sort. Fenton, you remember where the old mainframe is, right?" Landry asks.

Fenton nods, "Sure."

"I'll stick behind here and see what else I can dig up. Fenton, let's hook you up with a ComLink so we can stay in touch. Sound good?"

"Yup. Works fer me," Fenton agrees.

"Good. Before you're off, I think you should at least eat and rest first, though. It's getting late, and I bet you're not used to the sleep stuff yet, are you Runa?"

"We can camp out in the tunnels, Landry. I'd rather not waste more time than we have to," Trae says.

Kani walks to the kitchen table and takes a seat. "I will, however, never pass on your cooking."

Landry chuckles and whispers, "Don't say that too loudly around Fenton."

"Too late. I already 'eard." Fenton says, sticking out his tongue at the two of them.

13

RUNA

*L*andry hands Fenton a small, clear device the size of a thin wire, but arched in a semi-circle.

I lean in for a better look and ask, "What is that?"

"ComLink. I pu' this behind one of me ears and it'll bind with me skin, givin' Landry a feed to vitals and direct communication. Kinda like tha eLink. Unfortunately, ya got tha eLink already in yer 'ead, so they'd short circuit. Which is why I'm tha lucky one," Fenton says.

"Wow," I say, impressed, "Can you tap into the visuals, like the Helix does, or does this operate on word communication only?"

"My ComLink can do visuals, too, but sometimes they can be too intrusive. Especially when you need your own sight. The software will only trigger a visual response if you specifically request it," Landry says, "Personally, I think whoever invented the eLink shoulda considered this stuff more."

"Everyone ready?" Traeton asks, placing his washed plate

and silverware into the drainer. "Thanks for the dinner, Landry. Much appreciated."

"Eh. It was nothing," Landry says, shrugging, "Do you guys have everything you need?"

"Seems like we do," Trae says, "Fenton, you got the sleep packs?"

"Sure do," Fenton beams. His grin is broad as he turns to me and winks. "We'll getcha used ta this sleepin' stuff yet, Runa."

"Are the Archives really so far that we'll need to sleep again?"

"They're far enough that we'll need to rest before we get there, yeah, " Kani says, throwing some more supplies into her pack. "You should grab some water, too, Runa. You'll need something to drink."

Nodding in agreement, I fill a couple canisters with water and place them in the pack Landry's letting me use. The sound of the water reminds me of the first time I heard the voice in my head. Even now I can't quite figure out what to make of everything. If I hadn't just watched Baxten—I'd be seriously questioning my sanity right now. But everyone else saw it too. As it is, I still haven't come up with a good way of explaining all that's happening to me. What if my friends reject me because of the voice? Could I do this all on my own?

Trae walks to the door and holds it open, "Alright, let's get moving. I'd like to be outta here before anyone has time to question where we are."

Kani pats him on the shoulder as she walks out the door and says, "Running from Lane, huh?"

"No," He says, his eyes shifting from Kani to me.

"Don' worry, Trae. Yer secret's safe wit us," Fenton says, laughing, "See ya, bro."

"Careful out there, guys," Landry calls out to us as we all exit the building.

Trae leads us through the crowded streets, keeping his head low and a hood up. No one says anything, we all just follow along and try to keep up. We exit the city walls through a tiny side door meant for a person the size of a small child. A pathway winds away, leading into the black abyss on the furthest part of the large cavern opening which houses the Lateral. Staring into the depths, my eyes slowly adjust to the darkness as Trae flips on a microlight and puts it in ambient mode. The wide open space surrounding the Lateral is easily five times its size, but most is unusable. Gigantic mounds poke up all over, and massive spikes cling to the ceiling.

After an hour of silence and walking in darkness, my mind is screaming for stimulation.

"How much farther are we walking?" I ask, tapping Kani on the shoulder.

"Are you *two*?" she says, batting my hand away without even looking back.

"I thought there was supposed to be a pathway leading up and out of here?"

"Soon," she says, "We're all getting bored, okay?"

"Pathway's up ahead," Trae says, pointing the microlight at a specific spot on the rocky wall.

"*Finally*," Kani says, maneuvering closer to the wall.

As we get nearer, I pull up short and point to the tiny ledge-like pathway in front of us. "You don't mean—*that*? It can't be more than a meter wide."

My eyes drift upward.

With no end in sight.

"This is it," Kani says, her teeth sparkling brightly, "Our *only* way out now."

"You're not serious," I mutter.

"It's not as bad as it seems, Runa. Stick by me. I'll help guide you," Trae says, offering his hand.

Kani's grin widens, and I clench my jaw, taking Trae's hand.

"This is a piece of cake. Just don't look down. Keep your back against the cavern wall. Okay?" he says, squeezing my hand in his.

"Okay."

"I won't let anything happen to you."

I place a tentative footstep on the ledge and clutch the wall for balance.

"How's that gimpy leg of yours holding up? Kinda looking shaky from here," Kani says.

"It's *fine*."

My vision blurs in and out, and I wish more than I anything to burrow through the wall. Shadows below appear like sinister spikes of death and do little to help with depth perception. The weird orbs of light dance around in the open space of the cavern, making it hard to see anything else.

For a while, our jagged breathing and footsteps keep track of time. Sweat drips down my neck, but I can't bring myself to attempt wiping it away. Instead, it pools in the small of my back as we continue to shuffle farther and farther from the safety of the ground.

Without warning, something large and fast moves in my peripheral. It undulates in the darkness, rippling the rock. My muscles clench as I quickly twist to my right to get a better view. Unable to stop the momentum, my footing falters and I lurch forward into the black abyss.

Hands wrap around my forearm and the back of my NanoTech jacket, and I'm wrenched back onto the pathway. As I slam against the wall, a series of rocks crash to the ground below, echoing loudly as final punctuation to one possible end.

Exhaling terror, my eyelids slam shut and my legs give out. My back scrapes along the rocks as I sit straight down on the safe, hard pathway. Thrumming loudly in my ears, my heart could take off and fly.

"Are you okay, Runa?" Trae asks, his voice quivering.

"What the hell were you thinking?" Kani says, slapping my shoulder.

I swallow hard and stare into the vast expanse ahead.

That was close.

"Ya just abou' took a nose dive," Fenton says.

"Did you see it?" I ask, "The movement?"

"The only thing moving was us as we scrambled to pull you back," Kani says.

Trae takes a seat next to me and says, "Sometimes your eyes can play tricks on you in this kind of darkness. It's not uncommon."

I nod, but can't muster the strength to move.

"Do you think everyone in the Lateral heard?" I ask.

The dimly lit circle in the distance is so far away now, but the reverberations from the rocks falling continue to bounce around us.

Fenton tilts his head to the side and places a fingertip to his lips in a silent request.

"Landry," Trae mouths at me.

I sigh. *Of course.* The ComLink.

"Yep. Landry jus' confirmed yer theory, Runa. He wanted to know if we're alrigh'. I let 'em know ya tried ta take a swan dive, bu' we talked ya back," Fenton says, smirking.

"Great." I say, dusting myself off, "Well, I think I've wasted enough of our time."

Trae stands, holding his hand out for me. My legs are wobbly as I'm wrenched to my feet, but gain stability as we begin walking again. I hug the cavern wall, keeping my sight ahead to where the microLight shines.

"We're nearly done with this part. Hang on just a little longer, Runa," Trae says as he glances over his shoulder.

When we reach the end of the ledge and the start to the enclosure of the new tunnel, the space wraps around me in a delightful embrace. I run my hand along the walls, taking in the safety through my palms.

"I think this is good place to stop. We should get a couple hours of sleep before setting off on the last leg of the trip," Trae says, taking his pack off and setting it on the ground in front of him. He bends down, pulling out a lamp that expands outward and turns itself on. The light accentuates all the crevasses in the natural rock around us.

"So which one o' ya lovely ladies wants ta sleep in my pack?" Fenton says, wiggling his eyebrows up and down. He grins widely at Kani, sweeping his hand out in front of the two sleep packs on the ground. Kani steps forward and playfully slaps him across the arm.

"As if you ever had a choice," she says.

My mouth drops open.

"Fenton," Trae starts, "Why are there only two sleep packs? I thought you said you grabbed them all?"

"Wha' do I look like? A mule? I grabbed as many as I

though' we'd need," Fenton says, a smirk deepening across his features.

"Unbelievable," Trae mutters, running his hand absently through his hair, "Okay, it's settled, then. Runa, you take the extra pack. I can sleep without one."

"Wha' fun is tha'?" Fenton says.

Kani grabs the first sleep pack, unrolls it and slides inside, "Well, what are you waiting for? Get in," Kani says, patting the outside of the fabric.

The sleep pack barely fits around her, so I have no idea where Fenton plans to squeeze himself in. Without another request, he dives at Kani and disappears inside the sleep pack. It quickly becomes a lumpy mass with Kani erupting into a fit of giggles.

I shoot a lopsided grin at Trae, who looks conflicted as he leans down and grabs the other sleep pack.

"Well, here. Let's get some rest, huh?" He says, handing it to me.

I blink hard and cling onto the pack as he walks away.

"Trae, wait," I hold the pack out to him, "You should take this. You've done so much for me already. Really. I doubt I'll be able to sleep anyway."

He stops walking and shakes his head, "No deal."

"If you won't—I mean, if I can't get you to …" my heart thumps unevenly, "I think *we* should share. You can't sleep out in the cold. That isn't right, either."

"Yeeeaaahhh!!" A rumble emerges from the lumpy sleep pack, "Listen to tha woman, Trae."

I bite down on my lip to suppress a grin, but Trae remains unreadable.

My resolve falters, and I close my eyes, shaking my head, "I just thought …"

"I can't, Runa," he says, his eyes blazing, "It wouldn't be right of me. Let me be the gentleman here, okay?"

A wave of disappointment washes over me. A part of me really hoped to be nearer to him before he leaves. I don't understand this connection—but I wish I had more time.

"Fine. Okay," I whisper.

I spread the pack on the ground and slide in, rolling away from Trae and his rejection. Fenton growls, making Kani giggle again and I swipe at the tears on my cheeks.

Why do I have to feel so alone?

Trae shuffles around behind me and clears his throat. A second later he says, "Did you know those are called stalactites?"

I inhale and roll over. He's lying on his back with one leg bent, an arm behind his head. When our eyes meet, he points to the cavern ceiling.

"See, the things dripping down like icicles?" he says.

"Oh."

"The ones on the ground are called stalagmites," he says, an easy smile gracing is lips. The shadows play across his face, and his dimple deepens because of it.

"Trae, what do you think attacked my brother?" I ask, "Have you seen anything like that before?"

"I honestly have no clue. Never seen something like that before," he says, "Seems to be happening a lot since I met you."

"What do you mean?"

"Odd occurrences. Things I've never seen happen before. And believe me, I've seen a lot."

"What's the strangest thing that's happened since you met me?" I ask, not wanting to let our conversation fall into another uncomfortable silence.

"Hmmm … well, besides your attack, or the tree that spit us out … or your fast healing … the seismic activity—which we never pinpointed the source … your brother … the Morph that isn't a Morph. This hunt for a guy named Videus. I think a better question would be what's been *normal* since I met you," Trae says, chuckling.

"I'm guessing not much, then?" I say.

"Not really," he says, shaking his head, "You know, Runa, I'm sorry I didn't tell you about this mission I have to go on. I wasn't entirely sure how things were going to play out after I brought you in to the mix."

"Play out?"

"I wasn't sure if you were going to wake up at first. Then, when you did … " His voice trails off.

"When I did?" I urge, wanting to know where this is going.

"When you did," he pauses again, staring deeply into my eyes, "then I kinda didn't wanna go."

I bite my lip as my heartbeat thumps louder.

"Why not?" I ask.

Trae takes a moment, his eyes distant as he searches for his words.

Finally, he says, "Runa, I know all of this is new to you. Adjusting to life without the Helix methods. But for me … There isn't much I haven't done. Much I haven't experienced. Which also means, there isn't much that will make me pause or second guess myself. Since I've met you … I seem to be doing it a lot."

"I don't— " I begin.

"Runa, I like you. I like being around you and it's sorta messing me up," Trae confesses. "You haven't really had time to adjust or to sort out your feelings."

"I like you, too, Trae. A lot. You're the first one who's made me feel included or wanted. You never had to do that."

"I don't think you understand what I mean, yet— and I shouldn't push you. Hell, I shoulda never let things get complicated like this ... but I just feel— a connection with you. And I can't seem to shake it."

"And that's bad?" I ask.

"No, not bad. Just ... *complicated*," he says, looking beyond me to the now quiet sleep pack behind me, "I have this strange desire to protect you, to be near you. Then, the other part of me feels I shouldn't get too close. When I'm done here, I need to leave and I don't know when I'll be back. That's not fair to you."

"Let me be the judge of what's fair. Okay?" I say, raising an eyebrow, "I can handle myself."

"I know you can. I just don't want to make things worse for you."

"Well, you're not," I say, rolling onto my stomach and propping up on my forearms.

"You don't know that yet. Give me time," he says, smirking, "Well, I suppose we should get some rest ... Sleep well, Runa."

He covers his eyes with his free arm.

"You too, Trae."

I settle into the sleep pack, trying to relax. After a few minutes, Trae's rhythmic breathing sets the tone, and I will myself to give in to the darkness ...

Those hands ...

Strong arms wrap around my body, pulling me into his warm

embrace. The blood coursing through my veins sparks at the point where my fingertips trace the nape of his neck. He groans and angles his head to the side, leaving his neck exposed. My legs straddle his, so I rock forward and nibble my way from his ear to his shoulder blade.

With a growl, his hands leave my back and firmly cup my jawline as he guides my mouth to his. His lips burn on mine, and warmth radiates from deep in my belly as I press closer. My hands fly to his gorgeous hair, and I entangle my fingers in the soft waves. I love the way it feels. Our mouths move in rhythm with one another, a simple knowing beyond words. He tickles my tongue with the soft, fleshy part of his lower lip, and I lure it in, gently nipping.

He pulls back, hunger lurking in his dark eyes, "You think so?"

A wicked grin plays across his features, the faintest hint of his dimples appearing. I brush a strand of blue hair from his forehead and giggle. Like a predator on the hunt, he pounces, attacking my neck in a movement so swift, I'm rendered immobile. Returning a hand to the small of my back, he softly traces my jawline with his tongue ...

MY EYELIDS POP OPEN, and I blink, wide-eyed, at the cavern walls. The shadows flicker with the lantern light, and I shudder away the emotions rolling through me. My eyes dart to where Trae lies, sleeping. The mere sight of him restarts my pounding heart and I turn away, staring at the rocky wall.

What was—*that?* How can my lips still tingle from—*was it a dream?* It felt so *real.*

We were sitting on the bench at the Lateral—the same one where I watched the couple kissing— My fingertips brush against my lips, and I sneak another glance at him. He's facing me, his head resting in the crook of his arm. The concern weighing down his expressions during the day has evaporated, and what's left is the little boy inside. I roll to my side, facing him, and smile.

What was he like as a child? Was he adventurous? Was he like me, sneaking out into the woods? What were his aptitudes like? Where was he headed with his scans?

Still ... why *blue*?

With my right hand out in front of me, I rub my fingers together. The texture of his hair lingers in my fingertips—as if I'd actually run my fingers through those blue strands. His hair was longer in my mind—and more vibrant.

A strong hand drapes across his torso, and a tickle runs down my spine.

Shivering in his sleep, Trae's forehead furrows and he jams his hands under his arms. As he rolls onto his back, his exhalation billows in clouds as it escapes.

I bite my lip, and shift onto my back, staring at the stalactites.

What would he do if I moved closer? Would he be upset?

The sleep pack is wide enough for both of us to fit underneath if I unzipped it. Having a layer on top is better than nothing at all, right?

Peering cautiously at him through the corner of my eye, my teeth almost pierce the skin on my lip. I can't stand the thought of him being so cold. Not after everything he's done for me— not after his confession tonight.

If I'm going to do this, it's now or never.

Shifting to a seated position, I slide out of the pack as silently as possible.

Am I actually doing this? What if he wakes up? What if he freaks out?

What if he doesn't notice at all?

Trembling, I gather the soft, cool sleep pack in my arms, and move tentatively toward Trae. Within inches from him, the pull to him intensifies.

Before I have time to over-think, I place the sleep pack on top of him. He exhales loudly, making me pull my hand back, and freeze. When nothing else happens, I take another slow, deliberate breath, and slide in beside him.

His clean, earthy scent does little to level my head. It transports me to my early moments in his arms, and to the vividness of my dream. Inches separate us, but I shift uncomfortably. There's nothing to rest my head on, and lying here is anything but restful.

Would he wake up if I moved his arm? I've already risked so much to get to this point. Do I dare risk even more? At some point, he's going to know I'm here.

I take shallow inhalations and grab hold of his right wrist. It's held in place by his other arm, so I tug gently until it releases. Trae stirs slightly as I lay his arm on the ground beside us. Shaking, I slide my shoulder under his and rest my head on his broad chest. Fire burns through my cheek at our point of contact, but I move closer. Heat radiates from him, along the entire length of my body. He sighs, and my head rises and falls with the movement. From this place, his scent is stronger, and I sink into it. Relief floods through me, as though I've appeased an itch needing to be scratched.

It doesn't take long before his unconscious shivering subsides and a smile creeps across my lips.

This was worth it.

His heat, the way he smells … the rhythm and familiarity

… My heartbeats slow, and I close my eyes. Surprisingly, I don't think anything is more relaxing than this.

In the moment just before darkness consumes me, his hand wraps around my waist, gripping my back, pulling me closer.

"Thank you, Runa," he whispers.

*R*una lifts her head from my chest and props up on her elbow. Her face is inches from mine. Her scent, a subtle hint of vanilla, tickles my senses and makes it impossible to think clearly as I blink away the remnants of my uncomfortable sleep.

She's here? With me?

Why?

My hand smolders at its point of contact against her waist, but I'm too afraid to let go. Each place where her body meets mine is more alive than it's ever been.

Runa's multicolored eyes penetrate mine, and the corners of her mouth tug downward. She looks like a child who's been caught doing something mischievous, but with her mesmerizing lips—she's anything but a child.

"Please don't be mad," she whispers, "You seemed so cold."

She struggles, trying to sit up, but my hand reflexively pulls her closer and I tell her, "You shouldn't have, but thank you."

"Are you sure? Is this—okay?"

Alarm bells sound in my head. There is no way this is okay. I shouldn't be here, getting myself involved like this, but I can't bring myself to care.

"Are you comfortable?" I clench my jaw, partly hoping she'll say no.

The first real smile breaks across her face, and she nods, "Very."

An explosion of anxiety mixed with elation erupts in my chest, and I swallow hard, "Then, that's all that matters."

"Really?"

"Absolutely."

Runa's warm exhalation sweeps across my cheek. I can tell there's something she'd like to say as she hesitates, her eyes locked on my lips. I hold my breath as she bends in, her lips centimeters from the surface of my own.

What is she doing?

Suddenly, she pulls back, her eyes wide, "I don't know what I ... "

Unsure how to respond, my tongue sweeps across my lips, echoes of a near kiss left behind. I shiver but try to recover, "Uh ... the RationCap flush. Remember? Probably still ..."

"Oh, right," her eyes go distant, "I didn't think of that."

She frowns slightly and returns her head to my chest.

"So, uh ... no worries," I offer.

She inches closer and places her right hand above my heart. The tips of her fingers gently rest on my collarbone, and I take slow, deep breaths to center myself. My heart's pumping so aggressively, I can feel it pounding—everywhere. My eyes widen, and I fixate on a single piece of jutting rock above me. *Please don't let her notice.*

This situation couldn't get any more awkward and yet,

part of me is maniacally giddy about that fact. I need something to do. Something *physical*.

I remove my hand from her waist to stroke the tips of her hair. Runa snuggles her cheek against my chest, and her exhalation sounds like music.

Sleep. That's why she's here.

That's why *I'm* here.

Sleep.

Woodworking—yep. I'll think about woodworking. What project would I work on now, if I could? I stare blankly ahead and return my hand to Runa's back. The only wood that comes to mind is the burning kind. Hot and fiery …

This is so ridiculous. I've been attracted to other women —why is she so *different?* It doesn't help having all of Fenton's tales raging through my mind like a disease—I wish he'd keep his comments to himself.

Who am I kidding? I may very well be worse than Fenton. At least he's honest with himself. Sure, he's always been more flamboyant about his … desires, but at least he's never felt a need to hide from them. Damn, I envy that. I don't want these attachments … I don't want to hurt anyone else.

The enticing tickle of an alternative twists in my brain. What if Fenton's right? What if things can be different with Runa? What if I can find a place in her eyes? Her heart? What if—

Sighing softly in my arms, Runa sinks deeper into me. Sleep would be so much easier to deal with than reality right now. My forehead creases, and I press my lips together. She's so innocent. Even if we had kissed—she'd have no context. Maybe the Helix wasn't so far off by restricting these types of impulses, after all.

My eyes travel the length of our bodies, resting on the

rhythmic way Runa's head rises and falls. Oddly enough, it's relaxing.

Before Landry filled me in about the hormone control in the RationCaps, I thought I was going insane. But no—the Helix, for whatever reason, wants to control these … *urges*. Despite being uncomfortable at first with our conversation, I felt better afterward. Relieved I was normal. Not Helix normal, but *nature* normal. I wasn't going to die because of it. One day, this would equalize. It wouldn't be so … intense.

And for a while, it wasn't.

For someone who's never lived inside the Helix, Landry's been a fount of knowledge. Not everyone in the Lateral is as open to discussing things as he is. Hell, I'm not. I've just learned control. Focused my energies elsewhere. Runa's fingertips slide toward the edge of my neck, and another wave of heat washes over me. This situation—is completely different.

The physical attraction is obvious, but it's more than that. She can be open, despite the pain hiding in her eyes. She has this … gentle kindness about her. And she's been so accepting of our band of outcasts. Of me.

Runa shivers in her sleep, making me hyperaware of each part of her body touching mine.

I stiffen at the intensity— but I still wouldn't change a thing. I'll stay here, locked like this for as long as she likes.

———

The heat is intense, and beads of sweat drip down my back. I walk purposefully down the hallway, but the anxiety builds to a crescendo. She's down here, and I need to get to her. This was all my fault.

Now I need to set this right.

I turn the corner and creep toward the heavy wooden door. My footsteps are barely audible on the cold, hard ground, but I still hold my breath.

This door. I can feel her inside. There's no way to explain it; she's just in there.

The scorching metal handle blisters the inside of my palm, but I manage to pry the door open. Lying on a stone slab in the middle of the barren room is my sister Ava. Her emaciated frame is only a shadow of her former self. Dark hair is matted to her head, and large, pearly beads of sweat seep from her pores, puddle beneath her.

I clutch her shoulders, "Ava—Ava, I'm so sorry. I didn't know what I was doing. I didn't realize what I said would cause this—"

But it isn't true. I knew back when I'd turned her in I was being overheard, and at the time it didn't matter. I couldn't take the agony anymore. The constant hovering over her. The way we had to live our lives. The impending doom of what may happen. I wanted it to end. I needed it to end.

Deep brown eyes fly open, locking with mine, and Ava wrenches forward. Her skeletal fingers claw at the front of my NanoTech jacket as she tries to pull me in.

"You—you did this. Every last eternal pain I suffer … it should be yours."

Blood spews from her mouth as she rasps. Her tiny arms drop, and I reach forward to catch her.

Blue flames erupt from torches in all four corners of the room and the heat is incredible. Ava's head lolls to the side and her eyes begin to radiate, glowing like hot embers. In an instant, her whole body ignites, and she flails backward onto the stone slab. Her high-pitched scream makes me feel sick and the hairs on my neck stand on end.

"Ava! Please—"

I lean toward her. But what can I do? There's nothing in this room to stop it.

Ava's body melts, distorting and twisting into something else— someone else. The fires die out as if someone snapped their fingers, and a young man takes Ava's place. I step back, blinking wildly.

His face is so familiar—

"Do not stand by and let history repeat. If she dies, everyone dies!" Baxten's voice rings in my ears, and his bile spews outward.

"But I—" I sputter.

Waxy hands reach out for me. "No! Promise me you'll remember—she dies, everyone dies!"

Baxten's flesh begins to drip like candle wax, evaporating upon contact with the sizzling floor. Within seconds, all that remains is his mocking skeleton and his haunting words.

AIR. I need air.

Gasping, I try to roll over, but Runa's still nestled against my body. The dream was so real, *too real.*

"Well, would you look at this?" Kani snickers nearby.

My eyelids slam shut and my muscles tighten. The last thing I need right now is these two perverts making comments.

With a sigh, I rub Runa's back, hoping to wake her, but she doesn't move. The expressions on Ava's and Baxten's tortured faces haunt my mind, and I tense even more. Dammit, I need to get up—take a minute to myself. Being this close—it's suddenly unbearable.

"Don't you two look cozy," Kani's obnoxious grin hovers above us, and I narrow my eyes.

Runa rubs her eyes as she rolls over in the sleep sack.

"Yeah, too noble and all tha'. Right, Trae, right," Fenton's jeering comes next.

I cringe as Kani's smile widens. Last night had been both exciting and scary as hell. Now, all that's left is the scary part.

"I'm gonna … I gotta—" I release my arm around Runa and slide away from her. She clutches the sleep pack close and sits up, blinking her wide eyes. Wishing I could blend into the shadows, I back away until I graze the rocky wall.

What I need is a few minutes alone—a few minutes to sort all this out in my head.

"You can imagine our surprise," Kani jeers, "when we wake up and find Runa missing. Only … she wasn't missing at all."

Fenton smirks, and I run my fingertips along the deep groove of my forehead. Runa's eyes weigh on me, trying to get my attention, but I can't meet her gaze. Instead, I keep seeing Baxten's dripping flesh in the back of my mind.

"It's abou' time ya both got on wit' it," Fenton chuckles.

"Geezus, it's not like that," I glare at him. Shaking my head, I take off down the tunnel.

"He was freezing. I thought …" Runa's eyes catch mine as I turn the corner, but I keep walking.

When I can no longer hear them, I find the nearest alcove and slide to the ground. My back is pressed hard against the uneven rock, and the temporary pain feels good. It's what I need.

This attraction to Runa really muddies my mind and all my plans. I'm supposed to be heading out with Ash. I *should've* taken off already.

But now … Who is she? Could this dream mean anything

or am I just losing my mind the way Ava was? What if I've been idiotic to toy with the idea things were okay? I've tiptoed to the edge of believing. But what if I've been kidding myself to think things could work out with Runa. That we were meant to be together, and all could be right in the world. Here, people get hurt, and they hurt each other. Hell, in my case—even dead and gone. I'm not always going to be around. I can't always protect her. Especially if I have my missions to accomplish.

The nightmare may not have been reality, but the basis for it—all of it is real. It's my mistake, my stupid childish anger that killed Ava. Had I kept my mouth shut the way I'd been told—who knows where we'd all be right now.

Baxten's another matter. There's no way anyone could've saved him, I *know* that. But it doesn't stop me from wishing I could've. They should both be here.

Pounding my fist into the ground, I press my eyes shut tightly.

This is all my father's fault.

If he'd been a better role model, cared equally for his children, things would've been different. I wouldn't have felt the way I had back then.

My head throbs. I haven't thought about my father in so long. He'd cared so much for Ava. She was always his precious favorite, and no one else could ever match up. When she was captured—he let us go without a second thought. But she was already lost—we weren't. He'd left us all wandering in the woods without a way to keep us safe. We needed him.

I needed him.

I pull my knees close and rest my forehead.

Who am I kidding? I'm not any different from my father

in so many ways. I leave people behind, too. But I do it because I'm trying to rectify my past mistakes.

How selfish. I snort and press my eyelids tighter. Cecilina and my mother are in the Lateral, but I can't bear to see them.

How awful is that?

Runa should have nothing to do with me. These feelings —maybe I need to bury them and move on. She deserves better than me. She deserves someone as special as she is. Someone who can always protect her. I need to pull myself together and finish what we started. Fenton and I will scour the Archives for an explanation to what happened to Runa's brother and whoever this Videus is.

Then, I'll be gone.

She's better off this way. Never knowing just how much …

Latching onto my resolve, I lift my head to find Fenton standing a few feet away. His glasses are pushed to the top of his head as he observes me in silence.

"Ya can't beat yerself up like this, ya know?" He walks over to me and takes a seat.

"Fenton, don't start—"

"Trae, ya can't live life shielding yerself from everythin' tha's gonna bring ya pleasure in this world. You're a good guy—a grea' guy. But yer stupid."

"Are you trying to make me feel better?" I spit, "Geezus, Fenton. You don't know—"

"Pffft. I've known ya a long time. Yer no' mystery ta me. Here's wha' I mean. Life … is meant to be lived. *Enjoyed.* Why else are we here?"

My jaw tightens and I stare at him. What can I say? I don't

know what the hell the meaning of life is. I can barely manage to stumble through my own.

Fenton's face is serious, "Runa's awesome. Sure, a little naïve, but it won't last. She'll get things figured out."

I frown, "I don't need—"

He cuts me off again, "But she doesn't *need* ya. You'd be right about tha'. She'll survive because I think she's stronger than she realizes."

"First thing you've said I agree with."

Fenton's dark eyes set on mine, "But you—you *need* her."

I look away.

"The question is," he continues, "are ya strong enough ta admit it to yerself?"

He's trying to be helpful, and I can't fault him—but his words only make me feel sick. Staring blankly at my hands as they rest on the ground, I sigh.

Strength, huh?

He has no idea how much strength this is gonna take.

RUNA

*T*he moment the guys come around the corner, my heart sinks. Trae's face is guarded and his dark eyes lack their usual luster.

Have I screwed everything up?

Everything is so confusing … These feelings. Baxten. The voices. My *life*.

"Fenton, do you think you can do some digging on this Morph situation when we get to the Archives, too?" Kani's voice has an edge. "I, for one, want to know what the hell actually attacked Runa."

"Good plan, love," Fenton agrees.

The line on Trae's forehead digs deeper, but he doesn't say anything. Reaching into his bag of food, Fenton shakes his head and starts setting things out to eat.

Fenton hands me a small orange object and proceeds to peel back the outer layer of his own. "This's an orange, Runa. Ya'll love it."

The orange has a good weight and an interesting texture.

Clutching the round object in both hands, I bring it to my nose. It doesn't have much of a smell.

"I told you you guys Delaney's as bad as the Helix. Still can't believe she made everything up."

Trae is stoic, his jaw clenched, and his eyes on the ground in front of him. I dig my fingernail into the outer shell of the orange, as Fenton did, and a sweet, pungent odor entices my senses.

"Well, it is pretty clever, dontcha think? Gives 'em a cover while keepin' 'em safe," Fenton says.

"That's not the point, Fenton," Kani spits. "They're controlling the way people think the same way as in the Helix—through manipulation. How can they be trusted?"

I see what Kani means. However, when I was inside, I never realized we were being manipulated. Though I'm not sure how that makes it any better.

Somewhere farther along the darkened tunnel, a strange scratching noise makes us all freeze. Fenton's bread is lifted to his lips as his eyes dart back and forth. Trae even makes eye contact for the first time since we woke up.

A momentary silence falls before the scratching happens again. Trae stands, then heads down the tunnel toward the sound. I grab Kani's microlight and scramble to my feet.

"I'm going with you," I tell him, grabbing hold of his wrist.

Trae looks down with wide eyes and brushes my hand away. "No, stay here with the other two. I can handle this. It's probably nothing. Don't worry."

The top of my hand tingles from his touch.

"If it's nothing, then I should be able to come with you," I say defiantly.

"Don't be stupid, Trae," Fenton drops his bread and stands.

If eyes had the ability to stab, Fenton would be in serious condition from Trae's murderous stare. Through gritted teeth, Trae says, "Fine. Let's *all* go."

He takes the lead, walking with purpose down the dark pathway.

My chest swells and I exhale. Why is he being this way?

"This is the way out. What if someone found the entrance?" Kani's whisper wavers beside me.

"Let's hope no," Fenton mutters.

With the microlight in ambient mode, we barely have enough light to see where we're going. The sound starts again as we approach, but it's different—almost similar to fabric flapping in the breeze. We reach a bend in the tunnel, and Trae pauses, holding up a hand for us to stop.

When the sound happens again, it's clear how close it is— on the other side of the bend. Trae's fingers begin a silent countdown.

Five.

Four.

Three.

Two.

One.

Adrenaline floods my veins, and every part of me is hyper-focused on whatever is causing the immediate threat. We rush forward as a group, tumbling out one after the other.

Flapping around the middle of the dark tunnel is a single, disoriented junco.

With a white beak.

I step out in front with my hands raised. "Wait—wait!" Everyone stares at me unblinking. "He's my …"

The little bird shimmers eerily in the dim light, almost as

if he himself exudes it. Bending down, I reach for him. First petting his gray head, then scooping him up. He's so small, his body fits well in the palm of my hand. With my pointer finger, I stroke the place between his wings.

What possessed you, little bird?

I look up to a mixture of relief and confusion on everyone's faces.

Kani shifts and puts a hand on her hip, "Don't you even *tell* me this is the bird you were delirious over when you first got here."

"Wha' tha hell would it be doin' down 'ere?" Fenton leans forward, fiddling with the yellow band on his face.

"Clearly, flopping along trying to locate Runa," Kani snickers.

Concern creeps across Trae's face as he steps forward. His intense brown eyes investigate the bird in my hands.

"What do you wanna do? With the bird, I mean," Trae asks.

"Well, we can't leave him down here," I say, "He needs to come with us to the surface. As long as he's not hurt, I can release him into the trees when we get outside." Now nestled against my body, the bird is calm and collected. I gently stretch open his wings, and he allows me to examine him. "Nothing seems to be out of the ordinary."

"Yeah, because it's completely *ordinary* for a bird to be down here," Kani says.

Trae tilts his head and says, "Okay, enough. Time to head out. We gotta get into the Archives as soon as possible— especially since we need to get this bird to the surface. Everyone ready?"

Fenton rubs his hands together and says, "Yesssss! Let's doooooo this! Time fer some diggin'."

After gathering the remainder of our things, we prepare to head to the surface.

"Runa, the series of tunnels ahead will be difficult terrain, particularly with a bird," Trae says, "They were left pretty rough as a natural defense to the Lateral."

I glance at the junco in my hand. *How* did *he make it all this way?*

"It's fine. I can handle it."

"All right. Let's go."

We walk for almost an hour with barely a word spoken. I follow a few meters behind Traeton, with Kani and Fenton taking up the rear. Kani giggles behind me, and I glance over my shoulder to see her nudge Fenton with her shoulder. My eyes trail down to their interlocked hands. Waves of anxiety roll through me, and I face forward only to notice how Trae's hands are balled into fists. I concentrate on petting my junco. He doesn't seem to mind.

"I think I'm going to name him Rowan," I announce.

"You would," Kani chuckles.

I can even *hear* her roll her eyes.

Fenton laughs, "I dunno. Kinda nice name. Oof!"

Kani pulls her elbow from Fenton's rib cage and grins at me.

Trae doesn't seem to notice the exchange at all as he continues on the pathway. I didn't have many expectations about how today would go. But this—isn't even close.

At least Rowan has calmed down. In fact, the way he relaxed, it's like he *was* looking for me, and now things are put right.

I steal another glance at Trae's hands. So much has happened in the past week. There are so many things I can't wrap my head around, and he's one of them. He's comforted me when I needed someone— I'd like nothing more than to be next to him again. To feel his arms around me, to smell his skin. To know I'm not as alone as I feel. For the briefest moment, he looks over his shoulder and sparks crackle in my abdomen.

These feelings … they're so distracting—and consuming. I should be completely focused on my mission to get answers. To find out what happened to Baxten. To figure out where this key is. Instead, I'm more confused than ever.

Is this why the Helix felt it was necessary to diminish hormones? Honestly, I don't even recognize myself.

"Kani," I call back, "what made the Helix begin their genetic matchup program?"

I instantly regret my question, because a wicked smirk takes over Kani's expression, making me blush. I almost walk into Trae, who has become a statue in the middle of the walkway.

Kani snickers, "What an interesting … er … question."

Fenton's smile is huge and goofy.

"What?" I search their faces. It's too late to take the question back.

Trae uses his fingertips to smooth out the lines on his ashen forehead. "I, uh … why're you asking, Runa?"

"I was thinking about my parents' selection, and what it would be like. You know, having the geneticists pair you up without any say. The design and implantation process seems so … impersonal. My mother and father hadn't even met until after Baxten had been implanted."

"Well, actually," Fenton begins.

Trae's eyes could be laser beams, and he raises a hand, "Fenton, I got this."

Kani snickers again and erupts into a fit of giggles.

165

"Why is this so funny?" I round on her, "I want to understand."

Rowan flaps wildly, clearly unsettled, and I pet his head to calm us both down.

"No one's laughing at you, Runa. I don't know if you're ready for some of the information you're asking for. Or the information these doofuses are insinuating, anyway," Trae says.

I sigh. "If I'm going to be a part of this group, you have to trust me."

"Let's stick with your question for now, okay?" I stare into Trae's dark eyes as he continues, "Why did they start the program? Well, from what we've pieced together, when the first ships colonized the planet, it was less of a planned thing and more of a necessity thing. Earth had been destroyed, and the ships escaped with a few hundred people each. These people were hand-selected to be a part of a mission based on their genetic makeup and intelligence."

I wave my hand dismissively, "I know all that. It was a part of the history downloads."

He nods, "What you don't know is a pandemic swept through years after we colonized. According to the records in the Archives, our numbers dwindled so low ... had everything been left to nature, we would've killed ourselves off. The resurrection scientists intervened, and their program was redesigned to help the Geneticists instead of finding a way to make Earth's animals live here."

I shift to one side, "I still don't get it, though. Why would they need to intervene with whatever natural courses we had before?"

Trae rubs the spot under his lip.

"Because of the problems that arise when people," he

swallows hard, "*mate* with someone too close to their gene pool."

My head spins as I try to place the context. It makes no sense ... not in a human context. Kani stifles another giggle, and I turn to them for further explanation.

"It's called inbreeding ... or incest," Fenton chimes in, "Tha' genetic code of a human gets all garbled up an' we ge' walkin' monstrosities."

"Well, that seems ridiculous. Why would humans choose to do something like that? Wouldn't they know better?"

"Not really," Trae's face remains guarded as he shakes his head, "Anyway, the Geneticists were appointed to run through the genetic strains and choose the best genetic matchup for each person to avoid any of these monstrosities."

"And they've been doing it ever since," Kani says.

"But a hundred thousand people or more live across the whole Helix. How many people do you need to avoid this? Why are they still—" I begin.

"Precisely," Kani says, raising both arms in agreement, "If they can control the code—or at least, the way the code gets exchanged—they can control the masses. They tell you what they want you to hear. And because people can't think for themselves, they all go along with it."

Trae leans into me and says, "Kani doesn't do well with not being the one in control."

His close proximity, his earthy scent, spin up my senses. Unfortunately, he frowns and takes a step back. I hug Rowan tight, trying to shield myself from further disappointment.

"I heard you, Traeton. Maybe you'd like to explain to her how things are *supposed* to be done?" she says, crossing her arms across her body, "The whole mating thing, perhaps?"

Trae flinches. *Is he blushing?*

I reluctantly turn to Kani, "What do you mean, *supposed to?*"

Her eyes twinkle. "Let's just say boys and girls can connect in more ways than one."

For some reason, Trae's boots are suddenly very interesting to him.

"Well, ah ... trust me," Fenton chuckles, "once ya've go' experience, life itself will *never* be tha same."

"Ugh," Trae walks away from us.

"Is this about the kissing thing?" Heat creeps up my neck and flushes my face, "Kani's already explained that to me."

"Oh, she did, did she? How did I miss tha' exciting talk?" Fenton says.

"She was gawking. What was I supposed to do?" Kani points toward me defensively.

"Yeeaah," Fenton rumbles, "Tha's my girl! Didya 'ear tha', Trae? Runa here's been a kissin' detective."

"Would you three hurry up? We have more important issues to be dealing with here." Trae says, "I'm sure Runa will agree."

Rowan flaps again, probably reminding me to be gentle. I loosen my grip on him.

After nearly an hour's trek, we finally exit the tunnel system. I bask in the sun's rays and take slow, deep inhalations of the crisp outdoor air. My veins open and my head clears. I've missed these beautiful trees and the sun's constant presence. The halo around the sun is cut deeply into the sky and in the distance, the Helix arches through the sparse trees far in the distance. Rowan flutters about, but settles into my arms, not wanting to be released yet.

After scanning the area for potential hazards, Trae stands

off to the side, taking a moment to himself. His eyes are lit up like the sky and he has the slightest smile teasing his lips.

Kani and Fenton scuffle off to my right, throwing snow back and forth. A fluffy chunk splatters on Fenton's yellow band and Kani laughs as she dives behind a tree.

"Oh, ya think so, eh?" Fenton bends down, gathering more snow and packing it into a ball.

Squealing, Kani runs a few trees down.

Traeton shifts, kicking the snow and frowns, "Guys, let's get things moving along."

Rowan squeaks, flapping in my hands and I almost drop him. When I open them, he immediately takes flight—but only to the nearest tree branch. He cocks his head to the side, watching us.

"Go home, Rowan. You're safe now." I shoo my hands at him.

He sits and chirps.

"Did he jus' laugh at ya?" Fenton chuckles.

"We don't have all day," Traeton calls from fifty meters away, his face dark and impatient. "Come on."

"Uh-oh. Better appease Mr. Grumpy-Pants." Fenton pulls down his mouth into a mock frown. The absurdity makes me giggle.

Once we catch up, we don't have far to walk before we're all standing around a heap of snow.

"What's going on?" I search their faces, trying to figure out why we've stopped.

Fenton kicks at the snow, and reveals a circular stone door with a large loop handle.

Together, Trae and Fenton grab hold of the loop and pry the door open. It squeals loudly, landing hard on the ground. The opening is just wide enough for a single body at a time.

Peering down below, a series of large metallic handles are embedded into the wall leading into the darkness.

Fenton nods to Trae, who slips into the opening and swiftly descends. When he reaches the bottom, lights begin to illuminate the man-made tunnel below.

"Clear," Trae calls up, "Take up the rear, Fenton."

"Ya wish," Fenton replies.

Trae rolls his eyes and walks out of line of sight.

Kani laughs and points at me, "I think *you* should go next."

Swinging my legs over the way I'd seen Trae, I catch the first handle and start to lower myself down. The sharp coldness of the metallic bars seep through my NanoTech gloves, making my palms sting. As I reach the bottom, Trae steps up, grabbing my waist and lowering me gently to the ground. I suck in a breath, surprised by his sudden contact. His hands are strong and powerful in the brief moment they wrap around me.

"I— thanks," I smile, my eyelashes fluttering.

We stand face to face and my heart starts skipping beats.

"Yeah, uh … there's a big gap at the bottom," he says, running a hand along his neck.

Trae repels from me and leans against the wall of the tunnel. With one foot propped up, he folds his arms tightly across his chest and stares at them. Beyond him, the tunnel is illuminated its entire length to another door on the opposite end.

"Trae, what's going on with you?"

I stand in front of him, giving him nowhere to run. His downcast eyes don't move and I reach out, making him look at me. He flinches, but glances up anyway.

"What do you mean?" His eyes widen, softening his face slightly.

"I'm *sorry*. I didn't mean to embarrass you, or upset you," my shoulders sag, but I continue, "Last night— I thought I was helping. Please don't be mad."

He opens his mouth, but immediately shuts it again. Conflict brews in his eyes and I can't figure out what I need do to fix this. Kani comes bounding off the ladder and Trae's head snaps back down, his eyes locked on his arms.

"Oh, *please*. Would you two get on with it already?" Kani chides, walking by without a second glance.

Fenton hits the floor just behind her and the heavy door above him slams shut.

"Get on wit wha'?"

"*They* know!" Kani says, her voice reverberates off the enclosed space.

"*Yeah*. Get on wit it, already." Fenton's grin is bright as he pats Traeton on the shoulder.

Trae huffs, dropping his arms and rearing on Fenton. "You're such juveniles. Runa's brother just died yesterday, for phug's sake. Have a little respect. Can you two *honestly* think of nothing else?"

Instinctively, I take a step back. Traeton's hands are clenched at his side and this sudden outburst of anger is unexpected.

To my surprise, Fenton laughs him off, "Evidently *you* can't."

16

RUNA

*a*fter a few moments, I will my feet to move, forcing myself to catch up with the others.

The twinkling lights on the floor go out as I pass them, sensing I'm the last person in the tunnel. I peer into the darkness behind me with a pang of regret. Something in our dynamic has changed overnight and it's not for the better.

Ornate pictures are carved along the stone walls and they remind me of Kani's paintings in a way. Though, they've clearly been here a long time, their simplistic quality draws me in. I follow their deep grooves, touching the etchings with my fingertips. The cold, gritty texture snags at my gloves, so I relieve my right hand of its sheath and try again.

How old is this tunnel? Who created it?

I pull my hand back from the wall, and replace my glove as I continue on.

The others stop bickering as I approach. Fenton appears greatly amused, but Kani and Trae are ready to have an altercation.

"Idiot," Kani curses, staring hard at Traeton.

"Okay, guys. Let's cease tha 'ostilities, shall we?" Fenton cuts his hands between the two of them.

Trae continues glaring at Kani, and refuses to acknowledge I've caught up.

I search the space around us, trying to figure out our next move. There's no door in sight.

Fenton grins at me, answering my unspoken question, "As they used ta say on Earth, *Abra-DUHcabra!*"

He pulls a metallic disc from the pocket of his jacket, and spins around.

I take a step back, just in case.

Fenton waves the disc in front of himself in a wide, sweeping motion. The wall directly in front shifts aside and vanishes completely within another section of the wall. We all wait for the debris tickling the air in swirling clouds to subside before entering the Archives.

The sight on the other side of the wall is breathtaking. Stepping inside the Archives is like stepping into another world. Dark burgundy beams crisscross the light golden walls as they arc from the floor to the insanely high ceiling. At the apex, the beams create a repeating geometric pattern surrounding the windows—a five petaled flower.

The wall closes behind us and we're left standing in a room so vast there isn't an end in sight. Somehow, natural light cascades in sheets from ornate windows embedded in the ceiling.

Everyone is staring at me when I take a moment from absorbing the Archives. My cheeks burn under their scrutiny.

"This place ... is beautiful," I say.

"Yeah ... beautiful," barely audible, Trae agrees. He shifts his gaze to Kani, then to the floor.

Kani rolls her eyes in response, as we move forward as a group into the large open space. For as far as my eye can see, decorative shelving units adorn the space. They're arranged in half circle arches with a large open passageway through the center. Each one is covered in foreign objects. Some seem positively ancient, others—slightly newer. There are heaps on the floor, on tables, *everywhere*. It's so overwhelming, yet somehow—familiar.

Fenton walks to the circular table in the center of the nearest section and takes a seat in front of an older holographic screen—perhaps one of the first ever made, it looks so old. The rest of us follow him into the section. Trae sits next to Fenton, while Kani sits at the opposite end and props her arms up on the table behind her.

"Might wanna sit down. We have now entered Fenton's dream world. We'll be here *a while*," she says.

I do as she says and take a seat beside her.

"How did you ever find this place?" I ask, "How old is it?"

"We go' no records 'bout this place, or when it was built. Pure 'appenstance we found tha darn thing, if ya ask me. When Landry and I were out explorin' as kids, he stubbed his toe on tha door up top. Talk about 'stumblin' into it."

"Wow," I say.

"I know, righ'?" Fenton says as he starts sifting through the holographic data, "Leave it ta Landry to trip over summin' awesome."

"Once you get this system up and running, I think the first thing we should search for is the name Videus, again. I'd like to get a better idea of what might be going on here," Trae says, bending in.

"Tha' was tha plan," Fenton says, "I'll probably try to crack into the Helix and do some more pokin' 'round, too. I doub' this system will 'ave anything tha' isn't completely dated."

Too anxious to sit still and wait, I stand up and peruse the items filling the shelves. Maybe I'll be able to find something on Videus ... or this Tree of Burden. If nothing else, the distraction helps.

Everything has a distinct odor of something in a slow case of decomposition. I run my hand along the shelf as I peer into their depths. Each unit is packed and I wonder if these three even know what most of the items are for. Somehow I doubt it. The most prevalent thing I can make out are the mounds of antiquated electronic devices littering the shelves. I could spend my whole life down here and probably never understand what they all do.

Why would the colonizers bring all of these things with them? If they were fleeing Earth, wouldn't they want to take only the necessities?

Kani is suddenly at my side, tipping her head to where my hand hovers, she asks, "Have you seen books before?"

"No," I admit, "Is that what these are?"

I pull a rectangular item off the shelf and she takes it from me, "Yep."

She flips the object open, paper flutters about with scribbling. In some sections, even images. I lean closer, trying to make out the words.

"We come here a lot. Took some time to understand them, but books prove to be invaluable. They allow you to witness the world from different perspectives. Did you know, some of these books were written *for fun?*"

I look up at her. "Why?"

Shrugging, she closes the book and sets it back on the

shelf, then says, "To enjoy. To expand their minds. Over there, see those things on the floor? They're sculptures. I use paint as my creative outlet, but other people used to create with clay, wood, or even stone," She points to a large animal resembling a seated cat, "That one's made from melted gold —a chemical element we haven't even found on Pendomus yet. Then some sculptures further down are even made of bone."

My eyes widen at all the potential humanity has to create. My life has been so sheltered. I've never tried to tap into some kind of creative potential. I wouldn't know where to start.

Following Kani, we reach a section filled with items so unusual they stand out amongst everything else. One piece in particular calls to me and I pick it up, setting the object in my palm to examine a small metallic eye. It reminds me of my own, in the way a scar pulls down from the bottom. A series of circular items, some with jagged edges, and spirals scatter across the eye in differing metallic colors.

"You think this place is old, the thing in your hand is *beyond ancient,*" Kani's words make me jump and I nearly drop the eye. Smirking at me, she continues, "Anyway … This section is one of my favorites."

Her face is open and gentle for once.

"See these?" Kani points at a series of statues with people who are stiff and posed. Some have animal heads and I lean in trying to figure out their purpose. Did people look like this?

"These are Egyptian. Back on Earth, they were a revered society. Sorta revolved around a leader called a Pharaoh, but they had lots of myths about gods and goddesses. Very fascinating stuff. Anyway, they may appear a bit different, but humans haven't evolved much in the past four thousand years. Not on the *inside*, anyway," she sighs and points to my hand, "This thing is called an Eye of Horus. Or at least, I think that's what they called it. The old records don't show all of those gears on it, though," she points at the circular items scattered across the eye.

"Why does this one, then?"

"Your guess is as good as mine," she says, shrugging, "Here, I can show you what it's supposed to be like."

She moves to a series of heavy books that could fall apart just by thinking about them. Plucking one off the shelf, she brings it to the table in a cloud of dust. I wave my hand in front, trying to clear the air. She flips through the book quickly, as if it's not an integral part of humanity's history, and stops on a picture of the eye. She's right, the eye does look different.

"I'm not sure who added the gears to it, or why. Might just be another artist's rendition, though."

"A what?"

"You know, made the design their own. Throughout history, people take something they like and manipulate it. Then the object evolves."

"I like it," The metal of the eye glitters in the light, making me smile, "This sort of reminds me of my own eye."

"I get that. Scarred, but still kinda strong," she says, a mischievous glint in her eye, "Your eye is looking even better than it was yesterday, by the way. It's not even red anymore. Pretty soon, there will just be scars."

Without another word, she takes the eye from me and returns it to the shelf. I wish I could inhale the knowledge through my fingertips, as I flip through the pages of the ancient tome. Perhaps this feeling is why we evolved into using the eLink. There's so much I'd like to understand, but it would take lifetimes to learn in this manner.

Fenton continues to stare intensely at the mainframe while Trae paces back and forth behind him. His arms are crossed as he rubs at his lower lip with his thumb, deep in thought.

I frown and flip the page.

"Check this out," Kani sits down next to me with a tiny, black device. The object holds nothing distinguishable until she swipes her fingers across the surface. With a few flicks, lights flicker and moves through a command sequence. Kani smirks, rolling her hand in the air impatiently, "Gotta give it a second. This thing's a little old."

All at once, a tiny dot at the top lights up and she places her face inside a small scanner signal. A moment later, sounds flood from her hand, reminding me instantly of the night I woke up listening to Trae sing. From the corner of my eye, Trae stops moving and stares our direction.

"We never got introduced to music inside the Helix, and now I'm obsessed," Kani grins, "Music can be made from just about anything. A person using their voice, the tapping of your fingers, on an instrument—even a device like this," she tilts the screen to me. Tiny little pictures illuminate the surface. "Of all the devices here in the Archives, I like this one the a lot. It recognizes the user and plays back songs you've been most interested in before. Then it will mix and match similar songs. Of course, you can bypass this feature— which I do sometimes. I have a better one at the Haven. The music selection is based off chemical composition instead."

Surprisingly, the song chosen for Kani is slow and beautiful. I wish I knew what made the sounds. They mingle in a haunting way, reminding me of the wind and the way I feel when I'm outside.

"Here, you try it. Just hold on, like this," she sets the device in my hand and tips her head. "When the scanner comes on, place your purdy face in line. The first few times, it'll run through a test sequence. If you don't like the song, hit the red arrow until you find one you like. That'll start the recognition sequence to start compiling your list of likes and dislikes."

"Couldn't hurt, I guess," I say and allow the scanner to create a new profile setting for me.

After a few moments of flitting through the prompts, the hall fills with a new kind of music. The rise and fall of the words in combination with all the other sounds makes my heart beats grow louder—pounding in my ears and thumping unevenly in my chest.

"Can you hear the wind instruments?" Kani grins, "They resemble the wind blowing ... but really, people are blowing into them. The only one I really know about are flutes. Listen — hear the loop? Right here. Those are string instruments. Violins and cellos, I think," Kani smiles broadly, "They have these in the Lateral."

I smile, thinking of what it would be like to listen to something like this in person. I focus again on the song and the longer I listen, the less air I seem to have. Before I can control myself, my eyes blur and tears spill down my cheeks. The words are somehow able to make sense of my life, eons before I even entered this world.

The song is beyond haunting—it's *agonizing*.

"Hey guys, take a gander a' this— " Fenton's voice echoes triumphantly behind me.

Kani leans down and asks, "You ... okay? You're not gonna get completely sappy on me now are you?" she scratches at her forehead, "Because I don't do sappy well."

"I'm fine..."

"Alright, well, I'm gonna check on what Fenton's come up with. You comin'?"

So many questions percolate at the back of my mind. Have we been here long enough to find what we need on Videus?

"Give me a minute. Okay?" I say.

My smile is weak, but Kani pats my leg awkwardly and gets up.

"What's going on, guys? Did you find something?" she sets off around the table and I take a moment to center myself. With a final deep inhalation, I push off the bench and trudge toward the rest of the group. When I join them, my brother's face stares back at me from the holographic screen.

"What's going on here?" I ask, turning to Traeton, "I thought we were researching Videus?"

Trae stands a bit taller and says, "Right. And this is the latest entry we've found."

"What do you mean?" I ask, leaning in to get a better look. I follow Fenton's outstretched finger to a spot on the screen.

Beneath Baxten's current status, two words assault my eyes.

VIDEUS VASSALAGE

"Vassalage?" I ask, struggling to keep my voice even, "Is that his last name?

"Yer guess is as good as mine," Fenton says, shrugging.

"I think it's pretty clear, based on this, Videus was involved in the attack on your brother." Trae says, concern creeping across his face.

"Did you find anything else?" I ask, returning my gaze to the screen.

"Nothin' more in tha Helix side—everythin' we saw before's gone. There were a couple hits in tha old system, though. Lemme try an' bring 'em up," Fenton says, logging out of the Helix.

After a few minutes of searching, Fenton finally says, "Uhm ... seems there's somethin' ta this Videus Vassalage thing. If I'm righ'—and I think I am—Vassalage is not his last name. It'sa place."

"What does that mean?" I ask.

"I'm startin' ta think yer brother migh' no' be dead, Runa," Fenton says, fidgeting in his seat, "But you're not gonna like wha' I think is goin' on any better."

I tear my eyes from the screen and narrow them on Fenton.

He tilts his head and sighs, "I was curious, so I looked up tha word, vassalage 'cause I've never 'eard it before. Ta put things blunt, I think it's a kinda ... well, a slavery prison—"

"You're kidding, right?" Trae says, pounding his fists on the table and pushing away.

"How could he be in a ... prison? We watched him burst into flames?" I ask, my voice rising in panic.

"I dunno. Wha' if— wha' if tha's more like a portal or summin'?"

"A portal? What do you think this is? Science fiction?" Trae says, snorting.

"Look, man— after all tha's been 'appening, I wouldn't rule nuthin' out."

"So … he may still be alive?" I say, taking a step back.

"Maybe?" Fenton says, looking hopeful, "But I dunno where tha vassalage is. There's a couple references about an important Caudex wit information ta stop Videus. Maybe it's in there? Anyone know wha' a caudex is?"

"A caudex is a book, dummy," Kani says, rolling her eyes, "And I thought you were the smart one."

Fenton makes a face and continues, "Well, anyway, says 'ere tha original history o' Pendomus was imbued within tha Caudex. This … *book* was then 'idden from someone named Videus, who sought ta eliminate tha original inhabitants of tha planet and claim Pendomus fer 'imself."

"I thought Pendomus was devoid before we terraformed and initiated our gravity fields," Trae says.

"Tha's been tha story, ain't it?" Fenton says, "But says 'ere there was a war over tha planet … and Videus' side won. And you'll never guess who was on his side."

"Who?" Trae asks.

"Tha Labots," Fenton says.

"Of course," Kani says, tapping the table.

"This means the Helix is a much bigger problem than we ever knew," Trae says, running his hand across the back of his neck.

"Tha Caudex is 'posed ta 'ave a way ta reverse wha' tha resistance saw as inevitable. They started takin' precautions. Tha entry's kinda cryptic, but makes it sound like—nah, tha' can't be right."

"What?" Everyone asks in unison, enthralled.

"Says 'ere the planet's *rotation* was meant to be ceased

after tha war. Tha resistance was tryin' ta stop tha' from 'appening."

"Whoa," Trae says, raising his eyebrows.

I blink, trying to process what was just said. "Wait. You're telling me the tidal lock was ... artificially created?"

"Accordin' ta this," Fenton says.

"Wait a minute. Let's just say there was a war and Videus was the winner ... Who wrote this entry?" Kani asks.

"Doesn't say," Fenton says, shaking his head.

"Think about it, guys. If you were about to lose a war, you'd want to leave a trail to the old records, right?" Trae says, pacing behind Fenton's chair, "So the truth can be known."

"Sure. But if no one has access to these records anymore ... how would they ever find the trail to this ... Caudex?" Kani says, "This entry doesn't even say where it's hidden, right?"

Fenton leans forward and scans the entries. A moment later, he says, "There's no indication of a specific location, hu' it does mention ... a Tree of Burden. As if there ain't many trees on Pendomus," he snorts, "Bu' tha whole thing's unclear. Talks 'bout a blue crystal key ta open it. No' sure if it's meant fer tha Tree or fer tha book. Both?"

He points to an image on the screen. Clearly not real, the image is a drawn depiction— but there's no mistaking the shape —or the crystal. It's the same one I found days before my attack.

The one I left inside the Helix.

My mouth pops open and as everything starts to make sense. The key—the Tree of Burden—Videus.

"Fenton, is there a way to get inside the Helix undetected?" I blurt out.

Surprise flashes across his face, but he says, "Uh … I wouldn't recommend it. Why?"

"I need to know," I urge,"If Videus has my brother—I need to get him back."

"Wha' does gettin' in tha Helix— " he pauses as he takes in my expression, "You'd 'ave ta shut down yer eLink completely, but I dunno if tha's even possible."

"What would happen if I don't—or can't?"

"Then tha Labots would probably respond. Ya've been gone too long from tha system. If wha' we're findin' is righ'— the Labots are in league wit Videus."

"I don't understand why the hell you need to go into the Helix in the first place," Kani says.

"Because I know how the resistance were planning to illuminate the trail to the Caudex," I whisper, "Which means I may be able to find my brother."

All three of them look at me with intense fascination and I take a step back. My mind is reeling with all of this new information.

I haven't been losing my mind.

I pace for a moment, contemplating how to word things.

"Remember when I said this is all my fault? That Videus is after me?" I begin, "Well, I've been told these things … inside my mind. Someone's been … helping me. The voices started after my attack."

Trae blinks furiously and his forehead creases.

"What?" he says, an indignant tone hidden in the simple word.

"But tha's impossible. The eLink doesn't work ou' here," Fenton says, shakes his head.

"I *know*."

The room is eerily silent and I fidget with the cuff of my jacket.

"Something else is connecting to me. Sending me warnings about Videus—and the Tree of Burden. Whatever this is —" I circle my finger around my head for effect, "—whoever is doing *this* ... They need me to get to the Tree of Burden— and I know which one it is. But I need to go back to the Helix for the key."

I point to the crystal on the screen.

Their faces are completely blank and not one of them moves. Is it the revelation I'm *hearing things,* or I'm being warned of something that is quite possibly *real?*

After an agonizing minute, Trae walks over to me with clenched fists.

"Do you ... do you think this is *funny?*" he asks.

My mouth drops open, flabbergasted.

"Nnn—no."

He towers over me with his dark eyes flashing.

"I tell you about my sister Ava and you expect me to believe *you're* hearing things, now? That's sick, Runa. *You're* sick. Talk about delusions of grandeur."

Any remaining trace of oxygen is obliterated from my lungs.

Kani steps forward, pushing him hard in the chest as she says, "Back off, Trae. What if she's telling the truth? Think about it—"

Swiping his hand down in between them, Trae cuts her off, "Would you just stop. *Stop.* I *get* it. I know what you think should happen here and I'm telling you right now—it's *not.*"

I have no idea what he thinks is going on, but I can't take another second of this. I need to think—to figure out my next course of action. With or without their help, I need to get inside the Helix and get the key.

In an instant, I'm on my feet and running. Tears spill freely and furiously as I run to— *anywhere* else.

"Let her go, Trae. She won't get very far. She needs a minute," Kani says as I leave. "She's has a lot to process. Hell, we all have."

I've never been more grateful to her than in this moment. My sobs are uncontrollable and I can't catch my breath. It doesn't take me long to reach the wall where we came in and I pound my fist in disgust.

Why me? Why am I the one? Because of me, my brother's been taken—and it's not fair. I jump back in surprise as the wall slides aside without the disc Fenton used, revealing the tunnel beyond. Not questioning my luck, I run as fast as my feet can carry me. At the far end of the tunnel, natural light streams in and I pick up speed.

Forget them, or their help. I need to go to the Helix—*now.* I'll figure things out when I get there.

The time it takes to reach the other end of the tunnel seems like a blink of an eye. I scramble up the ladder on the wall and out the door, hoping I have a good head start before they come after me. The cold air knocks into me and I begin my sprint to the Helix.

Behind me, the heavy door slams shut and I spin around, my heart throbbing against my rib cage as I face whatever's behind me. But there's— nothing there. No sooner do I breathe a sigh of relief— the hairs on my neck raise of their own volition. A low grunt nearby makes me freeze.

Oh ... no, no, no—

The Morph—whatever it really is—is here.

I should have known. Things were much too easy ...

Spinning in circles, a muted glow comes at me from the left side of the fallen door. My scream is squelched before it can be released because the lump in my throat won't let it pass. Scrambling in the snow with my tears turning to terror, I take off at full bolt toward the Helix. My lungs burn and panic claws at my insides.

The creature is so close. And I'm so far—

Snow blows in wide spirals, vibrating in the space around me. The creature suddenly snatches the back of my jacket and flings me on its invisible body. In the next instant, we shoot like a rocket toward the Helix.

As I lay, dangling across what I thought was certain death, I'm on the verge of passing out. The tingling sensation slams into me with force—then nausea, and the bright light. I don't have enough willpower to fight it off. There's no voice this time, but as the light dissipates, I can clearly make out the shape of the thing I'm riding. But more than that—I have a clear sense of who the creature really is.

Her body is huge, like that of a bear—her eight strong legs moving swiftly, manipulating the snow as she runs. The edges of her body glow in a shimmering iridescent rainbow. Dreams flash through my mind of a time spent with this animal. Or are they memories? The water's edge. Her gentle protection.

Tethys.

The information and connection to her flows through me like the water surrounding her. She's no Morph—I know this animal.

I *trust* this animal!

My terror washes away and peace settles over me like a warm breeze. Her attack on me was never meant to hurt me —she had been trying to open my sight to the things I

187

couldn't see, but would need to. It was her healing saliva that saved my eye, allowing me to see—her.

The light fades, settling somewhere inside Tethys' body and I know things will be okay. At least, for now.

Tethys is, after all, *my guardian.*

*R*una's hearing things now? That's how she knows people are after her?

Why would she say something so ludicrous?

She, of all people, should know what saying something like that would mean to me. This has to be Kani's idea—trying to get me to lower my defenses. She's been at me all damn day to talk to Runa. What the hell's in it for Kani, anyway? Even Fenton's teamed up with her. As if I need to feel worse than I already do—even if this is for the best.

Runa's face when I yelled at her continues to streaking through my memory—she was so hurt. I pinch at the spot between eyes, hoping to erase the painful expression some-how. It does absolutely nothing to ease my conscience.

The only problem is, my anger isn't even meant for her. It's mine and mine alone. I'm angry at myself for letting things get so jumbled up. I'm angry I'm hurting her when all I want to do is kiss her. Hell, I'm even angry for wanting that.

On top of everything, I'm furious at Kani and Fenton for continuing to push. I'm so close to the brink of losing my resolve without their constant assault. Runa needs some time and frankly, so do I. A few minutes isn't going to kill either of us, despite what my insides are telling me.

"Uh, Trae. Ya migh' wanna take a look a' this," Fenton says.

Taking a deep breath, I walk back to the screen. Fenton has cracked into the Helix's system again and Runa's hProfile is loaded. Her beautiful face smiles sorrowfully at me. She looks the way she should look—white hair and all. Though her eyes aren't right—both the same fiery amber color.

"What's up?" I ask, trying to figure out what he's wanting me to check out.

Kani leans in, searching the screen.

"What else do you see? I don't get it," she asks.

"Look *closer*. Under 'er paren'al status," Fenton says, his eyes widening, "I had ta pull up Runa's hProfile ta find 'er brother's ... and stumbled on this doozy."

We both lean in as Fenton taps a section on the screen and leans back.

MOTHER: Absala Cophem
FATHER: Genetic Match Unknown

"What in the hell?" Kani says, taking a step back.

"How can her father's genetic match be *unknown?* She told me about her dad. He died when she was really young," I say, gripping the edge of the table until my knuckles turn white, "She ... has *memories* of him. What are they playing at?"

"I dunno know wha' ta tell ya. Bu' I didn't wanna say anythin' when Runa was— "

We all jump as the grinding of the main wall shifting aside cuts off his words.

We exchange confused glances and Fenton says, "Tha's impossible. I 'ave tha control right 'ere."

Fenton holds up the small device we use to activate the wall.

"There seems to be a lot of impossible going around lately," I say, stepping forward.

Kani smacks me aside and says, "You stay here. You've done enough damage. I'll go check on her. The door probably glitched or something."

She stomps off in the direction of the commotion.

Kani doesn't understand, but at least she's turned her hostilities toward me, instead of Runa. I pace the floor, waiting impatiently for Kani to come back with Runa. How am I gonna handle things when they come back?

"Damn, I can't find nuthin'," Fenton curses.

I stop pacing to glance in the direction Kani disappeared, but there's only darkness.

"What are you looking for now?" I ask, absently.

"Couple a things. None of 'em panning out."

"Please tell me there's not more— "

"Whoa— " Fenton cries, putting his hands to his head and closing his eyes.

"Fenton, what's wrong? What's going on?" I ask, rushing to his side.

Fenton's features take a blank expression, as if he's completely shut down. I shake him hard by the shoulders, but nothing changes.

Then, just as quickly as it had come, Fenton relaxes.

"Trae—we've go' bigger worries," he says, his skin tone going ashen, "I think Videus jus' tapped inta Landry's ComLink. He knows everything we know."

My fingertips fly to my forehead as I pace. What could

this mean? He knows everything we know— Including the fact Runa knows where this Tree is.

"Dammit!" I spit, "We need to warn Runa."

"She's gone— " Kani rushes in, her face flushed and eyes wild. "Runa's *gone*."

"What?" My heart collides with the sickening pit in the bottom of my stomach.

"I mean her scrawny butt is *gone*," she screeches, reaching for my arm and attempting to drag me with her, "Are you deaf?"

I blink hard, unable to move. *How—*?

Fenton rubs at his temple and says, "We gotta go after 'er, Trae. This could be a trap Videus has set. Tha' hatch isn't gonna stop 'er from gettin' outside."

"Phug," I say, flying around the table.

So many things can hurt her out there.

The Morph—the thing we *thought* was the Morph—this Videus guy. A whole host of other things.

Dammit. What was I thinking?

If anything happens to her—

I run down the tunnel and launch myself up the ladder through sheer adrenaline. After propelling the door open, I scramble out, clutching at the snow as I scan the woods. The cold air assaults my senses as I spin in circles, trying to locate her, but she's nowhere to be seen.

"Where the hell *is* she?" I demand to the wind.

My heart pounds heavily against my ribcage as I squint toward the Helix. Runa's nowhere to be seen, but I know exactly where she's headed, and it's not good.

Kani and Fenton clamber up, one after the other, each out of breath.

"This can't be happening," I say, trying to devise a plan as quickly as I can.

If she's heading to the Helix, she's gonna get caught.

"Fenton, take Kani to the tree I found Runa at. Do you remember where it is?"

Fenton nods.

"Good. When you get there—stay nearby, but not too close. If Videus is tracking you— or has access to your visuals, we don't want him knowing which tree it really is."

"Understood." Fenton says, grabbing Kani by the hand and kicking the hatch door shut.

Without any more options, I leave the two of them in a cloud of kicked up snow. Somehow, I need to get to Runa before she triggers the alarms—before the Labots—

Even though the cold air threatens to burst my lungs, I run as if my own life depended on it—because in some form or another, it does. My agonizingly slow progress fuels my imagination and flashes of losing Ava to the Labots twist into Runa. This cannot happen, not again. Not because of me pushing her away.

When I finally reach the Helix, I clutch for the first door I come into contact with and set foot inside the Helix for the first time in nearly eight years. Once I slip inside, I stand in a vaguely familiar section of the Helix. Memories of living here flood back as I take the location in.

Everything smells exactly as I remember.

The smooth, sterile gray walls are still backlit in the ceiling, giving the illusion the hallway goes on forever. From both directions, there are non-stop doors as far as the eye can see, but no sign of Runa.

Which way?

I take a sharp turn to the right and start running, but

every couple hundred meters or so, the hallway constricts, as you approach a scanner checkpoint. I wish I'd paid closer attention to her Living Quarters address when her hProfile was up. Dammit, we had the entire thing up on the screen.

I stop running knowing there's only one way to find her. She's already in danger anyway, at least this way, I might be able to get to her first. She can't gain access to her Living Quarters unless she logs in and that means she can't disengage the eLink. I find a secluded corner to hide in and start the sequence to log into the eLink. The system will flag my interaction, too. With any luck, it should take a few minutes to sort through all the data being exchanged before action is taken.

Twenty minutes. That's all I need.

My brain crackles with the irritating, familiar itch as the eLink connects. Blinded by the stream of data coming at me, I lean against the wall, focusing on the relevant information I need to acquire. There are a series of commands I'm required to use in order to create a link with Runa. I close my eyes to concentrate, because it's been so long since I've used them. The process takes longer than I'd like, maneuvering through the prompts with my thoughts. Finally, the permission request to connect to Runa Cophem is initiated.

My eyes search the hallway again, hoping I can remain undetected.

~C'mon, Runa. Accept.

A few excruciating moments pass.

Maybe she's not logged in yet? What if she is and she won't let me in?

Permission is suddenly granted and I'm given access as her beautiful face flashes in mind, letting me know I'm connected to the right person.

~Runa... Where are you?

My voice is frantic, even in my head, and a part of me hopes she can't perceive it.

~What do you want, Traeton? *You shouldn't be here. I can do this on my own ...*

Hearing her response in my mind sends a shiver down my spine and cool relief washes over me. She's reserved, but I hear her. She let me in and she's still safe.

~The hell you can. Do you not understand what kind of danger you're in just by being here?

A few seconds pass and my insides are screaming to run to her—but run *where*? We don't have time for this—

~Actually, I do. I don't expect you to understand—or care—

I tap my forehead, wishing I could implant myself with the right words to convince her of the danger she's in—that we're both in.

~I may not completely understand, but I wanna help. Videus tapped into the ComLink Fenton and Landry were using. He knows everything we know. We need to be fast and I know you can't do this alone—Runa, please.

There's a pause and I hope like hell she's considering what I've said.

~I'm sorry, Runa. I never should've gotten upset with you. Please, just let me help.

After another long pause, I close my eyes, and lean against the wall.

~Hurry.

I stand straight, ready to bolt the second I know where to go.

~Where are you? Send me directions, but wait for me—don't touch anything.

My heart kick-starts as a series of directions get downloaded from Runa regarding her whereabouts. I turn around, heading the opposite direction.

~Stay out of sight and shut down your eLink. I'm on my way.

My feet fly, but the distance between us is still too far to handle.

I disconnect my connection to the eLink completely, hoping like hell it's enough to enable me to sneak by the series of brain scanners without tripping the force field doors. If everything goes according to our hypothetical, the Helix isn't equipped to track normal human presence. At least, if Landry's right.

Holding my breath, I walk slowly through the first checkpoint. I step between the arched door frame, waiting for the screeching sound of an alarm … When nothing happens, I rush down the narrow hall with more relief I've felt since we woke up.

My feet continue to pick up speed and I finally see Runa sitting on the floor with her legs pulled in and her back against the wall. She's near the far end, barely out of sight of the next series of scanners. Her white hair is tousled around her shoulders as she sits, waiting.

"Don't ever do *anything* like that again—" I growl at her and instantly clamp my jaw tight.

Those multicolored eyes of hers flit around the hall before she turns them on me.

"Do you know how to get inside, or don't you?" she asks. Her whisper is urgent as she stands up and taking a step toward me.

"We need to devise a plan quick. The retinal scanners are the only way to get into your LQ and with your eyes being the way they are— "

"We don't have a choice, then," she says, taking a careless

step toward the door. I grab her by the waist and swiftly shove her toward the corner.

"Runa, these—the retinal scanners are connected directly in with the Labots. They can trigger a full lock down just as easily as the eLink. They're already gonna be looking for us. Let's not make it completely obvious for them."

Her cheeks flush and her lips tremble as she glares back at me.

"Get off of me," she says through gritted teeth.

Runa's pulse hammers in my palms and her gentle scent of vanilla fills my senses. My head spins and I close my eyes, not willing to let go.

Why does she have to have this affect on me? Why does she have to be so damn beautiful— even when she's angry? Why can't I control myself around her—when I really need to stay focused.

"I said, get off," she pushes at my chest, barely making me move.

A little shocked at the strength of her outrage, my eyes fly open, and I break into a grin.

"What? Am I *funny* to you now, Traeton?" she fires at me, her eyes burning.

Where did all this fire come from?

"I was *trying* to make sure you didn't set off the scanner. See, right *there*?" I point sharply at the small disc on the wall. My words come out harsher than I intend.

This isn't going at all the way I want.

"No, really? I had no idea, considering it's the scanner I've had to use every day of my life—*up until the past week*," she cocks her head to the side and sticks her tongue out.

I cover up a snicker and glance at the doors surrounding us. "Alright, so this is your LQ."

"The one and only," she says jabbing her thumb to the door right beside us, "Thus the using one eye. I know exactly where the crystal or stone thing is. I can grab it and we can be gone in seconds."

I rub my hands together in anticipation, and nod. "Okay, then let's do this and get the hell outta here."

RUNA

*T*raeton's stupid dimples shine triumphantly—as if he can walk in here and simply take over.

Please. I could smack it off his pretty face.

His eyes run the length of the hall and he says, "Alright, here's the deal. No one can get into another family's LQ without specific permission."

"I know," I say, practically spitting venom in my words. *I'm not a complete idiot.*

He smirks at me again and I swear I'm on the verge of channeling Kani. I roll my eyes and turn away.

Why did I let him find me? Am I glutton for punishment? What on Pendomus was I thinking? Had to be the surprise of it all. Seeing his adorable fourteen-year-old face from the last time he was in the Helix flashes in my mind and interrupt my plans—he was the last thing I expected. His piercing brown eyes were so sad and his hair was still its natural color; a hint of red intermixed with brown.

How was I supposed to say no? I push away the memory to glare up at him. His earthy scent is heady in the sterile hallway and I can't think straight. I wish he'd back up or something. Give me some room.

He rubs his hand over his mouth and paces in front of the door. Finally, he says, "I really don't think you should work the retinal scanner. As it is, our eLink connection has gotta be setting off some alerts. It would be like giving them a GPS coordinate."

"If we do it fast like I said, we can be in and out before anyone knows. Don't you think? We can't stand here all day. I mean, I could have been inside and out by now. You interrupted me— "

"Alright. You're right. We don't got all day. Try it," he concedes.

"Just for the record, I didn't need *you* to come up with this plan—I figured it out all on my own."

"Yeah, okay," he says, waving his hand at the door. "But you might wanna close your left eye. Better the scanner gets a partial than flips out over the blue thing."

"Blue *thing*?" I say indignantly.

Since when does he not like blue?

"You know what I mean, for phug's sake."

I stick out my tongue and turn to the door. Its massive size impresses upon me the significance of this moment. We could be seconds away from certain death and yet, I'm standing outside the door to a previous life so far removed from where I am now. How strange.

Inhaling deeply, I step up to the small retinal scanner and close my left eye. The red light flickers on and moves from the top of my eye, downward. I take a step back, expecting the door to swing open, or an alarm to sound.

Nothing happens.

"What do we do, now?" I whisper urgently, matching the concern on his face.

"Damn," he mutters, scratching his forehead. "We're gonna have to take more drastic measures. Look out."

Without giving me any more warning, he pushes me aside and launches his foot at the door. The metal frame groans, but he kicks it again—hard. The construction isn't meant for such a direct violation and bends in, breaking into pieces and allowing Trae to kick it fully off its hinges.

"I can't believe you just— "

"C'mon. *Now* they're gonna know we're here," he says, grabbing my upper arm and yanking me inside.

I dig my feet in, dragging them against the floor as I claw at his hand.

"Let go, Traeton. Get your hand off of me."

"Shhhhh—"

Spinning me into the main hall of my Living Quarters, he drops my arm and pokes his head outside the door. Glancing both ways, he turns back to me and says, "You've gotta make this quick. Find your little trinket and let's go."

"*Trinket?*" I spit.

"Whatever you wanna call it. I don't care. Grab it and let's go."

"I thought you didn't believe me. I'm a liar— remember?"

"Runa, let's not do this now," he says, his nostrils flaring. Gliding past me, Trae stops partway down the hall, "Looks just like mine did."

I scrunch my face and start walking, "What did you expect, Traeton? We're in the *Helix*. They all look the same"

"Not what I—*Fine*. You know what, where's your space?" he rakes his fingers through his hair, making the blue spikes stand out crazily in every direction.

Stupid blue hair.

Biting my lip to keep from snickering, I walk by him and lead the way.

"What?" he grunts.

"Nothing," I say, waving my hand in dismissal, "Forget it."

Trae follows right on my heels and I shoot him a dirty look from the crease of my eye.

Out of habit, I stop at the end of the hall to look through Baxten's open door.

Baxten ...

Traeton follows my gaze and says, "Your brother's, huh?"

"What difference does it make to you?"

"C'mon, Runa. That's not fair."

"Whatever."

I wave my hand dismissively and turn my back on him.

Traeton sighs, but I cross the threshold of my Quiet Space not wanting to rehash the reasoning behind his hurtful words and betrayal. Instead, I shake away my upset to inhale the possibilities ahead. So much yet to accomplish. But there's something eerie about being home—inside the Helix. It's strange after all I've learned and experienced these past few days. Everything here looks exactly the same and yet ... I don't even recognize the world around me.

Has my mother even noticed Baxten and I are gone? *Does she care?*

I bite my lip, bitterly. Doesn't matter.

Stepping into the center of the room, I march straight to the window. Traeton props himself in the side of the doorway, leaning against the frame. His eyes flit from my Lotus Chair, to my hanging clothes, to the window and the woods outside. My hand stops in mid-air as I reach out. The stone—

isn't here. I search the expanse of the window seam and then drop my gaze to the floor.

Nowhere.

"What's wrong?" Trae asks, taking a step into the room.

"No, no, no ... has to be here," I whisper to myself, anxiety flushing through my veins, "It's ... ah ... I'm sure I—"

I finally give in, dropping to my hands and knees, feeling along the bumpy carpeting.

"You lost it?" he says, his voice accusatory.

"I didn't lose anything," my jagged words squelch out through clenched teeth, "I left it on the window seam."

At least, I'm pretty sure ... I took it out of my pocket, right?

"Oh, for the—okay. What does this thing look like?" he says, sweeping over to me and kneeling, too.

Resting back on my legs, I smooth my hair and take a deep breath.

"It's here. Has to be. Just—just give me a second. I'll go back through my data memory."

I can do this ... I can find it if I can pull up the right memories—

"What the hell are you doing? You can't log back in to the eLink for memory access— "

In a fury, all caution is thrown out the window as I stand up and scowl at him.

"Why did you even bother coming here?" I ask, my hands ball into fists and every muscle in my body twitching with anger.

He snickers and stands up.

"What the hell does that mean?" he asks, "You know why I'm here."

"I don't need you to protect me, *Traeton*," I say, my voice thick with contempt as I take a step toward him, "I could've handled this myself."

His eyes open wide, but he fires back, "What was I supposed to do, Runa? Let you run around the Helix without supervision. Do you gotta death wish? The Labots are everywhere and could be here in a blink of one of your *different colored eyes*," he flickers his fingers mockingly in their direction, "You don't even know what they look like—or what they're capable of, need I remind you?"

My jaw drops open and my blood burns, flushing my face.

Supervision!

"I didn't ask for your *supervision.* You chose to come along—in fact, you pretty much demanded to. I thought you were going to be helpful. Instead, you do nothing but insult me— "

My fingernails dig into my palms and tears are stinging in the corner of my eyes. I struggle with the overwhelming urge to run from him and crumple into a ball on the floor. I can't let him see me like that—it would add to this notion I need his protection.

"I'm not insulting you. You're just so—*gah*— " he says, stumbling over his words as he walks away, "Why can't you be … *normal?*"

"Ooooh … Of course, I nearly forgot—I'm *not* normal," I say, frowning at him. "I suppose you're right— Yeah, okay … Take your pick. Which is worse? Runa, the-freak-with-the-white-hair? Or how about the crazy eyes?" My fingers dance in the air near my head, to prove my point, "No? Not enough? What about, Runa-you-shouldn't-be-hearing-things? Oh, I know … it's Runa, you're-not-already-a-big-enough-abnormality, so why not make stuff up for *fun?*"

It feels good to allow my frustration with him to manifest into words.

His eyes darken and he wets his lower lip before saying, "That's not what I meant."

"Oh, really?" I say, making a face and chuckling maniacally.

He sweeps across the room and clutches my shoulders. His fingertips dig in and I suck in a quick breath from the shock. Those dark brown eyes burn into mine with such intensity—it's all I can do not to look away.

"There's this—there's a—No, you really don't understand," he growls, "You don't—you're not *in my head*."

His jaw clenches, and his lips press into a tight line.

I've never seen him so angry—but I refuse to give him the satisfaction of intimidating me. I jut my chin out and stare him straight in the eye. Besides, I *do* understand. I'm nothing more than a girl he has to protect. A stand-in for his sister because he wasn't able to protect her. I can even see and hear things that aren't possible—like she did, right?

"You're just—so..." his jaw clenches and unclenches, "Dammit—"

"Crazy?" I offer, making a face.

Before I can jump to any more conclusions, the warmth of his hands radiate on the sides of my face, and his lips crush down on mine. He pulls me into him with such force— his earthy scent surrounds me, permeating everything. My lips tingle, and my mind swims in a sea of red and orange.

I push against his chest, trying to gain space between us, but he pulls me in tighter. Suddenly, I'm kissing him back, my body connecting to something so intense, so *primal*, I surprise even myself. I don't tell it what to do; wisdom beyond my years lights the way. Lingering on the salty taste of his lips, I allow my hands to roam free. They slide up his broad shoulders and rest on his neck as I tug at the back of his blue hair.

This stupid, beautiful blue hair!

All the ice frozen in my veins melts into a puddle at my feet, and I'm absorbed in a flame so powerful I'm afraid I'll consume us both.

A rumble erupts from somewhere inside Trae's chest, adding fuel to the fire. He lifts me up and I wrap my legs around his waist. In response, he surges forward, pressing our bodies to the wall as we continue our exploration of each other. We can't get close enough and we desperately need to find a way to get *closer* somehow.

I break our kiss to tilt my head to the side and he takes my offering—electrical impulses scatter throughout my whole body as he places kisses along my neck and shoulder. Then, he traces my jawline with his mouth, just as he had in my dream— until he returns his lips to mine. Sparks fly behind my eyelids, but he pulls away from me.

"I—I can't. We need to stop, Runa. Stop," his voice is gruff and his lips quiver, "The Labots— we need to— "

I try to return to our kiss, try to ignore his words. I'm not ready. *Not yet.* Taking his head in my hands, I kiss his jawline below his left ear, then switch to the other side, kissing his dimples and he shivers under my touch. He doesn't make a move—he stands perfectly still, waiting.

When I stop to question him with my eyes, he gently places his forehead against mine and lets out a soft sigh. I weave my fingers in circles in his hair, desperate not to return to the people we were moments ago.

I can't go back to that. Not after this. Not now.

"*Please ...*" I murmur, bending his face upward. I kiss at the outer corner of his eye— his long eyelashes tickling my lips. I inhale the smell of his skin, kissing the rough stubble along his cheekbone. He groans, his head tilting back and he closes his eyes.

An easy chuckle escapes his inviting lips and he whispers, "You have no idea … how much I *wish*. But we need to get out of here. We've stayed to long already."

"I know …"

"What have you done to me?" he says, contentment hidden in his voice.

My heart sings and I can't help but laugh.

"The same thing you've done to me," I say.

His eyes open, a hint of curiosity playing at their creases. I stare into them, admiring their depths. They aren't *just* brown—they're unfathomably complex, like he is. In the center is a star of green, which fades out into a rich, dark brown. But other colors are in there as well. Colors I have, as of yet, no words for.

I know we need to hurry—we need to find the crystal or leave, but I bend in for one last kiss. Electricity sparks between us as our lips barely come into contact.

Beside us, someone gasps in the doorway. I immediately drop to my feet, scrambling back as Trae shifts in front of me, once again my protector. We turn to face our intruder as she stands in the doorway, gripping onto the edge with shock clear across her pale face. The RationCap Chemist badge on her arm is blinking furiously— a holographic alarm.

Oh, no. This is worse than Labots.

It's my *mother*.

*W*ith Runa safely behind me, I step toward the intruder. A woman with remarkable resemblance to Runa clutches at the edges of the doorway, gaping at us. Clearly older, her dark hair and eyes stand out in stark contrast with her daughter. It's been so long since I've had any parental attachment—the idea Absala Cophem would be the first notified never crossed my mind.

I shoot a tense glance over my shoulder and wide eyes blink back at me. One amber, one blue—*both incredible.* I haven't even begun to process the last few moments—everything's still vibrating, humming. A slow rumble moves through my body as I try to regain a semblance of control. The sensations still flooding through me are unlike anything I've ever felt before. All I could think about during our kiss was what I wanted from her. What I *needed* from her.

What I hoped she needed from me.

The shock across Absala's face flits from horror, to concern, to deep consternation as she fixes her dark, piercing gaze on the places our bodies touch.

"How *dare* you," Runa's mother says. Her smooth, fluent voice is damn near perfect as her eyes turn into horrifying slits, "Either of you."

You can see it in Absala's eyes—she *knows* things—

"You remember how to speak?" Runa says, confusion clear across her face as she steps around me.

"Runa, we need to get moving," I warn.

"I know. I'll make this fast," she says, reaching for my hand and squeezing, "I just need a minute with her. She might know where the crystal is."

I nod, but lean against the wall, watching the body language Absala puts off. She continues to watch me; her lips pursed and her glare intense.

"I always knew this day would come," Absala says, turning around and walking away from her daughter.

"What does that mean?" Runa asks, following her mother into the main room.

I kick off the wall, following the two women. Runa's mother paces silently in front of the large table in the middle of the room.

When she finally turns to her daughter, she says, "Runa, you've always been different, but now ... Now look at you. Your face— "

Runa lifts her hand to her eye, running her finger tips along the healing wound.

"I was ... attacked," she whispers.

"Of course you were. From the time you were a child, you've always been too curious for your own good. You always wanted to do the things no one else wanted to do— You always cared more than you should."

"More than I *should?*" Runa says, indignantly.

Absala sneers over her shoulder, but continues, "Yes.

More than you *should*. I knew from the moment you infected me with your presence that you would be the demise of everything I held dear. I should have gotten rid of you then."

"Whoa— Hang on there," I say, taking a step between the two of them, "What the hell's wrong with you?"

"And you—you think you can walk in here, as strange looking as she is—and *speak* to me?" she spits, pointing to my hair.

"This is ridiculous. Runa, your mother doesn't know anything about the crystal. Forget it— let's go," I say, turning on my heel, "We'll find another way."

Runa's face is ashen, and tears brim her eyes, but she doesn't say anything. Instead she stands there, like she was pierced through the heart by her mother's words.

"Yes, that's right. Get going. There's nothing for you here. There never was," Absala jeers, "Especially not a little blue crystal."

I round on Absala and peer down at her tiny frame. She stands firm, jutting out her chin, and her face red with anger.

"If you have the crystal, you better hand it over now," I say, my nostrils flaring.

"Even if I had it, I wouldn't give it to you," Absala says, the corner of her lip peeling upward. She maneuvers her body slightly, blocking the door behind her and it becomes clear to me she knows exactly where the crystal is.

"Runa, check the room behind your mother," I say, tipping my head to the closed door. "I'll make sure she stays put."

Runa looks confused, but starts walking.

"Don't you dare go into my space, Runa. You know you're not allowed. I don't want the stench of you lingering in my only place of solace from you," Absala says.

"I thought people in the Helix aren't meant to reveal their emotions, Absala. You seem to care an awful lot to me, even if it's only disgust," I say through gritted teeth. My fingers clench tightly into fists and Absala shrinks back, ever so slightly.

"Who could abide such an—abnormality?" she says in rebuttal.

"Abnormality?" Runa says, stepping toward her mother, "Who are you to say I'm abnormal? You live, locked up in your own bubble of a world. You're supposed to be knowledgeable, esteemed, but you don't even know what humanity is meant to be like— You don't even know how to really live."

"Oh, believe me, I know better than you think," Runa's mother says, giving me another dirty look, "You think fornicating with him is living?"

"Ah— Is that why Runa's father has no genetic match?" I fire back, "You spent your time away and decided it wasn't worth the effort?"

Absala's eyes widen and for the first time, her resolve falters.

"What are you talking about?" Runa asks, confusion and hurt mixing in her expression.

"Do you want to tell her? Or should I?" I ask, turning to Absala.

Pressing her lips in a tight line, Absala crosses her arms over her body and sneers.

"Have it your way," I say, returning my gaze to Runa, "When you ran, Fenton was hacking into your hProfile looking for more information on you and your brother. Runa, the Helix has no genetic match registered for your father. Your mother's been lying to you all these years."

"Is this true?" Runa says, stepping forward and getting tight in Absala's personal space.

Her mother looks away, her gaze dropping to the floor.

"Never should have been …" Absala mutters.

"I don't understand …" Runa says, gripping at Absala's shoulders, "What does that mean?"

"It means your mother has spent time outside the Helix, too," I say.

I take a step back, chuckling to myself. This makes things so much clearer.

Absala's lips tighten, but she says, "If you think I'm going to tell you anything— "

The sound of Runa's palm as it makes contact with her mother's face surprises all of us. Rubbing at her hand, Runa blinks feverishly while Absala holds her face in shock.

"You disgust me," Runa spits, staring her mother in the eye.

Without another word, Runa pushes past her mother and marches straight into the room behind us. Absala makes a tiny gesture to follow and I stand directly in her way.

"Don't think so," I say.

"Found it," Runa says, exiting her mother's space.

Runa holds out her hand. The small blue crystal shimmers in the light and something about it makes Runa's presence radiate. Closing her hand, she clutches the crystal tightly.

"Excellent. Let's get outta here," I say, making a move toward the door.

"You're out of time," Absala announces, a menacing grin spreading across her lips. Suddenly, her face twitches, flickering like a holographic screen gone bad. Before our eyes, her features melt away until her face is wiped clean and standing before us is a Labot.

"What the— " Runa says in shock.

"Phug— We gotta go!" I yell, grabbing hold of Runa's arm and yanking her out the door.

Runa's eyes are wide as she continues to look behind us as we take off running down the desolate corridor.

"What just happened?" she cries.

"Your mother's been taken over. She's a Labot now—we need to run."

"Will she be okay? How did that happen? D—Does that means Videus is near?" Runa asks, scanning the halls as we make our escape.

Absala's faceless form rushes out after us, her arm poised out in front of her as the ear piercing sound of her weapon, the Seize Scanner, fills the narrow hallway of the Helix. She only needs to be within range and we're done for. The eLink will take over our brains and seize them in an instant. With my ears trained on the danger behind me, I pick up speed, holding Runa's hand as she keeps up.

"Whatever you do—don't let your mother get close enough to seize you," I say, forcing my legs to go faster.

Our footsteps reverberate off the barren walls and door-ways along the corridor start opening as curious onlookers poke their heads out.

"Oh, no— Someone's trying to connect to me, Trae," Runa says, "It feels like they're trying reinitiate the eLink."

"Phug, can you stop it?" I call out.

"I'm trying," she says. Runa's footing falters, as she fights off the intruders in her mind. "It's Videus. He's somehow talking through my mother's eLink— he's saying he won't stop. That I should turn myself over."

"Forget that. Don't you dare stop. We aren't giving Videus the satisfaction of taking you."

Runa's hand flies to her temple and she says, "Videus' gone. What does that mean?"

"It means be careful—any one of these people could be turned," I warn.

No sooner do the words tumble out, than a man at the door up ahead begins twitching. His features melt away as he steps out in front of us.

Screeching to a near halt, we scramble around him as he raises his arm and initiates his Seize Scanner embedded in the cuff of his NanoTech jacket.

"They're going to just keep coming— How are we going to get out of here?" Runa cries. The footsteps of our pursuers edges closer, running right on our heels.

"Dammit!" I curse, wishing I had something—anything to fend them off.

Wait—I have Jane!

I grabbed it as we left the Haven, but I've never used the sonic resonator in a situation like this. I hadn't given it a second thought. Releasing the small device from my side pocket, I push the button, allowing the sonic resonator to extend open to its full size.

"Keep running, Runa. I'll try to fend them off," I say, dropping to my knee and taking aim.

Runa's footing falters and she slows down when she realizes what I'm doing.

"Trae, we need to go together. Don't waste your time— " she says, running back to me.

I take aim for the male Labot closing in. The resonator bursts through the hallway, blasting him back a few steps. His face flickers between human and Labot until it maintains resolution as a Labot. The high-pitched fluttering of his Seize Scanner is temporarily disrupted, but Runa's mother gains momentum, closing in. Taking aim again, I fire at Absala, then fire again immediately after. Absala is knocked backward, landing hard on the floor.

"Go— That will buy us some— " I say, turning around to run.

Behind me, Runa stands ramrod straight as a faceless little girl no older than eight-years-old stands behind her. The Labot child's hand rests gently on Runa's back. The front of her NanoTech jacket flashes red—a silent warning that she's been seized in a different manner.

"Trae, I can't move," Runa says, her voice trembling.

"I know Runa. Hang tight," I say, working through the options.

The paralyzer requires contact to work. If I could disengage the child …

Behind me, the other Labots regain operation and the fluttering of the Seize Scanners claw at my ears. If I fire Jane at the Labot, I could risk hurting Runa in the process.

I take a quick step toward the two of them. The child remains motionless, a sentry holding its captive until backup can arrive.

"Sorry, kid," I say, whipping the butt of the sonic resonator upward in a swift movement. It makes contact across the young Labot's jaw, making her tumble back into the wall. The contact on Runa's back is temporarily broken and her body relaxes, once again under her own control.

Looking over her shoulder at the young Labot on the floor, Runa says, "Sorry."

Without looking back, Runa and I take off running again. The Helix hall floods with people, as if a silent order has been given to block our progress. Dodging their touch and watching their faces, Runa yanks me down a side hall.

"This way, I know a faster way out," she says.

We stop in front of a typical maintenance panel, but scratched lightly on the surface is a five petaled flower.

"I hope you know what you're doing," I say, looking over my shoulder.

Placing her palm in the center of the flower, Runa pushes outward. We both jump back as the panel falls with a loud clang to the solid floor meters below.

Glancing back the way we came, people with faces flickering between human and Labot start flooding down the offshoot after us.

Without a word, Runa grabs hold of the opening, lowering herself inside and letting go. When the soft thud of her boots hit the ground, I look inside to see how to follow. It's only a short drop to the floor of what looks like large utility room. A giddy feeling, almost high on adrenaline, washes over me.

We might actually get away with this. I can't believe it—

We've just outsmarted the Labots.

I shoot a warning blast, knocking those closest to us back before securing the sonic resonator on my back. I follow behind Runa quickly, hitting the ground with a muffled thud.

"There— " Runa points and an outer door—our door to *freedom* is just meters away. Her small frame surges forward, reaching the door well before I do, and she starts working to get it open. Footsteps pound behind me and I spin around, reaching for the sonic resonator and preparing to protect the woman behind me.

Three faceless bodies close in fast—

Runa continues to struggle with the door as the all too

familiar fluttering of the seize scanners warming up saturate the air.

"Runa—" my voice wobbles and I take a step toward the Labots, sonic resonator ready.

"I know—" she calls out over her shoulder.

The Seize Scanner reaches maximum volume, and I take a shot—but Runa finally throws the door open. I twist around to follow her. As I lurch myself forward an inky darkness takes over my vision. Realization dawns—left with no hope for myself, I use every ounce of strength I have left to shove Runa out the door.

2 0

RUNA

*T*rae thrusts me out the door with such force, I slam into the side of Tethys' large body. Her agitation has been palpable since I entered the Helix and she's more than ready to make a stand in the interest of my protection.

I hope Trae can trust me—there's no time to explain her.

The deafening sound, like strange mechanical wings, dies out behind us and I swivel around to reach for Trae's hand. To my horror, his beautiful brown eyes dim and his body descends right in front of me.

The way his hair flickers in the sunlight—the heaviness of his eyelids as they close—the way a billowing cloud escapes his lips—even the sound his clothing make as they ruffle in the wind's resistance—*everything happens in slow motion.*

I reach for him as he hits the snow with a soft thump, completely motionless.

"No— " I cry, fumbling with his hands and wrenching him the rest of the way out of the Helix.

In a flurry around us, Tethys manipulates the moisture

from the air, and the snow beneath us. Droplets glisten, congealing in mid-air as she connects to her source, to her element of water. A rainbow of illumination ripples across the top of her body and the phosphorescence surrounding her shimmers in the low light of our sun.

Three Labots close in; their tall, masculine statures race toward the exit with such ferocity, my mind goes blank.

Their faces ...

Just like my mother and the others inside—they have no cheekbones, no noses, no mouths or eyes—nothing to focus on but the glistening void on top of their shoulders. Trae's description is nothing compared to the actual experience of witnessing them. With a surge of adrenaline, I scramble backward in the snow, pulling Trae as far away from the doorway as I can get. The Labot in the lead reaches the entrance, with the other two following immediately on his heels. Locating us, they use the command sequence on their NanoTech suits to reinitiate the weaponry they used on Trae and the strange sound it makes rings out again.

The second they exit the building, Tethys is ready, pitching forward with her enormous claws extracted.

Even if the Labots had eyes, they wouldn't see what's coming.

But I do.

A gash opens wide across the first Labot's chest and his blood sprays the snow in a low arc. The smell is repulsively sweet and I fight the bile it provokes when he's flung backward into the other two. Their bodies slam into the Helix with a sickening crack that reverberates through the open air, and echoes off the trees behind me. A tangle of arms and legs crumple onto the snow in front of me, not one of the Labots making a move.

Without time to waste, Tethys leans down, nuzzling the top of Trae's forehead. She sweeps her long tongue across the top of his head, leaving a trail of saliva in his hair. All around his body, the snow vibrates, suspending him in a cocoon of animated frozen water. I take a step back, watching everything unfold. All at once, the vibration halts as the snow melts into water droplets and barrel through him. Trae writhes as steam escapes his body from the processes she's creating. I can only hope this is a part of the same healing touch she was using on me. Trae's eyes flicker, and for a moment open, but he sinks back into unconsciousness.

I kneel down and run my hand along Trae's hard jawline.

"You're going to be okay," I whisper. With my thumb, I rub his lower lip, "I promise."

Tethys takes a step back, sending me the impression it will take a little time to undo whatever the Labots have done to him. Inside the Helix, footsteps echo not far from the exit. Moving swiftly, Tethys positions herself between us and the doorway as she lowers herself so I can climb onto her strong back.

Running my hand along her muzzle, I look deeply into her crystalline eyes, sending her the impression of the Tree. She already knows—but I need to let her know I'm ready. A fierce determination settles over me like a warm blanket.

I need to finish this.

Tethys grunts in acknowledgment, preparing for the fastest course. There are no words exchanged between us, only a simple knowing back and forth. Everything about our connection is so fluid—natural, though in many ways, not unlink the eLink.

I step around Trae and pull myself up. Tethys' soft, iridescent fur tickles my cheek as I lean forward and wrap my arms around her thick neck.

Tethys bends forward and with her mouth, lifts Trae by the front of his jacket. In the same instant, the outside world pushes away—like being inside a bubble as her protective shield engages. It's a strange feeling, as though I'm somehow an observer, but no longer a part of the world. Under us, the snow trembles, humming as it merges with her shield and propels us forward. I close my eyes, willing us to get to the Tree quickly, but Trae's blank stare as he fell plays over and over in my mind.

Suddenly overwhelmed by everything, tears threaten, brimming in my eyes and I blink furiously fighting them back. After everything that's happened, I need to stay strong.

"He has to be okay ..." I whisper to myself, unable to accept the alternative. I don't know what they've done to him —but he has to heal from it. He *has* to.

The edge of dismay cuts deep and I shiver uncontrollably against its grasp.

Tethys' mind is focused on the Tree, the outline of it is etched in her thoughts, pulling us in an invisible line. Inside my trouser pocket, the tiny blue crystal emits an energy all its own, as if there is an anticipation of what comes next embedded within. I only hope I'll be able to figure out what needs to be done when we get to the Tree.

I continue to watch over my shoulder, but no one is pursuing us. However, the halo around the sun seems ominous as we zip in and out of trees toward a destiny thrust upon me. Right now, I'd give anything to be a normal girl inside the Lateral—not someone being *hunted*.

What if Videus has found the Tree first?

I still have no idea who he is—or what he even looks like.

So far, he's only hidden himself behind the facelessness of others. Things aren't adding up and my heart thumps unevenly in response.

As if in a time warp, we reach the location of the Tree in a matter of minutes. Kani and Fenton are huddled together in the distance, clearly watching for signs of danger as we approach. Hidden to their eyes by Tethys shield, they don't see or sense us as we pass right in front of them.

I give Tethys the instruction to bring me to them first, but she shudders, ignoring the request. She has no intention of going to them when we are this close to the Tree. Something in her energy tells me they're better off where they are for now.

We weave around trees of all shapes and sizes, finally stopping in front of one on an enormous scale. On the ground nearby, my blood is splattered and frozen in the snow; a suspended memory in time.

As Tethys' shield disengages, my eyes flit to the large gash carved in the surface. The once hollow tree is frozen solid with ice—just as Trae had said. However, superimposed over the natural opening, is … a doorway. Intricate and beautiful, just like in my dream.

This really is it. *The Tree of Burden.*

I tuck a strand of hair behind my ear, and gaze at the Tree with bewilderment. The massive wooden door is staggering, the likes of which I have never seen. It appears to be *ancient,* but unbelievably as though it's timeless. The outer edge housing the door is decorated with etched stones, some large and small. The door arches to a point at the apex and is hinged with black metal plates decorated in ornate spirals, reminding me of water. To one side is a large, black metal loop meant to open the door.

We're so close …

Sliding off Tethys' back, my feet crunch in the snow as I hit the ground. As an experiment, I close my left eye. Only the normal, natural tree stands before me. Then I switch eyes, and only the doorway exists.

Beyond seeing her, this was why—this moment was what Tethys had been trying to prepare me for when she attacked my vision. It's no wonder Videus has hunted for the Tree, but has never been successful. He has no way of seeing it for what it really is.

Everything around us vibrates. The Tree, the ground, the crystal in my pocket. What's more peculiar, I feel the vibration—under my skin. This tree emits something powerful, making me want to touch it.

In the distance, Fenton calls out, "Runa? Tha' you?"

I turn their direction as both Kani and Fenton stand up from their crouch. No longer watchful for enemies, they start running our direction.

"Where'd they come from?" I hear Kani ask, "Did you see them arrive?"

"No, I didn't. Wha's goin' on wit Trae? Is he hoverin' in mid-air?" Fenton says, astonishment in his tone.

"I'm going into the Tree, guys. Take Trae and get out of here— " I call out. I sweep my hand toward Traeton as I turn back to my mission. I still have to figure out where the crystal goes.

"Jus' wait a minute, Runa. Wha' tha hell 'appened in tha Helix?" Fenton yells, nearly tripping over his feet as he runs.

When Videus had control of my mother's mind, he had somehow triggered by extension, access to mine. He had tried to take my mind over, but I was able to push him out. I couldn't find the words to tell Trae, but I felt the creeping sensation being triggered in the back of my brain, like a buried code come to life. When he couldn't gain full access, he said he would kill me and anyone I care about if I don't give myself over in the Helix. I have no doubt that if my eLink connection had remained open much longer, I would have been taken over the way my mother had been.

With only a matter of minutes before the two of them reach the Tree, I don't have much time or I'll have a lot of explaining to do.

Tethys slowly sets Trae down in the snow and he stirs slightly. Quickly, I drop to my knees and run my hand along his cheek. He groans, and raises a hand to his head.

"I have to go Trae. But I'll be back as soon as I can," I whisper. I wish I knew whether I was telling him the truth or not.

All of this, getting to know Trae, our connection, our kiss—it brings me a sense of hope that if I succeed in figuring all this out—maybe I'll have something worth returning to.

Walking up to the Tree, I run my hand along the wood frame, wanting to make sure the door is real. The texture is not unlike the bark of the Tree itself; rough. The wood pulsates under my touch, beckoning me to open it. No longer frightened, I take a deep breath, and set my hand on the large metal loop, and pull.

Of course, nothing happens.

What was I expecting?

I let go of the loop to stare at the space above it. A small, five-petaled flower is etched into the base of the handle. The middle of the flower is hollowed out in a pentagon, the perfect size for the crystal. Somewhere in the back of my mind, the symbology of the flower is embedded—but I can't fully access it yet. Perhaps one more thing to learn once inside the Tree.

Tethys follows behind me, silently encouraging me to go inside without any further hesitation. Pulses of energy vibrate off the crystal as I pull it from my pocket, ready to place it inside the space meant for the key.

As I reach out to the door, the field behind me suddenly ignites in a burst of yellow and orange. I spin around to see flames quickly dying out, leaving behind what appear to be a sea of enormous, black salamanders. Strange red and orange markings are distinguishable across their backs as they huff ominously.

The ground sizzles beneath their feet as the snow flees the place where their flesh touches the ground. The moment the salamanders burn through the snow and make contact with solid ground, electricity arcs, zapping back and forth between the group as a whole, connecting them—grounding them. The sound makes my skin crawl, reminding me of the moment Baxten was taken. None of them make a move— instead, they maintain their position as if waiting for a silent command not yet given.

"Runa are ya— Whoa!" Fenton cries, coming to an abrupt halt beside me. He stares in the direction of the salamanders, breathing heavily from running.

Kani nearly slams into Fenton as she rounds the Tree behind him.

"What the— " she says, scrambling back at the sight of the salamanders, "Are those what I think they are?"

"Yes," I say, refusing to take my sight off of the black mass.

"We gotta ge' outta 'ere, then. Don'tcha think?" Fenton asks, backing up slightly.

Trae moans, setting himself upright in the snow.

"My head's killin' me," Trae mutters, shaking his head.

"Trae, now's no' tha time ta be sleepin' on tha job." Fenton mutters, kicking Trae in the leg.

Scrambling to his feet, Trae stands shoulder-to-shoulder with me.

"How'd this happen …" Trae asks, his voice trailing off as he takes in the gravity of the situation around us.

A gathering of large birds darken the colorful sky. Their unfamiliar groans reach us far in advance of their physical bodies. These birds don't have the same calming effect as the juncos, instead, it feels like all the light in Pendomus is extinguished with each caw.

As they grow nearer, I feel Tethys trying to be omniscient, spreading her awareness through the snow. But there are too many enemies to focus on at once. The salamanders stomp from side to side, their energy arcs widening and brightening. My heart thuds unevenly and I fumble backward, my hands searching for the Tree.

The sense of urgency reaches a fever pitch and the weight of the pressure is a heavy burden. If I go for the Tree, I leave my friends behind to deal with this alone. Which is precisely what I don't want for them.

Tethys moves in front, stomping the ground and directing her energy to her shield as the large birds are drawn in, converging with her. The invisibility that would normally protect her doesn't seem to hinder them as they dive in two at a time, taking swipes. The air across the surface of her shield crackles as their talons purposefully graze the outer edge, testing her. Tethys groans, but stands her ground, prepared to protect us.

"What are they doing?" Kani asks, her voice a high-pitch.

"They're attacking," I say, frozen with terror.

"Attacking *wha'?*" Fenton says, trying to see over my shoulder.

A shudder ripples through me as I gape at the bird's large black bodies and long necks as they circle Tethys and all of us. Their underbellies are a bright, flaming orange and I can't help but marvel at the way they remind me of a distorted Earth vulture.

"No time to explain— " I say, knowing now is not the time to get into everything.

Without warning, lightening explodes behind the curtain of birds and the majority disperse to oversee us from above. A few of the largest birds continue to circle us in an ominous captivity hold. The salamanders, however, spread out; their electrical zapping more pronounced and fervent.

Tethys moves out further, pushing the salamanders back as she stomps the ground.

"Runa, you need to get in the Tree," Trae urges, stepping out in front of me, meters behind Tethys. Removing his sonic resonator from his back, he flips the switch, readying it.

I reach forward, pushing the barrel down.

"Please, Trae— don't use this," I plead, "There's more out there than the enemies. You just can't see, but you could hurt her, too."

Confusion crosses his face and he says, "How am I meant to protect you?"

"You don't have to. Keep yourself safe."

I hold his gaze, hoping to transfer the feelings I have— my trust, loyalty … my love.

He lowers the sonic resonator, the silent question written in his expression.

"When I'm gone—she'll protect you," I say, sending my final request to Tethys and trusting she'll follow through.

Fenton takes his place beside Trae and says, "Hate ta break it ta ya, doll. Bu' we ain't here fer ourselves. We came all this way fer you. So ya better ge' on wit it."

Kani ducks down as one of the birds bounces off Tethys' shield, flinging back toward us.

"Hurry up and get in the damn tree already!" she yells, arming herself with a knife in each hand and standing beside Fenton.

Surrounded by my friends and my guardian, the time has come.

Dazed, I turn to the Tree, reaching for the crystal again. As I wrap my hand around the tiny, pulsating stone, the hairs on the back of my neck prickle.

The breeze carries the subtle, but inescapable sound of a chuckle. The close proximity of it makes me freeze.

"*Runa* ..." A voice lulls. "There you are, my little *everblossom*. I've been searching for you."

*B*linking wildly, I turn around to I face everything I've been warned of—*Videus*.

Instead, the golden strands of Fenton's hair flicker like flames as they reflect the sun and its halo behind him. His yellow glasses no longer frame his face. Instead, his face contorts, flickering oddly until his eyes become impossibly dark, empty black pools. What takes me aback the most is the expression he's exchanged. No longer his normal goofy self, his nose crinkles as if the way I smell offends him.

A slow, creepy grin spreads across his lips and he dusts the snow off himself.

Trae stands directly between me Fenton—clearly having pushed his friend away from us as soon as he realized what was happening. Kani scrambles backward, her mouth agape and speechless. Her knuckles are white as they grasp the handles of her knives.

"Fenton, you can fight this," I say, my voice weak as I try to figure out what to do, what this could mean, "You're stronger than he is."

I can't take my eyes off of him, as I look for a sign, any sign, the real Fenton is still in there.

Kani's face tells me everything I need to know, however. A mixture of shock, horror and determination are rolled up into one powerful expression as she raises her knives.

"Get the hell outta him," She spits toward Fenton's form.

"Fenton, man—come back to us," Trae says, reaching out for his friend.

Fenton arcs an eyebrow and says, "Call me Videus. Fenton's not here right now. But I'll be sure to pass on the message."

"How can this be happening? Fenton's never been inside the Helix—he doesn't even have the eLink installed," Kani says, edging toward Trae.

"I don't know— " Trae says, bewilderment creeping into his voice, "The ComLink— Did he ever remove it?"

Kani shakes her head.

"No, with Runa being the focus, he didn't think he'd be a target any more. He was keeping Landry filled in on our plans," she says, her eyes opening wider.

"What are you talking about? *Again?*" I ask.

Trae leans back, whispering urgently, "Videus tapped into Fenton's ComLink. He knew everything. Where we were going; why."

"Alright. Enough chatting amongst yourselves. It's rude," Videus says.

Kani steps forward, her knives raised as she says, "Screw you."

Videus chuckles. "You always were one for the melo-dramatics."

"You don't know anything about me," Kani spits back.

"Ah, but I know more than you think," he says, tapping his temple.

Fenton's features contort in odd ways and for a moment, I completely forget this is our beloved friend.

"Videus," I say, trying to decide if I should still take my chances with the Tree. Tethys' energy insists I do—no good will come of staying here, "Leave them out of this. It's me you want."

I clutch the crystal until it digs into my palm.

"Runa ..." Trae says, shooting me a determined look, "Tree."

"You know, Runa ... I'll tell you about your *brother*," Videus says, his voice taunting me.

"Ignore him. He's trying to stall you," Kani says through gritted teeth.

"What about Baxten?" I ask.

A triumphant grin spreads across his face and he says, "I can take you to him, if you'd like."

Black tendrils sweep across the sky as a mass of juncos descend. Most circle the area to perch in the gnarly branches above. Their calls echoing across the snow as if they'd like nothing more than provocation. The hint of relief at the sight of them is dampened by the way the trees undulate in the sunlight, suddenly making me feel trapped. Videus barely considers their arrival, taking the moment instead to smirk.

"Where's the Waterbear? Using her parlor tricks, no doubt? *Come out, come out...*" he chides, tilting his chin upward as he surveys the landscape.

Tethys tenses at his prodding, her instincts teetering on the edge. She doesn't like this any more than I do.

Shrugging to himself, a wary amusement flashes across this false Fenton's face before he returns his cold gaze to me.

"No matter. She'll make herself known soon enough. She's no match for all I'm capable of. I can be anywhere and nowhere all at the same time. Ponder a bit on that. Besides, *you're* what we're here for."

"You're gonna have to go through us first," Trae says, reigniting the sonic resonator.

"Damn straight." Kani huffs.

"Kani, you would never hurt the man you love. You and I both know that. Put your weapons down," Videus says, peering down his nose at her.

As if struggling to retain control, Kani slowly lowers her knives.

So close, the vibration of the aquamarine crystal is intense, as if the air around us is super-charged. Taking a deep breath, I center myself for what I have to do, knowing no matter what happens, I need to be ready. My mind races and every part of me is hyperaware one wrong move could be my last.

Suddenly, my juncos enter the fray, leaving the trees to circle the scene. Their agitated calls add to the cacophony around us and I blink away the tears blurring my vision.

"Are you going to come with us? Or are we going to *play* a while?" Videus asks.

With a swift hand gesture, the largest of the birds not already circling us dive in from the trees. The additional birds come in waves from all directions. Tethys snorts as she stomps the ground, preparing for the attack. This is what she was anticipating. Feeling useless, I watch in disgust as everything unfolds.

Tethys extends her shield, encompassing all three of us inside. This time, as the vulture-birds hit, things are different —this is not their *play*, this is their *real* attack. Without care for their own lives, they slam against Tethys, each point of impact makes her shield bevel inward, releasing a black substance that creeps over the outside like a puddle of blood. Their bodies crumple to the ground and the next wave of birds take their place. The black substance begins to bind, sparking like the salamanders from puddle to puddle. I'm suddenly lost without air—the bond between Tethys and I has grown quickly and I take in the sensation this attack causes in her.

Videus' eyes blink as he steps back, searching for our location.

"Clever," he spits, pacing back and forth.

"What the hell is going on here?" Kani screeches, ducking down as the birds continue to attack.

"We're being protected—that's all you need to know," I say, readying myself.

Kani and Trae both look around, wide eyed as the attack continues from all sides. Tethys' shield holds, but she won't be able to keep up against this forever.

In an accelerated energy burst, she releases a thunderous reverberation which disburses the substance from her shield and slams the birds back fifteen meters or more. They recoil, some landing on the ground with a sickening series of scraps and thuds.

"Let me out, Tethys. Please— " I say, pushing toward the back edge of her shield.

She ignores me, holding her ground and searching for the next threat. The large birds lay motionless, their razor sharp talons grope at the nothingness in the air. Tearing my eyes from their carcasses, I swallow back bile. With the black substance disbursed, Tethys' shield pulls from the snow nearby, melding back into a cohesive unit. Unfortunately, it isn't enough, and a gray cloud contaminates the surface until her shield bursts like glass being shattered.

"Ah, there you all are."

The full weight of Videus' cold stare pierces through me.

Tethys groans from her exertion, summoning the snow around her again. The vibration is audible as it moves in accordance to her will. I take a step toward the Tree—but Tethys urges me to wait. This is still not our moment. She needs to regain some strength because I'm not the only one she'll have to protect once I'm gone. Struggling not to let impatience and fear get the better of me, I clench my jaw. I trust her instincts, but I don't like the wait.

"You'll pay for this Videus. Fenton was my friend …" I spit.

"Funny thing about friends … They can be so *fickle*. Wouldn't you agree, Caelum?" Videus purrs. A smile quirks in the corner of his mouth, but his eyes stay fixed on me.

Tilting his head to the sky, he turns his view to the trees. I watch in disbelief as a small junco lands on his shoulder. Its white beak glistens in the sunlight and for a moment, even the breeze stands still.

My bird—*Rowan*— no.

No!

Pendomus feels sideways as recognition begins to dawn. Nothing is safe. No one. I'm supposed to see everything with new eyes, quite literally—and I've *still* been so blind.

My memory races back to the event that started this all. Deep inside my mind, I've ignored the obvious flaw niggling at me. Even though I know better, I haven't given myself time to resolve this moment. With Tethys' attempts to keeping me near her, the way she slashed at my face to open my sight—gift me this vision … All was done knowing she could accelerate my healing. But she had been disrupted—Things happened the way they had because she'd been trying to save my life—trying to keep me away from the *real* attack. The one from the *birds*—the juncos.

Rowan.

All this time, I thought the birds had been trying to save me—

Catching my expression, Videus narrows his eyes and the corners of his mouth curl upward.

"Still so clueless about the world, aren't you? You know—you're just a child attempting to play a game without knowing any of the rules. Silly, really," he chides.

Raising my eyes to look at the dark gray bodies all around, the peace they once brought is transformed into treachery. Zeroing in on Rowan, my stomach churns over. How could I have been so wrong? Around his edges, a soft glow becomes evident, like he's emitting intense heat radiating off in waves. How did I not notice this before?

Stroking Rowan's back from his shoulder, Videus looks around again. "What do you say, Caelum. Shall we try one more time ... just for *giggles*?"

With another signal, a few dozen juncos catapult themselves with such a velocity my eyes can't even follow them. Tethys struggles to pull her shield up again, but the dome's weak. As they hit, the shield not only bevels, but the water holding it together scatters for a moment before Tethys is able to—drop by drop—pull herself together.

"Stop! Stop hurting her— " I yell, my scream piercing through the bird cries.

"What can we do, Runa— I don't know what to do," Trae says, watching in horror as the birds bounce off of the dome protecting him. The dome he can't even see.

Surprisingly, Tethys manages to send out a pulse of water, shooting out like tiny daggers. They create a rainbow effect in the sunlight as they pass through the bird's bodies. Juncos drop from the sky, lying motionless on the ground. At the same time a blue flame ignites in front of Videus and his salamanders, protecting them from the projectiles. The water sizzles in a quick burst and evaporates away.

The ground is now peppered with more of the fallen.

As the blue flame dissipates, Videus doesn't even seem phased at all. The salamanders, however, stomp forward. Their electricity arcs zapping up and over Videus and toward us.

"Runa ... This is not how the game works," Videus says. He smirks, no remorse at all for those he's lost, "Now, I suppose that was ... *better*. But not quite good enough." Looking over his shoulder at the salamanders, he turns back to us. When he turns back around, his face is completely deadpan until one corner of his mouth twitches upward, "Three."

Puffing his chest with anticipation, he clearly thinks he's won this. Three of the salamanders begin to stalk their way forward, each with a sense of purpose. Every step they take releases the fleeing snow in the form of steam until they appear to emerge from an electrical fog. Mesmerized by their movements, it takes me a second to break free from their hypnotic quality and come back to myself.

"This doesn't look good," Trae says, pushing me back as far as I can go.

Tethys shudders, unsure of her abilities against the salamanders. The time to get inside the Tree is nearing because we must be running out.

Before the three salamanders can take their places, the

236

crystal in my pocket vibrates more violently and I reach my hand inside, clutching it. I'm suddenly overwhelmed with the urge, not only from Tethys, but from inside myself, to go—

Go *now*.

For the briefest of moments, Tethys' shield lowers and goes on the offensive, intending to attack the salamanders first.

Not able to look back, I run at full bore to the Tree. Everyone I care about, their safety all hinges on this. I hear Tethys' attack happening behind me and based on the sounds of distress, I'd say she's been at least somewhat successful. Kani and Trae take up the fight too, because I hear their exertion.

"Enough! Forget the Waterbear! Gather *her*!" Videus cries out.

The remaining vulture-birds swoop in, while others circle in a wide berth around me and the Tree. One of them screeches close to my right side, swooping down and slashing open my right shoulder with sharp talons. Groping at my wound, I bite down on my lip, refusing to satisfy them with a scream. Instead, I force myself to take the last few steps and thrust the crystal into the center of the flower shaped locking mechanism without so much as a second thought.

With my hand still touching the door, a bright blue light shoots out the tips of my hair and lights up my skin. The light travels in an accelerated pace down my right arm, then continues to descend until finally escaping through my fingertips. In an instant, it merges with the crystal and the keyhole. The outer edge of the five petals slowly turn white, as if an invisible hand were drawing them one by one. Resonating across the snow, the Tree itself begins to hum—

low at first, but getting louder. Peace washes over me and I'm momentarily swept away by comfort.

However, the others continue to struggle behind me and I'm pulled back into the severity of the moment. I'm certain I can hear more salamanders advancing. Dodging another swooping bird, I don't waste any more time. As soon as I'm safe, Tethys will find a way out with the others. I know she can even save Fenton—

Grasping the cold handle on the door, I yank back hard, desperate for solace and safety. For answers. But more than anything, to put an end to Videus' control over my future.

To my horror, the door still won't budge. Conjuring as much strength as I can manage, I give another frantic pull. The ground comes up to meet me as I fall backward, landing hard in the snow. I duck and roll over quickly as the birds closest to me shriek, bending the wind with them as they fly by.

"No!" I yell, slamming my fist hard into the snow. Exasperation and desperations mingle together in a potent mix.

The door's supposed to open—it's *supposed* to be our answer!

Videus laughs in the distance, making my skin crawl.

I turn around, struggling to my knees to face Videus' vengeful eyes. The ground is red and steaming around the three salamanders Tethys attacked. A fourth salamander lay in pieces at Videus' feet, clearly having died protecting him from my guardian. The steam from its flesh rolls in a strange dance with the heat he radiates. Three additional salamanders have come to the aid of their fallen, caging Tethys within a circle of lightening.

Kani and Trae both have salamanders around their feet, squeezing tightly. Their bodies are locked stiff, as if they can no longer fight back and dark purple and black flames lick their bodies.

In complete disbelief, I shut my eyes tight. Any hope I'd been foolish enough to cling to is now replaced with complete emptiness.

Everything I thought I could give wasn't enough.

Videus has won.

My chin quivers and my hands shake uncontrollably at the thought of what Videus will do to us now. None of us know what he's capable of doing and it's clear he has more resources than we even knew. Certainly more than we have.

I bow my head, wracking my brain for any other possible way out of this—but nothing comes to mind. This was as far as my plan had brought me.

To top it off, Tethys' energy irritates me. Regardless of my despair, she's illogically anticipatory—practically excited and I can't believe she'd accept this fate so easily. Didn't she see nothing happened?

Nothing!

"The Tree's here, isn't it?" Videus says, his gaze searching the space around me. There's a peculiar sliver of consternation in his voice as he looks from tree to tree, completely missing the one he's most interested in. Holding my breath, I inspect his every movement, not sure when or where he'll strike next.

For a moment, he says nothing, but his dark eyes lock onto me.

"What did you do to it?" he questions, annunciating each word deliberately.

"N—nothing." I say, clenching my jaw, "What are you going to do with my friends?"

Trae's eyes move between me and Videus as I ask the question. I'm acutely aware one wrong move could mean they'll be taken the way Baxten was.

Pushing myself to a stand, I feel horribly exposed. The birds, have taken to the trees, but each and every one of their eyes is on me—waiting for their signal. The weight of their stare is palpable and the woods close in on me.

"How curious ... Why can I not see it now?" Videus mutters to himself, surveying the ground at my feet with wide eyes, "Was here a moment ago. It's all here inside the blonde one's his head. The Tree as to be here. The blood—of course. The blood's here."

Still holding onto my hurt shoulder, I cast my gaze downward. Surrounding my feet, I stand in a frozen puddle of my own blood, with more joining as it drips through my fingertips.

How ironic. This where my new life began—and where Videus would like to end it. It was also where I thought I could find answers and put an end to all of this madness.

How foolish.

The wind picks up, blowing strands of my hair across my face. I look up, staring my friend deeply into eyes that don't even remotely resemble the face they inhabit.

"Whatever you want to do ... Don't hurt my friends, Videus. *Please*—just take me. I'll go wherever you want me to," I say.

Videus lets out out an exasperated sigh and waves his hand dismissively.

"You *would* be the kind to sacrifice yourself. You know the irony in this? I would have jumped on the chance to take only you a while ago. But now look what you and your critter have done," he sweeps his hand out at the snow in front of him, "No, I think instead ... You'll get the pleasure of witnessing the eradication of each and every one of the entities you hold dear and you can carry the memory with you—for as *long* as I want the burden to be yours." His jaw sets, not dropping his gaze from mine as he calls out, "Start with the Waterbear."

Widening her stance, Tethys prepares herself to fight again, but there's nothing to prepare me.

At his command, the salamanders push forward, encircling Tethys and begin to flick their electricity across the surface of her shield like a whip, leaving seared markings where they touch. The water she holds dear, instantly boils away from her.

I let out a shrill scream as I grope at the snow, feeling each lash as if they were my own.

"Please. *Stop*— " I plead, gasping for air and groping at the snow.

If Tethys' shield goes down, I know he means every word. I'll watch as he kills everyone I care about without any remorse.

If only the Fenton I know and love was still in there. If only some semblance of his humanity was clinging onto him ... How can someone be taken over so completely?

"Ah ha ... You're feeling this, aren't you? Sharing her pain?" Cocking his head ever so slightly, Videus' finger circles toward Tethys and he snickers, "Well, this is better than I'd hoped. Not only can you relive her death from your memory banks—you'll have extrasensory memory. Brilliant. What a juicy little tidbit about the infamous *Daughter of Five*."

In response, the expanse of birds screech in excitement. Some of them swoop from tree branch to tree branch—their horrifying calls filling the air.

"Stop this. *Fenton*—think about Kani," I plead, pointing to her restrained form feet away. The knives she fought valiantly with lie in the snow near her feet.

Something flickers across Videus' face—a momentary flash of Fenton maybe—but he shakes it off, snarling to the nearest salamander, "Shut her up—and keep her on standby."

Tethys' agitation is heightened when the salamander huffs toward me. I stumble backward, trying to get away, but it's no use. In a lightening quick movement, the salamander slinks around my feet, biting its own tail before squeezing in on itself. I feel the flames well before they ignite—as if they were placed underneath my skin as they slowly creep up my legs.

The purple and black flames flicker at my clothes, but I don't burn. As they rise higher, I'm imprisoned by them—the air becoming unbearable stifling, making my head light and my body lock. Anger burns under the surface at all that's happened—everything which is *going* to happen. Videus is right—I've barely begun to understand myself, let alone my place in this world.

This is all wrong.

If I was so important, there should have been something I could do—something that would've stopped all of this. Why would I be urged to come out here? To seek the Tree for answers, to open the door—only to be met with this? Perhaps that was the point?

My jaw drops open. What if this had always been the plan? Lure me here to the Tree? *To kill me?* What if the door was never meant to open? Am I too trusting?

Defeated, I look into Videus' twinkling black eyes and he sneers in return.

"Are you ready? About to be pandemonium on Pendomus," he says gleefully.

Ripped from my internal anguish, I fight inside my mind against my imprisoning fire as the three salamanders shift the focus of their arcs at the ground around Tethys. A rippling band of lightning undulates like waves over each other at her feet. For a moment, I lose sight of her when a cloud of electric fog envelops her. Once it finally lifts, the ground is barren and exposed down to rock in a large circumference. They've removed her contact with the water.

"Fenton ... *please*," I beg, one last broken attempt to will my friend back to his body.

Lightening flicks furiously across the remainder of Tethys' shield—her body quaking as she tries to hold on, but simply can't. With the last remnant of her water spent, there's little fanfare as her shield disengages with a soft burst, exposing her.

The birds cackle an almost human-like laugh and the little juncos sweep in. It seems the birds have always been able to see her and now is no exception as they take purposeful swipes, clawing at Tethys' back in a victory lap. The salamanders shift from side to side, excitedly waiting.

"Excellent. Now the fun begins," Videus says.

Tethys' energy is impatient, again oddly anticipatory, despite her pain. I press my lids shut. I don't want to see this —he can't make me *see*.

Instead, I focus on Fenton. On the person I *thought* he

was. No, the person I *know* he is. If this is the end—I refuse to give in to having the memories Videus demands. I refuse to play this on his terms. I will make my own rules.

In my head, I conjure up Fenton's goofy grin, the yellow band that is so much a part of who he is to me. Even his strange manner of speaking—his accent. I miss that the most. He could always make me laugh, even when I had no clue what he was saying. I focus on the way he helped Trae research my brother, research for me—he'd really come through then. In the short time I've known him, he's shown such ingenuity. Not to mention, gentleness … The way he cared for his friends, for Kani.

I remember the surprise I'd had when I found out they were together. The touch I'd seen him share with her in the dining area my first day. Looking back, their touch started to wake me up from the hazy dream I'd been living inside the Helix. That touch in some minor way, led me to Traeton.

"Stop—" Videus snarls, his voice breaking through the birdcalls.

Jolted from my memories, I open my eyes.

Videus' hands are clutching at the sides of his head. Bewilderment casts a glow across his face as he glares directly at me.

"Now, *that's* new. How did you make me see those things?" he spits.

Suddenly, the humming from the Tree behind me switches to a thunderous roar and the world around me goes white. I'm completely blinded by it like all those times I'd been connected before—but there's no nausea, no voice. The snow on the ground flies upward, a blizzard surrounding us all.

The lightening stemming from the salamanders becomes

more ardent, and I watch the glittering white turn into a sheet of water, particularly around the salamanders near Tethys. But she doesn't have this kind of power—at least not without direct physical contact.

The melting snow extinguishes the salamander's flames momentarily, causing Traeton, Kani and I to be released from our prisons of fire. Though mine holds tight at my ankles, the salamanders holding Trae and Kani slink away, merging with the sea of others to create unity between them. Kani immediately drops to her feet, scrambling to grab her knives. Without hesitation, she throws one at the nearest salamander. The blade sinks into the salamander's head, causing it to slump forward and severs its connection with the others.

"Runa— look at the Tree," Trae yells, pointing over my shoulder as he runs toward me.

I twist around to find the entire Tree is a brilliant crystalline white and emanates an intense energy both powerful and reverent at the same time. Snowflakes fly feverishly from the tips of each branch as if the Tree is commanding them from within itself. As the snowflakes gain momentum, they swirl together, winding around like twisting white snakes— until they merge into a single monolithic serpent.

Gasping for air, I stumble backward. The serpent flows with intention, shimmering with an unearthly quality—a force to reckon with as it takes control of the scene. The salamanders surrounding Tethys are the first to be hit by the spiraling blizzard. They try to hold their ground, heating the water to the point of evaporation, but the bare ground beneath them seems to move on its own accord, encasing the salamanders's feet, and snuffing out their flames. More importantly—cutting off their ability to summon their lightening.

"Hold your ground," Videus calls out in determination to the rest of the salamanders. "You're not afraid of a little water, are you?"

Trae and Kani run to my side, standing back and watching as the snow serpent wraps around the first salamander at Tethys' feet, then instantly breaks itself off to arc around to the other two. Squeezing tightly, it slices the salamander bodies in half with a sloppy scraping squish and redirects itself to envelope Tethys.

Though the serpent doesn't linger with her long, Tethys' strength returns and I realize *this* is what she was anticipating. *This* was what she was hanging on for.

Holding my breath, hope returns—*almost*. I will the serpent to come to me, to get the salamander at my feet so I can get to Tethys—I want nothing more than for my guardian to get her shield around me and find a way for all of us to get out of here.

As I follow the serpent's movements, I realize the field isn't nearly as full of salamanders as it once had been. Videus swaggers awkwardly but manages to send out a hand signal.

Having all but forgotten the birds, they dive in, attacking the swirl of snow. When they collide, I cover my ears at the thunderclap that follows. The birds manage to call upon the wind around them, twisting the snow away with an almost tornadic quality. The snow serpent pushes back, blinding the birds and they struggle to maintain their place in the sky.

In an odd combination of relief and despair, Rowan —*Caelum* takes flight. He's the first to flee and a handful of birds follow after until they're tiny specs in the distance.

Others are not as lucky as they appear to freeze in midair. Too many to count begin to drop like a stones to the ground.

Through the blinding snow, I search again for Tethys and find the sliced salamanders have begun to shrivel away. Almost nothing is left of them but the steam they seemed so intent on creating.

Suddenly on the move, Tethys stomps toward me, not yet able to summon her shield.

Videus follows her progress and screeches, "Runa— Take her! Now!"

Heat and flames erupt at my feet, surrounding me again and shifting to an unbearable temperature. The wall of fire consumes my entire line of sight. When my vision beyond the fire returns, I'm in a long hallway with large metallic looking doors going off on either side. Moans escape the tiny slits above them. The heat in this place is intense and I know immediately where I've been taken.

The vassalage.

As the gravity of my situation catches up with me, I'm ripped from the scene. Staring Tethys in the face, I blink in confusion. I look downward to find her massive claws lodged in the head of the salamander at my feet. In a swift movement, she pulls back. With a disgusting squish, its head severs clean from its body in four neat chunks, and sizzles in the snow.

I reach a trembling hand out to Tethys' head. My heart throbs unevenly and with wobbly knees, I step around the disintegrating salamander to get to her.

Swallowing my trepidation, I take a look around. Trae rushes to my side, fear and concern mixing in his face.

"Are you alright?" he asks, breathlessly.

Suddenly, Delaney and a small team are on the scene,

rushing to our aid. Two of the men, Ash and Patric, are armed with special weaponry that incinerates its prey on contact—killing off five of the salamanders in the blink of an eye. Kani is taking advantage of the confusion and is working her way toward Fenton's overtaken form.

Behind me, the Tree of Burden shimmers white, casting a glow onto Tethys—and a brilliant white light seeps from the doorway. Its hazy white tendrils reach for me and begin to fill with a swirling of color—white, blue, purple, green, pink — They reach for me gently, caressing my face, lifting my arms and urging me to stand. Beckoning me.

Slowly, the light pulls back from the tips of each branch, summoned to return to the core of the Tree. As the last inklings of light pull back, leaving the cool sensation of the mist, my eyes rest on the wooden door carved on the side of the Tree. No longer locked tight, but instead, open wide. Inside, the light remains, pure and bright. It whispers in my veins, calling me forward.

"The Tree—it's materializing. Now. Burn it—burn the Tree!" Videus screams, pointing at the remaining sala-manders.

"Runa, you have to go. Find your answers, we've got your back," Trae says, planting a quick kiss on my lips and turning to face Videus and the remaining salamanders.

With my jaw set, I dash for the open doorway. The breeze ruffles my hair as I race to the Tree before Videus can stop me. Each determined step forward gives me strength as I reach for the door. My fear of the unknown lies dead on the ground as I grip the rough edge and thrust myself inside. The light is blinding and there's nothing to see but radiance.

Videus may know more than I do, but I need to rectify

that. It's time I figure out who I am and why I'm so important.

My foot leaves the safety of the past, entering the blinding chasm of the unknown as the gigantic wooden door slams shut behind me.

23

TRAETON

*R*una doesn't hesitate. She takes her opening and heads straight into the tree's doorway—vanishing before my eyes. The moment I turn to defend against anything wishing to attack her, the tree sends out a shock wave, knocking me and everyone in the vicinity to the ground. As I scramble to my feet and turn back, the tree seals the natural gash along its trunk, erasing the opening and making itself whole.

Will I ever see her again? I shake my head.

Of course I will. *I have to.*

A cry of panic breaks out and I twist around to find the source.

Delaney's expedition team has come at the most opportune moment, but Kani has completely lost her mind. Fenton's possession by Videus has evidently caused her to act rashly. My best-friend's features contort into a wicked grin as he takes a step back, gripping Kani by her neck. Delaney, Patric, and Ash all stand by, ready to make a move if an opening arises, but I seriously hope there isn't one.

"Whoa guys—" I say, holding my hands out in front of me, trying to be the voice of reason before things get out of hand.

"Let go or so help me—" Kani says, clawing at Fenton's arm. However, Videus stands perfectly still, as if her efforts don't even faze him. With a deliberately slow maneuver, he plucks the knife from Kani's hand and presses it against her throat, making her instantly still.

"I do believe everyone needs to take a moment," he says, his voice ice-cold as he tips Kani's chin upward with the blade, exposing her neck even more, "Traeton, call of your guard dogs, or Kani will die. It will be slow and painful and it will be done by me."

As if conflicted, Fenton's face flickers momentarily from being completely encompassed by Videus' possession. His eyes flash from black to his natural brown—but the effect doesn't last.

Trying to seize the possible opportunity, I say, "Fenton, this is Kani you're talking about. You don't want to hurt her— "

"Eh, eh," Videus says, shaking his head, "C'mon Traeton. You know better than that. Let's not get confused."

I shoot a glance at Delaney, who nods her agreement. None of us want to run the risk of hurting Fenton's body, or getting Kani killed.

"Everyone, put down your weapons," I tell them.

Setting down the sonic resonator at my feet, I kick it forward a bit and stand back with my hands raised. Delaney and Patric follow suit, but Ash quickly takes aim and fires. The shot clips Videus in the ear, splattering Kani in Fenton's blood.

Kani's scream is abruptly cut off as the knife in Videus' hand sinks into her skin and opens a thin line in her neck.

Blood pools in Videus' hand, dripping down Kani's neck and onto her white jacket.

Videus touches his ear with his other hand and takes a deep, calming breath as he surveys the area around him.

"You really shouldn't have done that," he says, maintaining the pressure on a very still Kani.

"Ash," Delaney warns.

Ash lowers his weapon, keeping his eyes trained on Videus the entire time.

The field of salamanders have been annihilated down to two survivors, which hover near Fenton's feet, huffing menacingly. The birds have all but abandoned their master to save themselves and I know this is Videus' last stand. If he's painted into any more of a corner, he's going to lash out and the result will be the loss of Kani, and likely Fenton. We can't let that happen.

What we need to do is capture Fenton and find a way to kick this Videus guy out of him—or something—but if he makes a move to harm anyone else, I know Delaney won't hesitate to take him out.

"Now then, we were in the middle of something when you so rudely interrupted," Videus says, narrowing his eyes at the tree behind me, "Fortunately, the distraction allowed the Tree to make a rather unremarkable reappearance."

With a single hand gesture from Videus, the remaining two salamanders slink from his feet, streaking past me and taking opposite sides of the tree.

"Don't you dare touch the tree— " I warn through gritted teeth.

If the tree is destroyed, everything will be for nothing. Runa's in there somewhere and everything inside me is screaming to put a wrench in Videus' plans. But how?

"Stop them, Trae," Kani yells, "I'd rather die than live in a world where Fenton is taken by this *monster*."

Videus chuckles, "Do you know nothing, Kani? Good, noble Traeton—risk your life? He won't do it, even if it means giving up on ... what was it? *Love? Lust?*"

Kani twists to the side, slamming her elbow hard into Videus' ribcage. Blood streams heavily from her neck, but she wrenches the knife from his hand and immediately turns it on him. With her free hand, she covers her wound, but sways slightly. Her complexion has gone a ghastly white.

Videus takes careful consideration of his situation, slowly raising his hands.

"Kani ... think carefully," Delaney says, using her most calming tone, "Don't do anything rash."

"Shut it, Lane," Kani says, anger and defense encompassing her entire makeup.

Videus stands, using Fenton's features to try to break Kani's resolve. He lightens his expression and takes a step forward.

"You wouldn't do anything to poor Fenton's body. Now would you?" Videus asks, wide eyed and direct, "He loves you, you know. And wants desperately to get back to you."

"Don't do that—don't you *dare* do that," Kani says, jabbing the knife towards Videus. "You don't care about Fenton. If you did, you'd get the hell out."

The control over Fenton's appearance flickers again, but the impenetrable black eyes remain.

"Of course I care. You are my people— Everything I've done ... I've done for you. This has always been about keeping the sanctity of life," he says.

"Sanctity of life? You have to be kidding me. After all

this?" Kani says, splaying her arms out wide, "All this death is because of you."

"He will not come around to your understanding, Kani," Patric says, stepping forward and regaining hold of his weapon.

Ash and Delaney also bend down, picking up their weapons and taking careful aim.

"Fenton's still in there somewhere. He has to be. What if we can get him out?" Kani says, her hand shaking.

"Hold onto that thought. Let it be your compass," Delaney says, giving Kani a significant look.

"Hmmm … You know, I kind of like this body. Young, agile. Lots of memories of this resistance of yours buried in here. No … I could get used to this," Videus taunts.

It's clear to me, he's hoping to agitate Kani into making a mistake and in her state, it just might work.

A ferocious snarl erupts behind me and Videus' eyes widen as if he remembered something important.

"No—she's still here," he mutters, his eyes distant.

I take a glance around, but of course, nothing can be seen.

Is the Morph here? Or whatever we thought was the Morph …

It certainly seemed like something was helping us through the mayhem.

Hoping the distraction will cause enough confusion, I launch myself forward and roll to where I kicked my sonic resonator. Before anyone can stop me, I prop myself up on one knee and face the tree. I flip the switch, readying Jane, just as flames ignite at the salamanders' feet. A burst of electricity erupts from the center of their bodies, creating a conduit that wraps around the tree and connects the two of them. In a flash, they start running in a counter-clockwise fashion, burning away all traces of snow the base of the tree. Due to their motion, it's hard to take aim as they ring around and around.

"What are you waiting for? Shoot—" Patric calls out, firing a shot of his own before I get the chance.

The shot misses its target, instead, hitting the tree and splintering a huge chunk from the side. Ash and Delaney also fire, but the sheer speed of the salamanders makes it hard to pin them down.

Centering myself, I take a guess as to where one of the salamanders will be next, and I fire two shots. There's nothing standing between me and the salamanders, and yet they ricochet in the opposite directions as if being parted by an invisible force.

As I try to figure out the cause, my sonic resonator is abruptly flung out of my hands and lands in the snow beside me. Directly in front of my face, a piercing howl of pain and anger makes me cover my ears to protect them. I duck down, covering my face with my forearms expecting to be attacked, but nothing happens.

Runa mentioned before there's more here I can't see—and that I could hurt *her*.

Did I just shoot *her* by accident?

A moment later, one of the salamanders is flung backward of its own accord as if being yanked by its tail. The fire at their feet and the electrical arc between the two severs. The salamander howls in agony, thrashing on its back as it tries to right itself. The second salamander abandons its post, rushing to its companion and slinging itself at the attacker. Stopping in mid-air, it latches onto the creature we can't see as it reignites the fire at its feet. Another ear-splitting howl of pain erupts, but it's not from the salamanders.

I fumble with the sonic resonator, unsure what to do—if I try to help I could hurt all of them.

"Delaney, can your team get a good shot? Take out the salamanders," I yell.

"What the hell is it attacking?" Delaney asks.

"Just do it— "

Two shots are fired, one making direct contact with the salamander on top of the creature. Blood bursts from its shoulder as it tumbles off the invisible creature and lands in the snow. Immediately, the other salamander flings itself at its enemy.

"Claws—watch out for Tethys' claws," Videus screeches.

"Shut up," Kani yells, stepping forward with the knife, "Just keep your mouth shut.

The shot salamander slinks around, trying to get on the other side of the invisible creature while the other attacks. The movement is ineffective as the invisible creature flings off the salamander on its back. It knocks into the other and with a loud squish, a head of one of the salamanders is pulverized before our eyes.

Without any further hesitation, the remaining salamander launches itself at the tree. It reignites the flames at its feet, slinking upward in a spiraling dance. It leaves behind a trail of fire until the entire thing has gone up in flames. The sky darkens with the smoke and there's nothing I can do but stand there in horror as the last salamander destroys the tree right before our eyes.

"Yes— I have to admit, I almost didn't think I'd accomplish this," Videus says, laughing manically, "You have no idea how long I've waited for this moment. To think—the *Daughter of Five* led me straight to it. After all this time, she was actually its undoing."

The heat from the raging fire becomes unbearable—even from this distance, but the salamander perches itself inside the large prongs of the tree as if it's its second nature to be alight. Even from here, I can see the wound on its tail healing itself in the flames.

"We have to find a way to stop the fire," I yell, running toward the tree and throwing heaps of snow into the flames, "Runa's still in there."

Delaney and Patric run to my aid, while Ash stays behind with Kani—keeping Videus under control. We throw armful after armful at the tree, but it doesn't even make a dent at the extremity of the blaze.

"It's beyond your control, Traeton. You can't stop it now," Videus says, "The prophecy will never come to pass. You and your Daughter of Five will never take this world from me."

Suddenly, the snow on the ground all around us vibrates and rises in the air on its own accord. As if in a reverse avalanche, snow hurls itself at the tree from every direction. The salamander hisses, flinging itself out of the tree and fleeing in the opposite direction. At first the snow sizzles, burning away as steam, but the force of it is too strong and eventually, it melts into a massive wave.

Patric and I stumble backward, watching in awe as the fire fights with the water, battling for dominion over the tree. Finally, the water begins to win out and the flames start to extinguish.

"Okay, I think we've had our fun," Videus calls out, "We need to go. *Now.*"

In a huff, the remaining salamander quickly slinks through each of us, trying to get back to Videus. A howl from the invisible creature makes me wonder if she's the one behind the water's attack.

"Don't let it get to Fenton," I yell, rushing after it.

Reaching for the sonic resonator, I fire at the salamander. It takes a direct hit, but shakes itself off and keeps running.

Kani holds her ground, training her eye on both the salamander's progress and Videus. As the salamander nears, she takes a swipe at its back. The blade scrapes across the top of the salamander, like metal on metal—impervious to the blade.

"It will take Fenton the way the other one took Baxten if we don't stop it," I yell, "Shoot it!"

Ash fires a shot and misses, hitting the snow between Kani and Videus.

The small salamander doesn't waste any time. It slinks in, curling quickly around Videus' feet and biting down on its own tail.

Videus' face briefly flickers back and forth between his agitated features and the scared expression I know only to be Fenton's.

Sneering, Videus takes control.

"Don't be fooled. These intrusions are not your saving grace. They buy you time and nothing more. Watch your backs. I'm coming for all of y— "

With the flick of her wrist, Kani releases the knife in her hand. Before anyone can react, it embeds itself deep into my best friend's chest. Blood gurgles from his mouth as he clutches at the intrusion.

"I'm sorry, Fenton," Kani sobs, dropping to her knees.

"No— " I scream, rushing to Fenton. After all that's happened—not this. Not this way.

The inky black in my best friend's eye color pulls back, leaving them clear of Videus. For the briefest of moments, Fenton is with us so Videus could flee to save himself.

"Tha's me girl," Fenton says. Blood spatters from his lips as he coughs. "Shoulda done it sooner, though."

"Fenton— I'm sorry, so, so sorry," Kani cries, scrambling to her feet and reaching for him.

Flames erupt at the salamander's feet and burst from the center of its body, engulfing Fenton the way we witnessed with Baxten. Before I can reach him, both he and the sala-mander vanish.

Cupping my hand over my mouth, there's nothing I can do to stop the severity of emotions—I fall to my knees.

I barely care when the tidal wave in the distance crashes down behind me. As quickly as it came, the wave becomes a surge of new snow creating a blanket to cover up the grizzly past. The scene is so calm, yet I'm forever changed. Videus has done this—wreaked a havoc I'd never in my wildest dreams imagine. All for what?

I stare numbly at the bloody, charred ground directly in front of me.

Delaney is suddenly by our side, wrapping her arms around Kani. Ash and Patric remain off on the periphery—giving us all a moment.

"Kani, I'm sorry— " Lane offers.

"He came back. Just for a second, he came back," Kani murmurs.

"Landry was working on removing the hold on Fenton's mind. We were hoping— "

"You knew? And you didn't tell us?" I demand.

Lane holds my gaze, trying to convey some sort of sympathy in her expression. But I can't find the strength in my to care.

Reaching for Kani's shoulder, she says, "We knew if

Videus was aware—the consequences could be dire. He would have killed Fenton there and then."

"They were dire, Lane," Kani says, the spark in her completely gone. Tears cling to her eyelashes as she reaches out, touching the bloody snow.

"We thought … if we could get to your coordinates quickly, we could buy ourselves some time. We had no idea just how bad— "

Shaking my head, I stand up and walk away. I can't hear any more of it. I can't stand the thought of how close we were to having it all—only to lose Fenton and the Tree anyway.

I face the charred remains of the now infamous tree. The blackened surface sizzles and the smell makes me sick.

We've lost the battle entirely. With the tree gone, how will Runa make it back to us?Fenton's gone and we have absolutely nothing to show for his loss.

An eerie silence falls when all that's left is the fluttering of snow and memories of people I love that I will never get back.

Runa, I'm so sorry I failed you.

24

RUNA

*W*armth. Like stepping through a shower of water, the light hugs my body, enticing me forward into its protection. For a few moments, I'm lost in it —unable to distinguish the separation of where the light ends and I begin. Sounds resonate through the luminescence.

No, not sounds … *songs.*

Quiet at first, one note blends into the next until my entire being is surrounded in harmonic resonance. I am a part of the song, forgotten and reborn in its melody. Suddenly, the songs become words, both foreign and familiar. Then the words become sentences until I'm comprehending all being said. The first voice is soft and masculine, a warm embrace from someone just on the edge of my memory. The second is a woman's, intertwining with the man's but rivaling no other. Their song is one of rebirth, love, and trials. As quickly as the voices arose, the song melts away.

The woman's voice rings clear, as if standing before me.

"Runa, Daughter of Five, we welcome you home. There is so

much to discuss ... Your place in this world is more important than you've ever been led to believe and we will do everything we can to prepare you for what comes next."

I wait, my mind holding a breath my body can't feel.

The light pulls back and I am suddenly standing in a lush meadow full of beautiful white flowers. In the center of its five petals is a burst of purple. I reach out, plucking a single flower from the ground. The petals are exquisitely soft and I bring the flower to my nose.

Home.

Yes, this is home. Something about the gentle fragrance of vanilla triggers memories that are not my own—but instead passed down to me from the ages.

A woman dressed in a simple white gown emerges from the distant woods. The gown flows ethereally at her feet, as if she doesn't even touch the ground she walks upon. Sunlight cascading through the trees radiates her presence and I know without a doubt, she is the one who has been in my mind warning and guiding me. Her long, white hair falls in voluminous curls around her shoulders and her inviting blue eyes sparkle. She stops directly in front of me, her graceful smile reassuring and gentle.

"We have waited a long time for you, Runa," she says, reaching out for my hand, "It's so good to see you."

"I know. I'm not sure how I know ... but I do," I say, taking her hand.

"My name is Adrian," she says as she guides me along a footpath through the flowers, "You must have many questions."

"I do," I say. But for the life of me, none of them are coming to mind.

We walk in silence for a while, finally pushing our way

through long, dangling willow branches to the edge of a large pond. The sun's rays filter through the trees, reminding me of music in the form of sight. Steam rises from the water's surface, creating a curtain of mystery. Large, majestic birds swim at the water's edge—*swans*, my memory recalls.

Adrian takes a seat on the ground and puts her bare feet into the water.

Patting the ground next to her, she says, "Sit. Let us discuss the things past and the things yet to come."

I nod and take a seat beside Adrian, casting my gaze out over the water. Bending forward, I release the flower, watching it float away on the water's surface.

"Why me?" I ask.

"Long before the universe presented you, we have waited patiently for the signs. One of the most important pieces of information I can bestow on you is this ... Our world, Pendomus, was never meant to be locked—the rotation was halted for the gain of one and he wants to ensure balance is never reinitiated. It would mean power has been given back to the planet, to the true inhabitants. This was once a peaceful planet. One of harmony and abundance. Now, for centuries, we have silently awaited a child to be born who will have the power necessary to return us to this harmony. The child was you, Runa.

This is why you've always had a calling to the outdoors. It is also why your professional appointment made no sense to you. Videus had been watching your progress, as he has with many who came before you, and felt the need to take action on your behalf. Cremator is the category he gives those who will be assimilated and transformed into his murderous agents—the salamanders. They are the children with the makings of greatness, with uniqueness. Make no mistake, he was trying to dispose of you, like he has already done to so many before, in his effort to circumvent the prophecy."

"What happens now?" I ask.

"There is so much you are unaware of. So much we have to teach you—imbue you with," she takes a deep breath, intertwining her fingers and placing them in her lap.

"Then start," I say, turning to face her.

Adrian's expression darkens as her lips tug downward.

"As you know, truth lies within the eye, but do not mistake your inheritance for security. There are people, the ones perhaps closest to you, who will wish to seek you harm. They will come at you from ways you won't see coming."

My words come, tumbling from memories that feel so far away, though I know they happened only moments ago. His blonde hair and dark, dark eyes …

"You mean … Fenton," I say.

"No, Daughter of Five. There is another. Bound by blood and destiny. You must be mindful at all times, be aware. Videus will plot against you until you are finished. You must not let this happen."

Adrian's eyes are full of sorrow.

"Who? Who do you mean?" I ask. My serenity in this place evaporates like the burst of a bubble and I'm left floundering.

Considering, she finally says, "I am bound by the prophecy to let unfold what must. Only time can answer this question for you. Fate may not as of yet decide the form this treachery will come in."

Frustration seeps into my demeanor and I struggle to remain unfazed.

"Why was I brought here? For this? To accuse people

close to me? Why not just tell me this before? Why lure me here?"

"The answer to your questions are simple. There are three reasons you were required to enter this realm," Adrian says, turning to face me.

Her piercing blue eyes feel like they see right through me and I squirm in my spot.

"The first, to inform you to the best of my ability. Outside of this realm, nothing is sacred. Nothing is untouchable. No corner of your mind nor body is beyond Videus' limits. Remember that."

She pauses, letting me rest within this notion and it doesn't sit well.

"For many years Videus has sought the one who carries the gift to see what he cannot see. What *you* can see," she says, holding my gaze, "He wishes to exterminate the light you will bring to this dying world. Pendomus was once a planet teaming with life. When humans colonized, the original inhabitants tried to be accommodating, to share the world. Humanity had other plans. Runa, you have been called here because of your importance. We need your help to rectify what has been done."

"But ... how? What can I do?" I ask, "I'm only one person."

"You are the only one that matters," she says, matter-of-factly, "This will make more sense as time goes on. Another reason you were brought here is so I can guide you onward. There are many tasks ahead of you, but you must focus on one at a time. Your brother is in the midst of all that is desecrate. His link to you may end us all if we are not careful. His capture was most unfortunate. In order to fulfill your destiny, you must recover him and I'll do my best to show you the way."

She places a hand on my forehead and images flash through my mind. Terrain of Pendomus—starting with the entrance to the cavernous system I know now as the Lateral. It continues on in rapid succession, through trees and snow drifts until it moves beyond the snow's edge, exiting the habitable area of Pendomus to enter the desolate desert side —the one permanently facing our sun.

She pulls her hand from my head and places it back in her lap.

"Your destination lies beyond what you've known. Beyond what you're comfortable with. You must go to the place where the sun touches the land in order to find your brother. This task is very dangerous because the trek cannot be made with Tethys. You will be traveling to where any water would instantly vaporize. Because of this, you must go on your own, but you will not be without guidance."

With the memories gifted to me, Tethys has become an important entity in my life. As important as my brother, my friends, even Traeton. The idea of going without her feels daunting.

"I have friends—people I care about. Perhaps they could help?" I offer.

"Your friends cannot go with you and I cannot tell you why. They have their own roles to play in all of this. You must trust me."

Adrian's expression is veiled, and I nod. Something inside me tells me I can trust her implicitly—just as I know the same of Tethys. After everything that's happened, a part of me knows that by involving Traeton or the others, I would be further risking their lives. Which is something I won't do.

I cast my gaze out over the pond and wait for more. A small blue and purple butterfly flutters beside me until it lands gently upon my hand. Bringing my hand closer, the butterfly's wings open and close slowly, but it remains facing me as if studying me as much as I study it.

I glance up and find Adrian smiling thoughtfully.

"A symbol of your transformation," she says, nodding her head at the butterfly, "You are also here so I can prepare you of the tasks ahead. Your gift of sight alone will not be enough. When the time comes, you will have the resources you require to acquire your brother. New gifts lie dormant within you and could only be awakened by your presence here. They will not be awakened all at once, instead emerging over time."

"I don't understand. What gifts?" I ask, shaking my head.

"That will be up to you. You will know as the time comes."

I snort, pulling my legs up close to my body. "How is any of this *preparing* me? You're being too cryptic."

"I'm sorry, it is as much as I am allowed. Is it not more than you previously knew?" she asks, tilting her head knowingly.

"I suppose," I mutter.

"However, you're right. There is more."

Adrian pulls her legs out of the water, choosing instead to sit in a cross-legged position. Placing her hands face up on her knees, she closes her eyes. I watch her curiously, wondering what she's doing.

Right before my eyes an enormous book materializes in her open hands. The cover is bound with a dark fabric, with impressions scrolled across the top. Etched in the center is a perfect replica of the Tree of Burden.

Adrian holds the book out to me.

"This Caudex will be your only source to the histories of Pendomus and eventually to the prophecy. When you leave this place, the software hardwired in your brain will be destroyed to deter Videus from gaining access to your mind. Unfortunately, it will likely disrupt our communication as well. The Caudex has its own ability to sense when new information is required. When you're ready, details will arise within the pages," she says, tapping the center of the tree.

I accept the monolith and place it on my lap. Peering down, I run my hand along the Caudex's edge and attempt to open it. Though there is no clasp, the book is somehow locked.

"Because this book's essence is tied to the Tree of Burden, you must use the same key you used to enter this realm," Adrian says calmly.

I shake my head, confused.

"But I don't have it. The crystal was placed inside the door—"

A sleek smile creeps across Adrian's lips and she points to me.

I glance down to find the crystal bound into a necklace and hanging from my neck. The silver surrounding the crystal is shaped in the form of small spirals and reminds me instantly of water.

"Where—? How?" I ask, touching the crystal.

"The Tree of Burden could no longer exist in its previous form," Adrian says, "It has been reborn—for you, in exactly the way it was always meant to."

She again taps the cover of the book.

"You are talking in circles. You say you're here to help me, inform me … but I feel more lost than I was before I entered the Tree," I admit, "What if I don't want this burden. What if you have the wrong person?"

"Rest assured, there has only ever been *one* with the

ability to enter this space," Adrian says knowingly, "Runa, the Tree of Burden holds its name for a reason. Once chosen, you can not *unchoose*."

I close my eyes trying to make sense of everything, "You talk about a prophecy. What does it say?"

"When you are ready to know, the Caudex will enlighten you."

The wind picks up, carrying the songs I heard upon my arrival. A male and female voice intertwine—beckoning me to stand.

"It's time for you to go now," Adrian says, untangling her feet as she stands.

"This can't be everything. I need to know more … Why me? What else do I need to know? How is my brother involved in all of this? How can I even save him?" I ask, frantic to learn as much as I can before I'm pulled from this place.

"Remember, the Caudex will be your guide now—" Adrian's voice grows quieter, nearly a whisper at the edge of my mind.

The swans in the pond take flight, heading into the bands of sunlight until they vanish from view. Enormous wings sprout from Adrian's back, surrounding her in an unearthly glow. Shielding my eyes, the light grows brighter and with my free hand, I clutch the Caudex, not wanting to lose touch with my connection to the Tree of Burden, or this realm.

Encompassed by the light, I lose touch with my body. Hands and feet, body and self—for the longest time I do not exist beyond my essence blended with the light. Suddenly, I'm thrust from the realm inside the Tree.

There is no snow on the ground, instead, I'm surrounded by sand and sun. No longer in the middle of a field of flowers, I find myself sitting cross legged on the edge of a large crater. Beside me, the remnants of the once living willow trees.

This is the same place—the location of the pond. Only, it's no longer a pond.

I blink away my uneasiness and look down. The Caudex remains with me. Reaching up to my neck, I find the crystal still dangling in place.

With a deep breath, I unclasp the necklace holding the crystal. I turn the small stone over and it glows brightly in my palm. Though there is no space for a keyhole, a sudden knowing washes over me and I wave the crystal in front of the Caudex. The book creaks open and I flip through the ancient pages. The majority remain empty—place holders for information just as Adrian had said. I flip open to the only section with writing.

In the age of the elders, the acropolis served as the source of foundation for all of Pendomus—far before the invasion of dying Earth's humanity. The structure was the most beautiful in all the world, truly a spectacular sight to behold. All inhabitants of Pendomus kept the site sacred above all others. When humanity released its scourge upon the land, all of nature conspired to protect the acropolis, burying it deep within itself. Creation itself split apart into five equal fragments. Each held its own special gift, none more important than the other. They hid themselves away, awaiting the day their gifts could be resurrected to once again bring balance to Pendomus.

Beneath the passage, a five-petaled flower is drawn in glowing metallic ink.

The Everblossom—now the image to invoke the five is key to the one who can reclaim its purpose. Once known to grow even amidst the most frigid of storms, the Everblossom was finally destroyed when humanity laid waste with their misguided attempt to terraform the planet. All cycles of Pendomus were ground to a halt, as the planet was locked in place with the closest star in an attempt to exterminate the original inhabitants.

Moving images of trees shriveling back and dying without the sun's natural cycle follow the paragraph. I let out a sigh, my shoulders slumping as I take in the barren sights around me. This used to be a lush garden…

Somehow, I always knew the trees had been here long before humanity. It had always been so clear to me. Shaking my head, I read and reread these two passages over and over, trying to decipher their hidden meanings and what they have to do with finding my brother.

When I have burned the words into my memory, I close the Caudex.

Not everything is clear—in fact, much of my life has become ridiculously ambiguous. However, one thing is certain … by circumstances much larger than myself, I have been put on a path I must follow to the next destination. Lives hang in the balance. People I care about need me to be strong—to do what's right, no matter how difficult.

I close my eyes, my thoughts drifting from Baxten, to Traeton.

Though our time together has been brief—a part of him lingers with me. I would give anything to have him here for whatever comes next.

Wherever he is now—I hope Tethys is keeping him safe—keeping all of them safe.

One day, I promise I will find them again.
This is not the end.

———

Next up—

Polarities

Book 2 of the Pendomus Chronicles

AFTERWORD

Did you love **Pendomus**?
If so, please kindly leave a review. It helps others like you
find this crazy, beautiful series.
You rock!
Carissa

Pendomus is also available in audiobook!

———

Next up—
Polarities
Book 2 of the Pendomus Chronicles

MORE BY CARISSA ANDREWS

THE 8TH DIMENSION NOVELS

*The Final Five: An **Oracle** & **Awakening** Bridge Novelette*

***Awakening:** Rise as the Fall Unfolds*

Love is a Merciless God

The Complete 8th Dimension Box Set

ABOUT THE AUTHOR

Carissa Andrews
Sci-fi/Fantasy is my pen of choice.

 Carissa Andrews is an international bestselling indie author from central Minnesota who writes a combination of science fiction, fantasy, and dystopia. Her plans for 2021 include continuation of her Diana Hawthorne Supernatural Mysteries. As a publishing powerhouse, she keeps sane by chilling with her husband, five kids, and their two insane husky pups, Aztec and Pharaoh.

To find out what Carissa's up to, head over to her website and sign up for her newsletter:
www.carissaandrews.com

facebook.com/authorcarissaandrews
twitter.com/CarissaAndrews
instagram.com/carissa_andrews_mn
amazon.com/author/carissaandrews
bookbub.com/authors/carissa-andrews
goodreads.com/Carissa_Andrews

Made in the USA
Las Vegas, NV
27 January 2021

16584287R00164